Act of God

books by Margaret Kennedy

THE CONSTANT NYMPH

THE MIDAS TOUCH

TOGETHER AND APART

THE LADIES OF LYNDON

THE FEAST

LUCY CARMICHAEL

TROY CHIMNEYS

ACT OF GOD

MARGARET KENNEDY

ACT OF GOD

Rinehart & Company, Inc.
NEW YORK

to Charlotte Davies

PART I

The Storm

1

The thunderstorm frightened a great many people in East Head. It came after a phenomenal heat wave, and it reached the Bristol Channel upon a Saturday night.

During the afternoon it had rumbled a long way off, to the north-east, over the Welsh coast. At ten o'clock the thunder claps were coming fast upon the heels of the flashes. An hour later it was described by everybody as *right overhead*, although this hardly did justice to its menace. Had it remained vertical it would at least have kept to its own place; it became horizontal, a continuous glare, punctuated by short sharp cracks. It no longer descended from the sky, but sprang out of the earth, sizzling along the roads and blazing through drawn window curtains.

After midnight it subsided for an interval and went growling off towards Exmoor in a dissatisfied manner, as though nothing had been settled yet. During the whole of Sunday the skies were sulphurous, the air stifling. At night it returned again in full force, damaged the power station, and extinguished the lights all over the town for nearly an hour. It was not until Monday morning that torrential rain fell, and the sense of oppression lifted. The air grew cooler. By noon the sun was shining in a clear sky and it was possible to believe that no serious damage had been done. Nothing had been struck save a tree in the middle of a field behind the town.

In spite of the confusion caused by the temporary black-out, many people felt that Saturday night had been worse than Sunday. After twenty-four hours they had got used to it, but they had not liked Saturday night at all. It had reminded them too closely of the big raids on Bristol. For a short time they were all doing and thinking and saying identical things. There was a prevailing disinclination for solitude. Families assembled in whatever room was felt to be "safest," frightened children were brought down from their beds, and everybody had a cup of tea. It was, some declared, worse than a raid, because there was nothing to be done. The risks might be smaller, might be negligible, but there were no civic duties to protect the mind from panic. It was difficult to believe that nothing would come of all this; a terrifying force seemed to have broken loose, and it was universally felt that something must be going to happen somewhere.

Old Mr. Pattison, who lived in The Rowans, at the end of Battiscombe Avenue, felt no uneasiness of this kind. If he remembered the raids, it was to thank heaven for his present contentment. He had no impulse to put on a tin hat and a warden's overcoat, to go out and be doing something. He had no fears which must be kept at bay. The entire universe, for him, revolved round his son Dickie, who had been in danger and was now safe.

Things had been very different ten years ago, when the sirens set up their wail and Mr. Pattison scuttled down the

Avenue to his Action Station. In those days he could scarcely be persuaded to go home, even after the All Clear, so haunted was he by thoughts of Dickie up in the skies, Dickie shot down over Germany. Even on the night of the oil bomb, the flames which he had fought did not seem half as terrible as those other flames which he could imagine. And, when he went off duty, it was to meet the same fear in the eyes of Dickie's mother, as she rose from her violent knitting to brew him a cup of cocoa.

She was dead now. He missed her hourly. Yet he could not want those days back. Dickie no longer ranged the perilous skies. Dickie had got through it safe and sound. He had come home to follow the path appointed for him, to make the wills and guard the property of East Head citizens, to marry a sweet, pretty local girl, beget a son, and bestow upon his father an Indian Summer of thankfulness and rejoicing. So long as all went well with Dickie, the Crack of Doom itself could scarcely have disturbed old Mr. Pattison.

He felt, however, some sociable desire for comment and conversation. The storm was certainly phenomenal, and a prodigy is better appreciated in company. His housekeeper had gone to bed. There was nothing for it but to go out, in the hope of a word or two with strolling neighbours. Halfway down the Avenue he found two cronies, Dr. Browning and Sam Dale, a substantial building contractor, who had lately become Mayor of East Head. They were both talking at once, and Mr. Pattison, on joining them, began immediately to talk too, without listening to what they were saying.

The air was insufferably hot. Not a drop of rain had as yet fallen, and nothing stirred in the Avenue. Yet there was a sense of high wind, of a violent gale blowing some-where. Trees and houses sprang into inky relief, two or three times a minute, against a blinding sky. The splitting cracks ended as sharply as they had begun; their sinister brevity suggested some malign, unexpended force, some event still in preparation. The three men talking in the road were half conscious of this. They were waiting for something. Their minds were not on their words; they re-peated themselves and paid very little attention to one an-other.

Dr. Browning had a patient at an outlying farm to whom he wished to send some medicine. He had meant, he said, to drive up there after supper, but his wife was nervous and he did not relish the idea of a drive through this himself. He was waiting for things to get quieter, yet wondering if he ought to wait.

Sam Dale was worrying about a lot of metal scaffolding poles which had been left near the top of Bay Hill. All that metal, piled up there, offered a sure target for light-ning, and there was some timber close to it which might catch fire. But he could not imagine what he was to do about it, even if he did go up there.

The reference to Bay Hill attracted Mr. Pattison's at-tention for a minute or two, because Dickie lived there. He listened to poor Dale's lament just long enough to be sure that these poles could not endanger, or inconvenience, Dickie, Christina, and their son Bobbins. Had such a thing been possible he would have urged Dale to go up immediately and control the elements, at whatever risk to himself. But, as soon as he learnt that the poles were on the other side of the hill, he left off listening, and began to describe Dickie's experiences when flying through at-

6

mospheric storms. Neither he nor Dale paid the slightest attention to Browning and his pills.

Presently a car came crawling cautiously down the Avenue. It drew up; its owner got out and joined the voluble group in order to tell them, and to be told, that it was a nasty storm. He was a retired engineer, of some distinction, and his name was Pethwick. In East Head he rated as a newcomer for he had only lived in the district for three or four years. Everybody liked him, but nobody knew him very well, for he was troubled by lumbago and seldom left his house, which was at Brinstock, some miles inland. He was said to be a good talker, but he also had gifts as a listener, and was able to give Dale an expert's opinion upon the problem of the scaffolding poles. Nothing, he asserted, could be done and it would be very foolish to go up there. As for Browning's pills, he could quite easily deliver them himself, on his way back to Brinstock. It would be less than half a mile out of his road and no trouble at all.

Browning, relieved and grateful, went off to get the package, and it was old Mr. Pattison's turn. To be listened to by Pethwick was an agreeable experience, of the kind which is subsequently described as a pleasant chat.

"I believe," said Mr. Pattison, "that my son and daughter-in-law are going to have the pleasure of meeting you tomorrow night, up at Summersdown."

"You mean Conrad Swann's party?" said Pethwick. "Yes, I was asked, but I'm afraid I can't go. I have people coming to dinner."

"Pity!" said Mr. Pattison. "You'd have seen this new statue Swann has just finished. Apollo, it's called, I believe."

"Swann, eh?" said Dale. "Giving a party? Well . . ."

Had Pethwick not been present he would have made some jocular reference to Swann's good lady, who was not good, not a lady, and did not even trouble to call herself Mrs. Swann. But he stood a little in awe of Pethwick, and the scandal was, in any case, a stale one. All that could be said about that rummy pair had been said, two years ago, when they first came to the town. So Dale merely grunted and asked if Pethwick knew Swann well.

"Hardly at all," said Pethwick. "But I own a work of his. I expect that's why I was asked."

"What? One of his statues?"

"Well . . . a piece of sculpture. Abstract."

Dale stared and exclaimed, "I never thought. . . ."

But he left the sentence unfinished, because he was not quite sure what it was that he had never thought. That Pethwick was the type of man to buy Swann's statues? That Swann's statues were worth buying? Pethwick was not, surely, so simple as to waste his money on rubbish.

"I saw a photo in the *Gazette*," said Dale. "Something Swann did that got a prize in Venice. I couldn't make head or tail of it. I daresay I'm behind the times."

"Dickie's up in all that sort of thing," broke in the happy father. "Art and all that. You mightn't think it, Mr. Pethwick, but my son Dickie is quite keen on art. Went to Italy for his honeymoon, and Christina, that's my daughter-in-law, said he walked her off her legs, in all those galleries. Very intellectual in a quiet sort of way, Dickie is. You'd be surprised at all the books he's read."

"I don't think I should," said Pethwick, smiling. "I always enjoy a talk with him. One can see he's a reader."

This was true. He had taken a strong liking to Dickie

8

Pattison, whom he thought a most attractive young fellow, pleasant, modest, good mannered, but saddled with more intellectual ability than he quite knew what to do with.

"He got a scholarship to Oxford," proclaimed Mr. Pattison, "from the grammar school here. I can tell you, we felt proud of him, his mother and I."

"Did he?" exclaimed Pethwick, surprised. "Did he go then?"

"Well, no. It was in the war. He joined the R.A.F."

"Wouldn't they keep it open for him?"

"Yes, but it was getting a bit late in the day for that sort of thing. He'd a job waiting for him here, and his law exams to get through. I wasn't so much set on his actually going there, anyway, though it was gratifying for us, his getting that scholarship. No point in it. He wouldn't learn anything there he'd need for his job here. People round here don't go to Oxford and Cambridge. It might have given the wrong impression. Might have looked as if he was getting a bit big for his boots. No, no, I said to him. You're a man now. You come back home and get down to your job. You'll only waste time at Oxford. Here's your future all waiting for you."

There was a pause. During the past few seconds the thunder and lightning had halted. They stood silent in the stifling night, listening and waiting for something. Dr. Browning returned with a little package which he gave to Pethwick. Sam Dale, who had been pursuing his own train of thought, said suddenly, "He owes money all over the town."

"Who does?" asked Browning.

"Swann. That sculptor chap. He's in queer street."

9

Their voices sounded loud and harsh, in that strange hush.

"Oh, Swann!" said Browning. "He owes me ten and six, and I can whistle for it. I went up there . . . they rang me . . . you never saw such a set-up! One of the kids had a bean up his nose. Know what? Not a single solitary soul in charge. No sign of Swann or the lady. Just these kids. It was one of them rang me. Pint size. But had a head on her shoulders."

"I've heard a rumour," began Dale, "that those kids . . ."

AK-AK-CRRRACK-AK!

Dale's rumor was never revealed. All four were reeling and blinking, dazzled by the flash, aware that *it had happened.*

They remained for a few seconds longer in a silent group, until the dazzle had faded, and they could see one another once more in the wan light of the street lamp. Then the bond which had held them there dissolved. They separated, like a flock of birds which suddenly rises and flies away. Pethwick, with a muttered goodnight, got back into his car. The others returned to their houses.

Mr. Pattison trotted home to The Rowans. It was a large house, too large for one old man, but his father had built it, and Dickie would have it someday. Only for a few years more would it be silent and empty. To him it was already full to the attics and throbbing with life. The future was ever present in his mind, a future in which the central figure was always that beloved youth, who was never to grow bald, wear dentures, or develop a paunch. The boy . . . he thought, able to envisage everything save the inevitable disappearance of the boy, who had,

10

indeed, already taken flight. A stripling Dickie received Civic Honours, fondled grandchildren, and celebrated his golden wedding. I'd like to come back and see that! thought the father, undaunted by any premonition of a stranger, an interloper, another "old Mr. Pattison" trotting down the path to meet him.

2

Nothing had happened. Nobody had been struck. No damage of any kind was reported on Sunday morning.

For this, and for her own preservation, Miss Agatha Byrne, aunt and housekeeper to Father Byrne, gave thanks during High Mass to an assortment of saints, under whose protection she had put herself during the night. But her gratitude was a little distracted by curiosity concerning a shock-headed child who knelt just in front of her. A good Catholic child ought not to come to church in so unkempt a state, with no head-covering save a duster, positively an old, dirty, checked duster, tied over elf locks. Such impropriety must be reproved.

When Mass was over she waited in the street for an opportunity to accost the girl and ask her name. She was answered with a suspicious scowl and a mutter:

"Serafina Swann."

"A-ah!"

That explained everything. Those children! Miss Phipps, at the school in Harbour Street, had found "things" in their heads.

"And how old are you?"

"Ten."

"You're a Catholic then? Why haven't I seen you at church before? You've been living here some time."

"I don't know. I was frightened of the thunder."

She knew her way through the Mass, thought Miss Byrne. Somebody must have taught her.

"Who gave you that rosary?" she asked.

The look which she got in reply startled her. She had been reproved! By a child of ten!

"A dead person," said Serafina, with considerable dignity.

Miss Byrne was not accustomed to be snubbed by ragged urchins, but she had to pull herself together before continuing the inquisition.

"And you've got a lot of little brothers and sisters, haven't you? What age are they, now?"

"Joe's four. Dinah and Polly and Mike are seven."

"What! Triplets?"

"No. Dinah is the oldest. She is three months older than Polly, and Polly is half an hour older than Mike."

"Hck!" clucked Miss Byrne, unable at first to believe this.

After a moment's reflection an explanation occurred to her which shocked her so much that she gave another cluck.

"Hck! Well . . . I'm glad you came to church, Serafina. I'm sure you try to be a good little girl."

Serafina stared. Nobody had suggested this idea to her for a very long time.

"But, childie, you know you should tidy yourself a little before coming to Mass. It isn't very respectful to come to church in a duster, is it?"

"I haven't got a hat."

13

"Oh, dear! Is that so? Why, then . . . perhaps Our Lady might send you a little hat, one of these days. If She does, will you wash your face and comb your hair, dear?"

"Oh, yes. Oh, thank you!"

"Because you could have done that today, couldn't you, dear, even if you had no hat?"

Serafina scratched her leg and mumbled something about breakfast.

"You cooked the breakfast? All by yourself?"

"I do all the cooking."

"Ah, poor child!" cried Miss Byrne, quite softened. "You do your best, I'm sure. Quite a little mother to them all, I'll be bound! I'll pray for you."

"Thank you. When will I get the hat?"

Miss Byrne was about to explain that prayers are more important than hats when an acquaintance, coming up to greet her, distracted her attention. The child immediately darted off.

A little hat can mean different things to different people. Miss Byrne had in mind something rescued from the jumble sale cupboard. For Serafina the words conjured up a flowery vision with an eye-veil, like Mrs. Dickie Pattison's Easter bonnet. She skipped home in a transport of complacency, no longer frightened by the distant growling thunder.

A little mother! Never before had it occurred to her to think of herself in so romantic a light. She perceived now that it was well earned. Who looked after the others, if she did not? Who saw to it that they were fed? Who dispensed justice among them? Who rang up the doctor when Mike got a bean in his nose?

14

For grown-up people Serafina felt, as a rule, very little respect. She made an exception in the case of Mrs. Pattison, with whom they had all made friends on the beach one day, when Dinah had cut her foot on a piece of broken glass. That kind, pretty lady had brought some bandages out of her bag and dressed the cut. She was like nobody else. She told them stories and could play like a little girl; she had made a wonderful switchback in the sand for them, down which they had rolled golf balls. Once they had gone to tea with her in her beautiful sparkling house. Even her little baby had his own basket, lined with blue, for his powder puff and safety pins.

But she had never called Serafina a little mother. The commendation of Miss Byrne opened up new vistas. What a pity that more people did not know about this! How glorious it would be when everybody knew! There she goes, they would say. There she goes, that sainted child! Where? Who? Why? Serafina Swann, to be sure, in her lovely little hat.

The house seemed to be deserted when she got home. It stood up bleakly under the heavy yellow sky, a mean, small box of a house, in a garden choked with weeds. All the doors and windows were wide open, as if the inhabitants had just rushed out in a panic and deserted it forever.

She did not go in because she knew that the others would probably be up at the tree.

This great oak tree was their favourite refuge and hiding place. It stood higher than the house, in the middle of a meadow adjoining the back garden, and was more like a little town than a tree. Each child had a particular house, or branch; Serafina had even managed to contrive a sacking roof for hers. Their treasures and toys they kept in their houses, suspended in baskets.

The ascent was particularly enchanting. They could not have reached the lowest bough without the aid of a derelict ladder which they had found in the garage. Most of its lower rungs were gone, but they could achieve the upper by climbing onto an old green metal garden chair, which had been knocking about in the field ever since they came to Summersdown.

The greater part of their life was spent in this tree. Sometimes they fell out of it but nobody had, as yet, been seriously hurt. They would sit for hours in their houses, or climb slowly from branch to branch, visiting one another. They felt it to be a friendly place. Up there they were safe, especially in the summer, when the leaves were so thick as to hide them from anyone not standing immediately below. They were all, except Serafina, timid, low-spirited children, easily terrified, and with a mania for concealing themselves.

Nobody ever came to look for them in the field. Only cows gathered in the shade of the tree in hot weather, whisking their tails to drive the flies off, and sending up a reassuring cow smell to the children in tree town. Even Serafina, who had outgrown most of the tree games, felt a security and confidence up there which she missed in her wary, battling life below. And she was, therefore, a little unwilling to tell anybody about this refuge; Joe, in his innocence, had betrayed their secret to Mrs. Pattison, and invited her to tea in his tree house. There was nothing to be done, save welcome her when she came. Nor had the party gone off badly. She had admired it all very much, thoroughly appreciated the ingenuity of the chair and the

16

ladder, paid a visit to every branch, and brought with her a contribution of lemonade and chocolate biscuits. But she belonged to the dangerous grown-up world, which Serafina distrusted. The people in it were not reasonable. They got themselves into the most mysterious predicaments and then made more hullabaloo about it than any child would dream of making. They seemed to believe that somebody would come and put everything right for them, if they made a great deal of fuss. Even Joe knew better than that. The little Swanns yelled and roared sometimes, if they hurt themselves, but only to relieve their feelings. They did not expect redress. Mrs. Pattison, although she was so nice, did belong to that strange, untrustworthy race, and the tree did not seem so safe after she had been there.

The back garden was a long one, running up-hill to the meadow. Serafina had only got half way up when she heard Joe's voice, plaintively hailing her.

"Where are you?" she called.

"In the miggle of the pond."

She ran round a hedge of rambler roses and found them all huddled together in a tank which had once been a lily pond. To her angry enquiries they replied that they had gone there for safety, until she came home.

"You said—you said yourself," said Polly, "that *they* can't cross water."

The worst of raising bogies is the difficulty of dismissing them. Serafina sighed. She ruled by terror, as many another little mother has done. Reassurance was not so easy.

"Silly! They can't come out in the day-time."

Her subjects looked at one another.

17

"Yes they can," whispered Mike at last.

"There's one now in the meadow," said Dinah.

"He's spoilt our tree," said Polly.

"Spoilt our poor tree all quite dead," mourned Joe.

"And he's there still," said Mike. "We saw him. Hopping after us and shooting at us."

Serafina's spine began to crawl.

"You mean . . . there's a person in the meadow?" she ventured.

A fluttering sigh of dissent rose from the woebegone group. It was not, they gave her to understand, *a person.*

"Not . . . not . . ."

Far away a long roll of thunder seemed to answer her. Joe suddenly dashed out of the tank and butted his head into Serafina's stomach, yelling at the top of his voice, "An Arfitax!"

Everybody cried "Ssh!" It was extremely dangerous to refer to the Enemy by name. Grown-up people might babble lightheartedly about Artefacts, but they did everything differently.

"I don't believe it," quavered Serafina.

To believe it would bring the skies toppling down.

The whole mythology of the Artefacts had been, as she knew in her saner moments, her own invention. Of course she was afraid of the things; she always ran past the studio as fast as she could. Even grown-up people were afraid of them. A char-woman, who came sometimes, called them wicked looking things. And Dr. Browning, when he took the bean out of Mike's nose, had peered through the studio window and declared that he should not like to meet any of them in a wood on a dark night.

18

They looked very frightening, especially those which had some faint resemblance to human beings. But she knew, perfectly well, that they could not really think, and had no life. They were not *real,* as she put it to herself. Her father made them. People sometimes bought them; for what purpose she could not imagine. They must be very wicked people. It was not possible for Artefacts to get out of the studio and attack the Swanns. If she had ever encouraged the others to think that they could, it was only as a means of keeping order. The idea had presented itself when Mike once asked if they could be in the house; she had answered quickly that they might come, if he did not do as she told him.

From this beginning the cult had grown and ramified. It was half a game, half a religion, mingling enjoyment with terror, until they had almost come to depend on it. Perpetual warfare raged betwixt the Artefacts and the Swanns, and, in this drama, Serafina played the part of witch doctor. She knew the habits of the creatures; she knew how to propitiate and defeat them. She could distinguish between an Artefact and a milder type of demon, known as a Form, also an inhabitant of the studio, but less malign and sometimes actually upon the side of the Swanns. It was by her spells and incantations that these creatures were *sent to the shed,* a kind of condemned cell next door to the garage, which was the ultimate fate of Artefacts and Forms alike. Once they were put there, all was over with them. Within a day or two men would come with a van or lorry and drag the occupant of the shed away to his doom. Sometimes a great many men came. Last year six of them had been needed to remove

19

an egg-shaped Form, so large that the shed door could not be quite closed upon it. The Swanns had rather an affection for it, and were sorry to see it go off to execution. Dinah had cried until Serafina produced the theory that the men were good, and were secretly helping it to escape. One of them had said that it was going to Venice, which was a beautiful place, full of churches and holy people.

Mike and Dinah believed it all. Joe believed as much as he could understand. Polly, who was sharper than the rest, had lately displayed some signs of scepticism, but she was thoroughly frightened now.

"It really is," she persisted. "Go up to the meadow and look. He's there still."

They had all come out of the tank by now and they followed Serafina up to the field, lagging a little way behind her, ready to fly at a moment's notice.

The first thing which she comprehended, when she reached the meadow, was the ruin which had fallen upon their tree. It really was destroyed, split from top to bottom and partially burnt. It looked terrifying enough, in that strange yellow light, with the thunder always growling around the hills.

Then she saw the THING, and cried out in terror, "Jesus-Mary-Joseph!"

She could not run away. She could not move. She had to stand there, petrified. If this could happen, anything could happen.

It stood just beneath the blasted tree; it was the worst that she had ever seen. In hue it was a smouldering red and it was about her height. One long thin leg it had, and a great flat foot. The head was very small, a pear-shaped blob at the end of a twisted neck. It had no arms, but, as

20

Mike said, it was shooting at them. Spikes of different lengths stuck out from it, like wicked arrows.

At the moment it was motionless, but it was obviously just about to move. On its one long leg it could come hopping faster than anybody could run. It seemed to quiver slightly, as it stood there looking at them, jeering at them, boasting of what it had done—could do. It was the very embodiment of evil.

"Pray for us! Pray for us! Now and in the hour . . ."

But I've got my rosary, remembered Serafina. I've got the Holy Cross. God is stronger than the devil. If he comes at me, I can hold my Cross up.

Her panic subsided a little. This was only an Artefact. It was not real. It could not think. How it had come there she did not know, but it had not come of itself. Somebody must have brought it.

"Pooh!" she shouted suddenly. "I'm not afraid of *that!*"

Gripping her rosary, she advanced upon it. Her heart was thudding and she felt sick, but she forced herself to go on. Having reached it she gave it a little push. It wobbled and fell upon its side at her feet. Immediately half its malignity seemed to evaporate. It looked weak and silly, lying there, shooting its harmless arrows at the sky.

A yell of triumph arose in the meadow. Dinah, Polly, Mike and Joe rushed up and gathered round the fallen foe. They would not have touched it for the world but they danced and jumped, threw sticks and dirt at it, shouting shrill taunts:

"Stinking old Artifack!"

"Now you're dead!"

"Lousy old Artifack."

"Lousy ole Arfitax! We'll kill you, and we'll kill you, and then we'll come back and kill you some more!"

"We'll send you to the shed."

"Oh, yes! Yes! Serafina! Put him in the shed!"

This was rather more than Serafina had bargained for. She did not much like having to touch it. But she had a reputation to sustain. She compelled herself to raise it, whereat the triumphant clamour died away and the others drew off, eyeing the business uneasily. No help was to be expected from them. Alone she dragged the horrid thing out of the meadow and down the garden to the shed.

This turned out to have an occupant already.

"Why," cried Polly compassionately, "it's a poor Form. Shan't we rescue it, Serafina? It looks almost holy."

Serafina agreed. There was something benign about this flame-shaped object, which rose from a slender base with so much suggestion of movement that they all instinctively looked upward, to some point above it. They dragged it out, pushed it into the garage, and concealed it under an old car tarpaulin. The Artefact was then placed in the shed. Set upright it looked formidable again, as though it might come hopping out at any moment. They slammed the door upon it and took to their heels.

All except Joe, who had never really been frightened of it. He was too young to understand the game; he merely shrieked and ran when the others did. To his eyes there was a certain familiarity about the prisoner, a connection which had eluded the others, because their imaginations had been more strongly assaulted. He lingered behind, for a moment, to yell, through the key-hole of the shed, a final taunt: "You ole *chair!*"

22

3

The invitations to Conrad Swann's party had not been issued by the sculptor himself but by a Mrs. Rawson, who had constituted herself his patroness in chief.

This toothy, determined little woman believed that she was born to lead. She had inherited considerable powers of domination from her father, old Tom Skipperton, who had owned a fleet of pleasure steamers and made a large fortune out of persuading people that they liked to be seasick. But she lacked his coarse geniality; she suffered from a chronic unpopularity, a total absence of followers, until she took up the cause of Art. In this field she encountered inertia but little serious resistance. Her fellow townsmen were never to be convinced that she knew more than they did about politics, economics, religion or hygiene; few troubled to gainsay her when it came to aesthetics. Since nobody cared to stop her, she was able to accomplish a good deal.

She seldom travelled, but she did occasionally go to Paris and it was there that she met Don Rawson, a large, lazy, handsome American, several years younger than herself. He believed that Paris was his spiritual home, but, having squandered his patrimony in an attempt to become an artist, had failed to find a material home there. Had he

23

not married Martha he would have been obliged to return to North Dakota. He brought to the partnership a number of very small etchings and a gift of tongues. He preferred, more often than not, to express himself in rapid French or Italian, which Martha would translate to the company, with an indulgent smile.

Until Conrad Swann came to East Head she had been rather short of protégés. The biggest fish in her net had been an architect called Alan Wetherby, who lived in Bristol, and for whom, after some crafty campaigning, she had got the job of building a new Marine Pavilion. Swann, however, was more rewarding. He had an international reputation and he was easier to manage, since he cared only for his work and took little notice of anything which went on outside his studio.

Martha it was who stopped Dickie Pattison in the street one day, and asked him to come to Conrad Swann's house on Sunday night. A band of the Elect were to enjoy a rare privilege: a first view of Swann's Apollo. He was going to enter it for the Gressington Arts Theatre Competition; a prize of five hundred pounds had been offered for the winning entry, which was to have this title, although, as Martha explained, a representational treatment would not be expected, naturally. In addition to this, the prize work would find a permanent home in the vestibule of the Arts Theatre.

"Conrad likes you so much," she concluded. "He very much hopes you'll come. I'm sure you'll excuse this informal invitation. He's such a simple person. It never occurred to him that anybody would want to see the Apollo before it goes to Gressington. But I told him there *must* be a party."

Dickie accepted with delighted alacrity, not because he wanted to see the Apollo, which he did not expect to understand, but because he liked Conrad Swann, with whom he very much wished to be better acquainted. Earlier in the year a truck, turning in the lane in front of Swann's house, had knocked down part of his garden wall. Dickie had acted for him in the business of extracting compensation. And then, a few weeks later, they had met down at the harbour just as Dickie was hiring a boat for a day's fishing. Swann had come upon the same errand but there was no other boat to be had. He had looked so much disappointed that Dickie offered hospitality on his own. They had enjoyed a delightful day and caught a great many fish. Swann, in Dickie's opinion, was the best company in the world. Only diffidence prevented Dickie from suggesting another expedition; he did not want to thrust himself upon an older man, a celebrity. He hoped that Swann might make some proposal of the sort, but weeks went by and no word of encouragement came from the great man. This was the first indication that Swann liked or remembered him.

"We shall be delighted to come," he told Martha. "Though I expect the Apollo will be rather above our heads."

Her face clouded. She had her reasons for wishing to stand well with Dickie, but she had not intended to invite his wife. "Little Mrs. Pattison" would, she felt, mix badly with the Elect. Dickie thought that she was shocked at hearing that the Apollo might be above his head and hastened to assure her that he was ready and willing to learn more about contemporary art.

"If people want to learn," she said, "that's everything.

So many don't. I'm glad Mrs. Pattison can come. I was afraid she mightn't be able to leave the baby."

"Oh, for an occasion like this," said Dickie, with enthusiasm, "we can get a sitter."

"Splendid! Nine o'clock. Informal dress. Mr. Pethwick will be coming. You know him, don't you?"

Dickie rushed home to Christina with the news, and was disappointed when she made a face.

"How like Martha Rawson to give other people's parties for them," she said. "Why didn't Mr. Swann ask us himself?"

"I suppose," said Dickie, ". . . it might be rather awkward."

"You mean he hasn't got a proper wife to send invitations? What about the Cucumber? Will she be there?"

This was their name for Swann's lady. It had originated in some primitive joke about concubines.

"I suppose so," said Dickie. "But it would be awkward for her to be hostess, perhaps, so that's why Martha is running the party. You wouldn't mind meeting her, would you, Tina?"

"Oh, well . . . no. Though I'm sure I shan't like her. Married or not, she ought to look after those children better. Such pathetic little things. But what a funny sort of party! In aid of a statue! Will they put it in the lounge and bring us all up to shake hands with it?"

Dickie ignored this crude sarcasm and said, rather solemnly, that the statue would be in the studio.

"We must take care to say the right thing," she continued. "And we mustn't laugh, whatever we do, or they'll look at us as if we were the dog's dinner."

"Swann won't," said Dickie quickly.

She agreed. She also liked Conrad Swann, who did not seem to be at all conceited, in spite of being a genius. She had sat next to him, at the opening of the new Marine Pavilion, and had been frightened out of her wits, until she found how nice and human he was. When the Archdeacon walked into the fountain by mistake, Mr. Swann laughed his head off, and she had been quite as bad until he gave her some chewing gum. You can't chew and giggle, he had said, and that was perfectly true.

"How he puts up with Martha Rawson and her set I can't think," she commented. "Or why he does those awful statues."

"If we knew more about art we mightn't think them awful," said Dickie.

"Dickie! You do annoy me sometimes. We know about art. We've been to Italy and you're always buying Phaidon books."

"Bobbins may think the earth of Mr. Swann's work."

"Oh, no. Even at that age you can tell if a child is going to be mentally deficient."

She continued to scoff at the party until Dickie was secretly relieved when, on Sunday evening, she decided that she could not go. The sitter upon whom she had relied was afraid of going out in the thunder.

"It's you they want, not me, anyway," she said, as they sat down to Sunday supper. "So it's just as well that Mrs. Simpson has failed me, under the circumstances. Or *in* the circumstances, as you say I ought to say."

"Do I? Well, it's right, you know. Circumstances are all round us, not on top of us."

"*Under* is what everybody else says."

"Not everybody."

27

"Everybody we know, unless they're Martha. She just can't talk like other people. Do you remember the time she said she was something of a donkey-hoty? Nobody could think what she meant, except that we agreed with the donkey part of it."

"Martha," said Dickie gravely, "is a keyhotic type."

Christina laughed. She had a delicious laugh, soft and merry, which set her, in Dickie's opinion, above all the other women in East Head. They roared and hooted and tittered. He had begun to fall in love with her on the day when he first noticed that laugh, and told himself that Christina Forbes was not like other girls. She had turned out to be more like them than he originally supposed, but he still loved to hear her laugh.

"Keyhotic!" she said. "That's good."

She made a note of this witticism to pass on to her friends. None of their husbands would have thought of it.

"Thank you," said Dickie. "What is this we're eating? It's very nice."

Christina smiled complacently. She believed that her cooking set her above all the other women in East Head.

"I was wondering when you'd notice. Oh dear! That was quite a flash. It's coming nearer again."

"Are you . . . shall you mind being left alone?"

"Oh, no. Not really. I'm not nervous of thunder. And it would be a shame if you missed your old party. I won't tell you what this is because I can't pronounce it, but we had it in Milan and you liked it. I found the recipe in a magazine."

"It's absolutely delicious."

"It took me some time to get it right. I tried it out at lunch-time before I fed it to you. Ooh!"

28

"Don't sit facing the window if you don't like it."

"Oh, I know it's not dangerous. Only it makes me jump. You know, it's a funny thing, you remember Rita? This, that we are eating, was really the reason why I sacked her. I mean her attitude about it. Just watching her slouch around over her work was bad enough, but when it came to actually criticising *me* . . . 'Ow, Mrs. Pattison! I wonder why you bother!' Some people! The most awful thing they can imagine is having to take a lot of trouble over anything. How can you get anything good if you think saving trouble is more important than what you want to do? But people like Rita! As long as food isn't downright uneatable, as long as it doesn't poison you, they think: it's good enough! It'll do. It'll get by. They don't know what *good* is."

Dickie nodded amiably. He had heard this indictment of Rita before, and was a little tired of it. But he listened without protest, just as Christina listened to him when he complained of his clerk.

Chris was a lovely girl. Her sweet mouth, high cheek bones, and slanting eyes would, he sometimes thought, have delighted Botticelli. He listened and nodded, his thoughts straying elsewhere, while she chattered on. Anybody looking at them through the window, unable to hear the conversation, might have been excused for supposing that he hearkened to the siren's song.

"So I said to her, I said, 'Now Rita! Is there anything . . . anything in the world you *would* take trouble for? In your own house, I mean; or over your clothes or anything?' 'No,' she said. She didn't believe in ever taking any more trouble than she had to. And that meant just enough so that she could say, 'It's not too bad!' I can't stand people who don't even know they're lazy. So I said, 'Bye-bye, Rita! You needn't come after the end of this week.' So now she's washing up in the Blue Kettle. Which is why I never go there. I know what Rita's washing up is like, thank you."

Dickie nodded for the dozenth time, and tried not to see that she was frightened of the lightning, because, if he had to see it, he would not be able to go to the party with a clear conscience. He was still managing not to see it when he went upstairs to change into his best suit.

Bobbins slept soundly in his cot at the foot of their bed. He had kicked off his coverings and lay coiled up with his fists under his chin. Dickie wondered if he would get curvature of the spine, but when he called over the bannisters, to ask if it was all right, Christina said that it was.

"It's the ante-natal attitude," she called, as she carried a tray into the kitchen. "The book says so. Normal at his age."

She did not say that it might be a symptom of retarded development, if it persisted too long, because she did not want to have Dickie ringing up the doctor if Bobbins did not drop the ante-natal attitude on the very night of the correct birthday. "Dr. Browning! Dr. Browning! My son has got retarded development!" Dickie, she considered, took books more seriously than he need. He did not seem to realise that they all say different things, and are always changing what they say. Sensible people merely select what suits them, out of books; they use their own judgment.

She smiled as she shook soap powder into a basin. She was remembering the book which had accompanied them on their honeymoon. Mrs. Hughes, the minister's wife, had given it to them; it was a bright, aseptic little book about the technique of a happy marriage. Christina had refused to look at it, but Dickie read it from cover to cover with earnest attention. The wonder was that he did not actually take it to bed with him, and at last she protested. What could this book have to tell him which he did not know already? She was not the first woman in his life; conscience had driven him to confess as much, when they were engaged.

"I've never been married before," he explained. "This book describes how a girl feels when . . . when she's a bride. It says that some brides are very shy, and the man makes mistakes, and never finds out until it's too late. So the marriage is wrecked."

"Oh, dear! How sad! Poor things! Oh, I do think life is sad. Well, darling, next time you want to have a read in this sa-ad book, you must look in the waste paper basket, for that's where I've put it."

"Tina! The chambermaid might read it."

"She couldn't. She's Italian. And if she could, I expect it would give her a good laugh. If you ask me, she knows more about it than the people who wrote that book."

"I've thought that sometimes," said Dickie, who had caught Angelina's eye once or twice.

"You have? The idea! You've no business to go thinking anything at all about the chambermaid. On your honeymoon, too!"

They eventually got rid of the book by posting it to an imaginary couple, invented by Dickie, a Mr. and Mrs. Huntingtower, who lived in New Brighton and needed advice very badly. As the young Pattisons grew easier together, more secure in their own happiness, they got a good deal of fun out of the fantastic ineptitudes of this luckless pair. Dickie, in soaring spirits, was always inventing a new mistake for them to make, in order to hear Christina laugh.

Nowadays, she reflected, they did not seem to laugh so often. They were not in love, like that, any more. They had settled down. She realised it with a faint pang, the same kind of regret which she sometimes felt for the lost joys of childhood. It was a pity that anything delightful had to end, but she did not want to go back. The present was a great deal more satisfying than the past, for now she had Bobbins.

Yet the regret lingered in her mind. When she went upstairs she kissed Dickie, and told him to have a good time at his party. As she did so, an unusually bright flash made her wince and start. Involuntarily she clung to him.

"I oughtn't to go," he murmured, holding her closer to him, aware of her fear. "You don't really like it, whatever you may say. You hated it last night."

But she was determined not to be selfish. At the back of her mind she knew that Bobbins was not, for him, so complete a compensation for that which they might have lost.

"It was only that one awful flash and crack," she said. "I couldn't believe something hadn't happened. I don't expect there'll be another like that."

He still held her, stirred by the appeal of a frightened woman.

"Do I want to go to this party?" he whispered. "I'll come back early. Don't be asleep when I come back."

"Oh, Dickie! What moments you choose for feeling sentimental!"

At that he released her, chilled, as he often was, by the

32

limitations of her vocabulary. Had she always talked like this? Perhaps she had, in the days when they had laughed so much over poor Mr. and Mrs. Huntingtower, but he had not minded. He had not noticed. He had only heard the siren's song.

He ran downstairs and she stood by the window to watch him go. The night and the storm were closing in. Below her lay the town, cowering down, flattening itself beneath clouds so huge and solid that they seemed to be fighting for room. They piled up, toppling, one upon another. They were pushed earthwards to hide the hills and the sea.

Dickie came briskly out of the house. He did not know that she was watching, so gave no parting wave, but got into his car and drove off, under that menacing sky. He looked spruce and handsome and pleased with himself.

Poor Dickie! she thought.

For no discernible reason she suddenly felt sorry for him, as she sometimes did, when she watched him bustling about the business of life, especially if he seemed to be enjoying himself. That he should often be worried, anxious and disappointed, struck her as more natural. Then she was sympathetic and tried to help him. It was his cheerfulness which made him seem forlorn, which had some mysterious power to wring a sigh from her.

4

Every set has its hangers on, a sprinkling of non-descript enthusiasts who are suffered by their betters because they run errands and fetch the beer. These satellites may be useful, but they contribute no lustre to the constellation, and sometimes they bring it into disrepute. Within the charmed circle they are meek and mannerly; they sit upon the floor and air no opinions. Outside it they make up for this by assuming a borrowed prestige. They boast of their distinguished friends, and offer to the rabble their own version of the current dogma.

Martha Rawson had got three of them: Billy, Rhona and Nell. Billy was the most harmless, since he had a bad stammer and could repeat nothing that he heard. Rhona and Nell were both talkative and silly; they repeated, with considerable inaccuracy, everything that they heard. Rhona was a fat girl with a large nose; she lived near the harbour with a widowed mother, and worked in a folk weaving centre which Martha had inaugurated. Nell had the misfortune to be the daughter of Sir Gregory Manders, the principal landowner of the district, a notoriously disagreeable man. He came of a quarrelsome line and was, moreover, obliged to live in an age which had

divested him of nearly all the power enjoyed by his fore-
bears. Unable to tyrannise, he still did his best to make
himself a nuisance. Poor Nell had suffered all her life from
his universal unpopularity and had been very short of
friends until Martha took her up.

Sir Gregory disapproved of the acquaintance but could
do nothing to prevent it save deny the use of his car to
Nell, whenever she went to see Martha. She therefore
had to foot it on the night of the Summersdown party,
and got down the hill from Chale Park in a series of panic
rushes, since she was terrified of thunder. Rhona, whom
she met by appointment in the town, did not like it
either. They would not have missed the party for anything, but the walk up to Summersdown daunted them.
They staggered for a little way through the empty streets,
clinging to one another, and came to a halt outside the
Cellar Bar of the Metropole Hotel. Rhona suggested that
a drink might pull them together, but neither of them
had any money.

"Let's go in," she suggested. "Somebody might stand
us a drink. I can't go on without one."

"Supposing they didn't," suggested Nell. "We should
look so silly, just standing wistfully there."

Rhona, whose secret ambition it was to be thought a
little devil, decided to face this risk. She pushed Nell
down the steps into the bar, thrust her into the arms of
the nearest man, and announced that her friend was
fainting.

"Could be," he agreed, surveying Nell's white, chinless
face. "You want an ambulance?"

Nell had closed her eyes. She opened them at this
and shut them again hastily, for his ugliness was really

terrifying. He had a face like a gargoyle, crimson, pug-nosed, with abnormally protuberant eyes. Nobody in the bar had ever seen him before, but his appearance had already provoked comment.

"A glass of water . . ." she murmured.

"Water," he told her, "is dangerous in a thunderstorm. Siddown and I'll get you what the doctor ordered."

The prawn's eyes travelled round the room and spied two chairs behind a table in a secluded corner. Timmy Hughes, the son of the Congregational minister, sat in one of them; he always kept out of sight, as much as possible, in the Cellar Bar because his father had forbidden him to go there. The other chair was empty. Nell was brought over and put into it and Timmy was ejected, to make room for Rhona.

"Excuse me, George! Fainting ladies," said the stranger blandly.

"It's worked," whispered Rhona, as their cavalier went off to get drinks.

"But he's such a horrid-looking man, and he's got a cockney accent."

"Don't be so drear. Nothing can happen to the two of us."

Rhona liked to bully Nell, whom she would have had to call Miss Manders in any other circle.

Their friend returned with three double whiskies, sat himself on the table in front of them, and suggested that they were easily scared.

"Actually," said Rhona, nettled, "thunder happens to be the only thing I am scared of."

This should have convinced him that she was a little devil, but he merely asked what she would do if she met a boa-constrictor. Nell, who had swallowed some whiskey, and felt better, replied for her. "Actually I've always been rather fond of snakes. I had a grass snake once, but it got lost."

He started and gave her a sharp look. She said *bin* rather than been, and *lawst* rather than lost. His accent might be cockney, but hers was exceptionally aristocratic. After thinking it over he advised them to go home, as soon as they had finished their drinks.

"It's a fierce night," he said, "and you're both scared cuckoo. Where d'you live?"

Nell looked helplessly at Rhona.

"Here and there," suggested Rhona, with a mysterious smile.

"I see. Just a couple of little waifs. But you must be going somewhere. I've got a car coming. I'm waiting till they find one for me. I could drive you anywhere you want to go."

"Actually," said Nell, "we're going to a party."

"A party, eh?"

He surveyed them from head to foot, taking note of their slacks and untidy horsetails.

"*Gamine* get up," he decided. "A wild, wild party?"

Nell was affronted by his manners but did not know how to snub him when she was drinking his whiskey. She told him that it was not the sort of party he might expect in East Head.

"Me, Gertie? I expect anything, anywhere, any time."

Even Rhona began to feel that he must be sat on.

"You mayn't," she said coldly, "have heard of an Australian sculptor called Swann."

At this his eyes popped more than ever.

37

"Swann? Conrad Swann? It's his party?"

"You have heard of him? He lives here, you know. He's a great friend of ours."

This seemed to make an impression upon him. They told him all about the party. He listened with such an air of bewilderment that Nell kindly explained to him who Apollo was, and what would be wrong with a representational treatment.

"Nobody's seen it yet," she concluded. "Conrad never lets anybody see his stuff till it's finished. So we're all very excited."

"We?" He showed signs of revival. "Who's *we?*"

"His friends here. A few people of his ilk."

"Ilk? What's ilk? Some kind of shell fish?"

"His sort, I mean."

"No. Look it up in Fowler's 'English Usage,' I would."

Nell gaped at him, disconcerted, and exclaimed:

"I can't make you out. I believe you knew who Apollo was, all the time."

"You aren't at your brightest this evening, I expect. My fault, giving you whiskey. If I'd made *you* out sooner, it would have been a mild sherry."

"So you think you've made us out?" cried Rhona archly.

"I think so. At first I took you for a couple of mysteries as the wide boys say. Don't look so flattered. They don't mean what you mean."

Rhona decided not to ask what the wide boys meant, but Nell did. He answered sharply, "Silly kids, who don't know how to look after themselves."

"You aren't very polite," pouted Rhona.

38

"Nothing to what I might have been. You were lucky to pick a family man like me. Your friend's accent is a giveaway."

"Why! What's wrong with it?"

"Nothing's wrong with it. That's the point. Not like mine. What do you make of mine, by the way? Don't blush. A lot of people make the same mistake, but it isn't cockney, as a matter of fact. Go on about Swann's ilks."

"In Venice, last year," began Nell.

"He won a prize for an outsize egg. I know."

"It was a Form," she told him in shocked tones. "But he's getting rather out of that stage now . . ."

She rummaged in the rag-bag of her mind for a phrase and went on glibly, "He used to entirely surrender himself to his material, and let it do things to him. Now he's got much more dynamic."

"Loud cheers!"

"He imposes himself on it now," put in Rhona. "There's a sort of loving brutality . . ."

She broke off, uncertain whether Don Rawson had said this about Conrad, or whether someone else had said it about someone else. Neither of them would have used such a phrase in Martha's presence.

"How come?" asked their host. "What's changed him?"

"A more congenial atmosphere. He used to have a very stupid wife and a lot of children. But she's dead. And now . . ."

Nell kicked Rhona under the table. Rhona shut up.

"Children dead, too?" he asked with interest.

"I mean he has friends now who really appreciate him."

"Meaning the ilks. Who are they? Give!"

They would have liked to give, but whiskey had clouded their ideas and impeded their powers of description. They boasted a little about Alan Wetherby and his Marine Pavilion, and quoted Martha extensively.

"This Martha," he said at last, "is, I take it, Head Ilk. Money?"

"Why, yes," said Nell, surprised. "She has got a great deal of money. How did you guess?"

"Money talks and so does she, apparently. Is it from her you got this line about Conrad's loving brutality?"

"Couldn't I have thought of it myself?" asked Rhona.

"No, Gertie. You never!"

"Why do you call us Gertie?"

"Always call girls Gertie when I don't know their names."

A face appeared in the doorway and stared round the cellar. He seemed to be aware of this, although his back was turned to it.

"That's my car come, I think," he said. "They've taken their time finding one. Come along. I'll drive you there."

They rose and Nell swayed unsteadily. He glanced at her, put a hand under her elbow, and steered her out of the bar. His skill in doing so was remarkable; it looked like gallantry and masked the fact that she really needed support.

A large hired car was waiting outside, in the flickering street. The girls flinched; they had forgotten the storm. He pushed them into the car, sat down between them,

40

and put an arm round each of their waists. As they set off through the crackling glare he advised them to hide their heads on his shoulders.

"I can't make out," complained Nell, as she did so, "whether you're a gentleman or not."

"I'm what your old man probably calls a bounder, as you'll find out, before you're much older. But don't worry. I don't take advantage of mysteries in taxis, especially when they come in pairs. Are you quite sure, now, that you've mentioned everyone who'll be at this party?"

"There's a local yokel coming," said Rhona, "whom Conrad insisted on asking. Conrad does like the most ghastly people sometimes. He's such a simple person. But Martha is quite glad to ask him. She means to bend him to her will."

"Convert him to loving brutality, you mean?"

"He's just a little local solicitor, an utterly provincial type. Completely satisfied with himself and East Head and has no outside interests. But he's on a Committee with Martha, for buying a work of art with some money that was left over from the War Memorial Fund, because the site was presented, so they didn't have to buy it. The Committee eats out of his hand, so Martha thinks it's just as well to butter him up a bit."

"Unfortunately his wife is coming, too," put in Nell. "Martha didn't mean to ask her, but found that she had."

"We've all got to take turns to talk to her in words of one syllable," said Rhona. "She's got a baby and we can ask if it has any teeth, you know. People like that! They don't live. They merely exist."

"And that's everybody?"

41

"That's everybody."

"Swann lives all alone, does he?"

There was a pause. Nell said icily that they were not discussing Conrad's private life.

"So I've noticed. What's wrong with it?"

"Nothing. But . . . he's a very simple person. . . ."

"Is that the theme song of the ilks? Too right! He must be. Very, very, very simple, poor chap. Now open your eyes, because I think we're there. We've stopped at a gate and there's a lot of cars outside it."

He helped them out into the dangerous night. A flash revealed the house and the garden path. They felt their way towards the door.

"It's all dark!" exclaimed Rhona.

"Lights off everywhere," he explained. "The street lighting went off just as we started. You'd have seen, if you hadn't had your eyes shut."

"But it's so quiet," said Nell. "Perhaps the party has been put off. But then . . . all those cars are there!"

A faint glow from a ground floor window was now visible. He took a few steps that way, looked into the room, and then returned to the girls with his report.

"A party all right. All sitting round a solitary candle. Come along. We don't knock, or don't we? Walk in, I should think."

"Oh, no," cried Nell, drawing back. "You can't."

He insisted that he was coming too, and ignored their flustered protests, declaring at last that he had been invited.

"But you don't know Martha?" they both exclaimed.

"I know Conrad. I'm his oldest friend. Honest I am. I've known him since he was a babby. Don't you notice

the accent? I'd have thought you would. He's 'Austril-
ian' too."

"Oh! Oh!" shrieked Nell. "Now I know what you
meant . . ."

"When I said I was no gent? Too right! But don't
worry. You've told me everything I came to find out, and
saved me a lot of trouble."

"You gave us drink," stormed Rhona, "and made us
talk . . ."

A head was suddenly thrust through the lighted window, and a voice demanded:

"Who is that? Who is yelling out there?"

It was a hauntingly beautiful voice, but its exquisite
diction was a little blurred.

"It's Rhona and me . . . and . . . and a friend of
Conrad's. . . ."

"Go away! I don't want you. I don't want anybody.
The party is off, I tell you. Conrad isn't here. He's in
Mexico. Walked out on me and gone to Mexico," sang
the lovely voice. "If it's a surprise to me, why shouldn't
it be a surprise to you? No need for a lot of people coming
and insisting, and insisting, and sitting here, and sitting,
and insisting. I never asked them. But they won't go
away. If they insist, then I insist. We'll see who can insist
the longest."

The stranger moved quietly up to the window, and
asked if Conrad had left an address.

"No. I told you. He's walked out. Left me cold. After
I'd given up everything for him. My career . . . stuck in
this lousy dump . . . sacrificing my career. . . ."

"Why do you think he's gone to Mexico?"

"Why shouldn't he? Mexico is a place, isn't it? People

43

go there, don't they? Conrad's gone there. Why . . .
Frank!"

"Hullo, Liz," he said equably.

The head turned and announced to the room behind,
"It was Frank yelling out there. Frank Archer. My husband."

Then, turning again, it said, "It's no use, Frank. I'm
not coming back to you."

"I wouldn't have anywhere to put you if you did, Liz.
I'm living in two rooms over the shop."

"Why! What's happened to Cheyne Walk?"

"Up for sale."

"For sale? No! Not Cheyne Walk! Not my home!
Frank! You can't do that to me. Sell my lovely home! It's
not like you. It's mean and petty. You're a horror, but you
were never mean."

"All right. Just as you like. I've come to see Conrad's
Apollo. Where is it?"

There was a short silence. Inside the room somebody
coughed nervously.

"You can't," said the voice. "That's what I keep insisting and they keep insisting. It's in the shed, down by
the garage, and there's no light. Do come in, Frank, and
make all these bloody people go away."

He turned to the girls and said, "Come along!"

This time they followed him without protest. Curiosity had prevailed over any fear of what Martha might say.

5

It was only by prodigious determination that Martha had kept the party assembled. Upon learning of Conrad's truancy she had, after a rapid interchange with Don in French, forbidden the guests to disperse. Conrad, she said, could not possibly have gone to Mexico. He had no money and no passport. He might have told Elizabeth that he wished to go there, but this was no proof that he had gone. In all probability he had taken one of his long walks and had forgotten the time, as very simple people are apt to do. He might turn up at any moment, whatever Elizabeth might say to the contrary.

Between Martha and Elizabeth little love had ever been lost. Their smouldering feud now broke into an open contest, in which most of the party took Martha's side, since Elizabeth had always been extremely uncivil to all of them. There was only one rebel, an obscure disciple from Porlock, who, after waiting for a little while, insisted upon going home. Dickie Pattison tried to go with him, but was sharply called to order by Martha.

"No, Mr. Pattison! Sit down! Wait. We haven't seen the Apollo yet. I don't believe it can be in the shed. He would never have put it there, when he knows . . ."

"He put it there on Thursday," snapped Elizabeth.

"Are you sure?" asked Alan Wetherby. "You don't often take that much interest in what Conrad does."

"He got Lobster Charlie to help him carry it down there. He came and asked me for half a crown to give to Lobster Charlie."

This was convincing evidence. Lobster Charlie was known to hawk his wares in Summersdown on Tuesdays and Thursdays.

"Half a crown!" exclaimed Martha. "A shilling would have been ample."

"I hadn't half a crown or a shilling either," said Elizabeth. "I should think it's very heavy. If you like to rupture yourselves, lugging it up from there, I couldn't care less."

Dickie inwardly thanked heaven that Christina had decided not to come. She would not have liked this sort of thing. She would not have understood it. He neither liked nor understood it himself, but his disappointment at Swann's absence had been so great that he had, for some time, taken very little notice of anything else. Christina would have been quicker than he to perceive the truth about the Cucumber, whose condition he had at first ascribed to natural distress and anxiety. For a short time he was sorry for her, bewitched by her beauty and her haunting voice, as once, long ago, he had been bewitched when he saw her upon the London stage. For a scene or two he had thought her the most wonderful actress in the world. And then, as now, disillusionment had stolen upon him. The face and the voice were cheats; she was giving a bad performance. He tried in vain to blame the play. Before the final curtain he had been obliged to think that she could not act. She was no artist.

46

And now, as the evening wore on, he found himself once
again turning against her. Moreover he began to connect
her frequent absences from the room, her unsteady returns,
with his own thirst, with a craving for that refreshment
which had not been offered to her guests. The night was
torrid and he could have done with a drink when he
arrived. He grew quite parched at the thought of all that
Elizabeth must be drinking.

Martha kept him beside her and talked to him about
sewage disposal, a subject which she evidently imagined
would not alarm him. Whenever he grew restive she
promised to show him the Apollo, if he would only wait
a little longer, and he did not know how to explain, without incivility, that he had no wish to see it. Besides, he
was afraid that Christina would laugh at him, if he went
home without seeing anything at all. So he sat on grimly,
thankful at least that the width of the room divided him
from Wetherby's vitriolic ill nature, of which he had seen
quite enough, although their acquaintance was very slight.

Suddenly all the lights went out. In the subsequent
confusion he got away from Martha and went to look
out of the window with a poetess whom everybody called
Carter, although her name was Mrs. Hobhouse. His pre-
vious dealings with this lady had been purely professional.
She had thought that her agent was cheating her, and had
asked his advice. Dickie thought that the boot was on
the other leg and that she owed the disputed commis-
sion, but he could not persuade her of it. All "business
men" were rogues, in her view, and all artists helpless,
unworldly victims. She kept an agent to foil her pub-
lisher, wished Dickie to foil her agent, and would doubtless someday ask somebody else to foil Dickie. Her in-

tegrity, of which she had a good deal to say, by no means obliged her to come across with a ten per cent which she had previously agreed to pay, and she had been very much disgusted with Dickie for telling her that she was in the wrong. A really competent lawyer would, she obviously believed, have helped her to avoid her obligations. But the first rate could not, of course, be demanded in East Head.

She did not seem to have forgiven him. She took no notice when he joined her at the window, but talked to herself in a rapid whisper while they watched the storm. From Summersdown there was a fine view of the Channel and the distant mountains of South Wales. Every few seconds a scribble of lightning raced across the heavens, outlining that distant coast and tinting the water between to a strange shade of pale lilac. "Newport seems to be getting it," he ventured. "I think I see a red glow. It must be a fire."

"A fire," chanted Carter. "Lovely, lovely fire!"

She continued her muttered chant. He heard something about wretched little people, in their smug little bungalows with their lounge suites and television sets. She appeared to have a strong prejudice against them. The flashes revealed her freckles and the petulant sag of her mouth.

"There!" she said suddenly. "That must have hit something. Oh, this is meat and drink to me!"

Drink! thought Dickie. She's lucky.

He looked at his watch. The gesture was observed by Martha, who immediately despatched Don to question him, in English, about the rules of cricket. The evening took on the compulsion of a nightmare, from which he could not free himself. All sorts of strange things began to happen. Elizabeth, after shouting to somebody in the garden, announced that her husband had arrived. On the heels of a particularly loud thunder clap, this husband appeared in their midst, looking very like the demon king in a pantomime, and demanding something to drink.

"There aren't any drinks," snapped Elizabeth. "You take them all away to your house, Martha, and give them drinks there, if they're thirsty."

"There is plenty," protested Martha. "I had a lot sent up yesterday, and I believe some cases of brandy were sent here which ought to have gone to my house."

"We can guess where it's gone by now," muttered Wetherby.

"Billy. You go and find it, and bring glasses."

Billy uncoiled his long limbs from the floor. "W-w-w-w . . ."

"Where? Look in the kitchen. Nell! You go with him."

"I'll go," said Dickie, hastily following Billy from the room.

The house was in darkness, but the resourceful Billy had a torch. He led the way into an evil-smelling cavern haunted by voices, high and far off, raised in a kind of piping drone, like the drip of a gutter. Billy's torch finally came to rest on a sink filled with dirty glasses. He sighed and began to rinse them one by one under the faucet, but had nowhere to put them save back into the sink, since the draining board was stacked high with unwashed dishes.

"You l-l-l-look for the d-d-d . . ."

He vaguely indicated a door and proffered his torch. "But you can't wash glasses in the dark," said Dickie. Billy nodded. It was obviously easier to do so than to look for drink in the dark. Dickie took the torch and opened the door. He seemed to be in another passage. The voices, which had droned on ceaselessly, became much louder. Sometimes it was a single voice, sometimes a piping chorus, and the chant seemed to be coming from behind a small door on his left. He listened but could not at first distinguish words. Then he recognised a phrase in the soft Latin which he had heard in Italian churches: *Gratia ple-e-ena* . . .

"Look outside the back door," said the demon husband, coming from the kitchen. "It's thought that the cases have never been brought in."

"*In mulieribus et benedictus* . . ."

"Godalmighty! What's that?"

The demon flung open the little door. Dickie's torch revealed some kind of broom cupboard with a squirming mass of humanity at the bottom of it. The chant broke off. A cluster of small faces blinked up at the light.

"Scared of the thunder?" suggested the demon.

"No, thank you," replied a voice from the cupboard.

"Oh? Just here for a lark?"

"Nobody in this cupboard is frightened." The voice was beautiful but distinctly bossy. "This is a Holy Cupboard. People in this cupboard are protected by St. Rose of Lima. She saved a whole town out of an earthquake, and she won't let the thunder come in here. Only inreligious people are frightened."

At this moment all the lights came on again.

Everybody said, Oh! A grimy passage was revealed. It was also possible for the inhabitants of the cupboard to see something of their visitors. A fresh voice piped, "That's my daddy."

50

"Could be. Which of you is it? Polly?"

"Did you come in a train?"

"I did. Is Mike there?"

"Serafina's sitting on his head. He's frightened."

After some fresh squirming, another face appeared. It was, like the others, dirty and tear stained. But they were pale and this one was purple with the effects of near-suffocation.

"Hullo, Mike?"

"Hullo?" gasped Mike faintly, and vanished again with a squeal as a fresh roll of thunder shook the house.

"Kindly shut the door," commanded the bossy child. "You're letting a lot of unholiness get in."

The demon shut the door and the chant instantly began again.

"Godalmighty!" he repeated. "Must be one of Swann's kids. Of course, poor Maddy was a Holy Roman. Their mother. But I never knew they were here. They were living with a friend or somebody when . . . could this be the back door, do you suppose?"

He opened a door at the end of the passage. The storm flickered and blazed upon several cases of bottles which lay grouped about the back doorstep. He and Dickie picked one up and carried it into the kitchen, where they found Billy very little further on with his glass washing. In the dark he had been rinsing the same glass over and over again. He was sent out to collect the rest of the bottles, Dickie was put to work at the sink, while the demon mixed the drinks.

Dickie was re-arranging his ideas about the children. He had supposed them all to be Swann's, when they were pointed out to him on the beach one day. Such an exhibition of infant squalor he never wished to see at closer quarters. But it now appeared that four parents might be involved: Swann, "poor Maddy," the demon and the Cucumber? Yet the children seemed to be all pretty much of a size and age. The whole thing sounded very complicated, and the less said to Christina about it the better.

"You know Conrad well?" demanded the demon suddenly.

"No. I never was in this house before."

"Ah . . . You're a solicitor then?"

"Yes," said Dickie, in some surprise.

The demon paused in his drink mixing to stare at Dickie and then he said, "I'm exceedingly fond of Conrad. You may think that strange, but I am."

"I don't," said Dickie, on a sudden impulse. "I like him tremendously myself."

"You do?"

"I don't know him at all well," amended Dickie. "I don't understand his work. But . . ."

The two men exchanged a glance and understood one another immediately. Each had an instant belief in the other's regard for Conrad. It did not seem strange at all.

"I've known him all my life," said the demon. "Though I've not been in touch with him lately. He's ninepence in the shilling about looking after himself, unfortunately. Always has been. All this" —he gestured round the filthy kitchen— "he was quite all right till Maddy died. Snug as a bug in a rug. But she got appendicitis and they didn't catch it in time. Died on the table. Knocked poor Conrad all to pieces, that did."

"I know nothing of his family affairs," said Dickie.

"I'd better tell you. When Maddy died he came to us for a bit, in Cheyne Walk. He has a weak digestion, you know, and we had a good cook. I thought it the best idea, till he'd fixed up some way to live. The kids were boarded out somewhere. But then . . . if he hadn't been all in pieces it wouldn't have happened . . . he bolted with my wife. He must have been *non compos.* Maddy hadn't been dead three weeks. A man does very odd things sometimes when he's lost his woman. I've known other cases. I don't blame him in the least. But it doesn't seem to be working out, does it?"

Dickie's astonishment at these confidences was distracted by interest in the drink mixing. He broke in to say, "You've put one bottle of brandy into that jug already."

"I know. There's plenty of room for more. What we want to do, we want to make this party a howling success. We want to send 'em home so happy they don't remember if Conrad was here or not. These Rawsons . . . they're doing a lot for him, I gather? Mustn't let him quarrel with his bread and butter, till we find out what's happened. You take this tray of glasses in there and start pouring it into them."

"I really think," protested Dickie, "that I ought to be going home. It's nearly . . ."

"Help me to start 'em drinking and then you can go. They're all in filthy tempers and we don't want them to get sore with Conrad. Besides, you could do with a drink yourself."

Dickie felt that he could.

Later, much later, he realised that he had not yet told anybody what he felt about Conrad. This should be set right, since it was Conrad's party, although Conrad had gone to Mexico. Everybody was saying what a splendid fellow Conrad was. But it was difficult to secure attention. Carter and Elizabeth were quarrelling. Billy was asleep. Nell Manders was sobbing bitterly, after some savage snub from Martha. Don Rawson, with most of the party gathered round him, was at the piano, playing and singing the same song over and over again. Martha and Mr. Wetherby sometimes joined in the chorus and some-times argued angrily about existentialism. Frank (they had been Dickie and Frank for the last half hour) was still busy filling glasses. When Dickie approached him he said, "You can go home, now, any time you like, old man."

"The thing about Conrad," said Dickie carefully, "is the thing. He knows how to enjoy himself. Nobody else does."

"Too right, old man. But go home now, I would."

"I don't. So I got married. You got married."

> *"Au bout de cinq ou six semaines*
> *Les vi-vi-vivres ont manqué, qué, qué . . ."*

"A very good wife," said Dickie. "Christina. You know her? Only thing to do if you don't enjoy your-self. Get married."

"Your career!" howled Carter. "As if we didn't all know about that. Your career was packed up years before you raped Conrad. . . ."

Elizabeth flew at her.

Frank hurried to them exclaiming, "Now, now, now girls! No rough stuff!"

Dickie continued his harangue to nobody in particular: "Very good life, very good wife, very good job. Nice town. I like everybody in this town. Only I don't enjoy myself, somehow, solely and simply and solely . . ."

Words eluded him. He had not meant to explain why he did not enjoy himself. That was not mysterious at all, although it was better not to think about it. He had never wanted to come back to East Head and would have told his father so, if his mother had not died just as he was about to insist upon his freedom. He had found it impossible to deal a second blow to the poor old man. No, he did not want to talk about that. He wished to praise Conrad, and to explain that East Head would be quite bearable if such a man was living in it. Had he left East Head he could not have gone fishing with Conrad. He wanted to define the qualities which he had found so attractive, but all that he could manage to say was this:

"He eats because he's hungry and not because it's dinner-time. And if he doesn't want to be here he goes away. Quite right of him to go away tonight. He wouldn't have enjoyed it. I don't know anybody else like that. Very refreshing. I'm not like that. If Tina gave a party, I shouldn't go to Mexico."

He pondered for a while and added, "I shouldn't want to. Tina's parties . . . not so bad as this. Conrad," he told Frank, who was escorting Elizabeth out of the room, "is the only happy man I know."

"Don't you believe it," said Frank. "Steady, Liz."

"He eats when he's hungry," began Dickie.

"Does he? You've seen his kitchen. Right now I'm hoping he hasn't got gastric ulcers."

Frank and Elizabeth vanished.

Dickie continued, "I wouldn't go to Mexico. But I

think it's a very good thing to know a man who goes to Mexico when he doesn't like it where he is. I like to meet people who are like other people. I know too many people who are like me. That's why I get so bored."

Nobody answered. He looked round in surprise and saw Nell Manders crying. Poor thing, he thought, she wants to go to Mexico. He went and sat down beside her.

"Don't cry," he said earnestly. "You're quite young still. You haven't made any mistakes yet. Your life isn't settled."

"I've got no friends," sobbed Nell. "I'm so lonely."

"Nobody has any friends. I haven't got any friends."

"Haven't you? Why haven't you got any friends?"

"I don't know. I had no time when it was the proper time. I didn't mind it up there. Flying, I mean, where I was when I was young. I liked it. But it wasn't a place, and you made friends and they didn't come back. No. You have to be in a place. But after that I was too old."

"They don't really like me. I thought it would be wonderful to know a lot of wonderful people. But they are very unkind to me. They aren't my friends."

"In this place I haven't any friends I chose for myself. I never did anything in my life I chose for myself. All . . . shettled for me. I believe if I could make just one . . ." Dickie, with an effort, got the word out safely, "*decision* . . . about anything at all, I should know who I am."

"But they don't laugh at you. They don't think you're silly?"

"No. They think I'm . . . sen-si-ble!"

"*Le sort tomba sur la plus jeune,*

56

*On la mangea avec les on-on-onions fricassés,
    sés, sés!"*

"Mexico wouldn't make any difference," Dickie assured
her. "We could get it here. All we want is something
. . . first hand. Everything's been . . . done-before! I'm
a product. I'd like to . . . mean-what-I-say-sometimes.
I'd like to . . . do-things-for-reashons. Never thought it
out, or found any . . . rea-sons. Know-what-I-mean?"

"They didn't give me any education," wailed Nell.
"Did they give you any education?"

Dickie did not answer.

She continued, "I went to a rotten school. They were
all going to be Debs at my school, but it costs too much.
Daddy hasn't got any money. Our class hasn't got any
money any more, you know. So he thinks I can get
married without any clothes."

"A product," said Dickie, who had arrived at the answer to her question about his education. "I came off the
. . . ass-em-bly belt!"

He thought this very witty and laughed.

"How can I get married? There isn't anybody of our
class round here that isn't married already, or else they
marry a girl with clothes."

"Don't get married," Dickie warned her. "Great mistake. Ties you. Gets very dull after a bit."

"My own class bores me. I'm not a snob. Why do
people have to be gentlemen? Conrad's not a gentleman.
You're not a gentleman. I wouldn't mind marrying somebody like you a bit. I could have a little house and I could
cook."

"No. Don't cook. Mistake. Too much cooking. We are
not all but stomachs."

"He . . . was . . . herr . . . mayan!

And . . . he . . . done . . . herr . . . wra-ang!"

Don had changed his song, and shed his careful European accent. In spite of Martha's protest he had returned to his boyhood and a sing-song in his home town.

"No, Don! Not funny! Merely adolesh . . . adol . . . we don't think that's funny. No! Not-at-all!"

"Look at Martha!" crowed Rhona, coming up to them. "Ha, ha! Martha's pickled."

Dickie frowned. Even in his cups he was a good fellow. "Don't!" he said. "Not nice. Never like to see it. Not a woman. Mustn't laugh at her."

"She laughs at you. She calls you the local yokel."

Dickie shook his head slowly. "Mistake," he said. "Yokel's a farmer. Must be somebody else."

"She only asked you because she wants to sell Conrad's work."

"He wouldn't. A farmer wouldn't. Only in Holland."

"I'm not talking about farmers."

"Used to go to these fairs and spend thousands of pounds buying pictures. Farmers did. Dutch farmers. Dutch pictures. Not in this century though. Pity."

"You've got to tell all the yokels that Conrad is wizard. They'll listen to you."

"How would I know? Greatest artist in the world . . . very-bad-artist . . . f'rall I know. I couldn't . . . tell anybody anything."

Oblivion was fast advancing upon him but he made a last effort to explain himself:

"I don't know . . . anything-at-all. Don't know if . . . Martha-knows . . . any-thing-at-all. Don't know if any-

58

body knows anything. Except Tina. My wife. You know Tina? She knows . . . everything-she-knows. Quite sure of it. Got her own ideas, Tina. Where'd I get ideas? Do I . . . have-any-ideas? Ideas . . . off the counter . . . off the . . . chain . . . store . . . counter. . . ."

Rhona's face grew very large and shrank again. He suggested that they should go and look for some ideas as soon as it had stopped raining. *Good* ideas, not chainstore ideas. Very nice, the rain sounded, a soothing whisper everywhere and cool drops falling on his face. It was much better than the thunder and the singing.

He liked it, and argued with Frank about getting into the car, because he preferred to sit on the path in the rain and did not feel inclined to drive home. But the car was a very good car. It took him home of its own accord. He had only to get into the back with Nell and go to sleep, while she told Frank how to get to Chale Park.

"It isn't at Chale," he murmured. "It's in the shed."

"We're taking Gertie home first."

The car rushed forward into the rain which was roaring and drumming all over the world. It got to a place where the noise was fainter, a mere background to a loud ticking, like the clock in his hall. *Tick-tock, tick-tock!* Engine trouble, he thought, opening one eye. But it was really the clock after all. He was at home. He was lying beside the umbrella stand.

Tina's white face hovered over him. She was crying. Poor Tina! Nobody had told her that the storm was over. Nobody had told her about the rain.

PART II

Nameless

1

The rain stopped before dawn. The sun rose upon a land refreshed, upon harvest fields and bird song.

These first notes of joy roused the man. He groaned, sat up, and looked round him. The place was unfamiliar. He was sure that he had never seen it before. His glance fell upon rough wooden walls, a wheelbarrow, a scythe, and some birch brooms stacked in a corner. Through the open door he saw grass and sunlight. He had been lying on a hard earth floor, and how he came there he knew not. He knew nothing save that he was cold, hungry and weak.

For a while he drifted upon the brink of the dream from which he had awakened. He did not wish to recapture it, although he was aware that it held something important which he ought not to relinquish. Deliberately he chose to let it go, and, in a matter of seconds all memory evaporated. A blank curtain descended upon everything that had preceded this awakening. He was nothing. He had nothing save gnawing hunger and aching limbs.

Presently he rose and left the place. The early sun shone on wet grass and many tall thin stones which rose up on all sides, at haphazard, throwing strange shadows.

For a time the shadows occupied him, but he did not like the stones. Then, turning, he saw a building. The shed, in which he had spent the night, leant against it, in a net-tled hollow. This building also offended him. There was a solid squareness about the main part of it which ac-corded ill with the stumpy cone above it. He turned his eyes away. A picture came into his mind: bacon on a plate. He wanted that, but in this place of stones and grass there did not seem to be any.

A cock crew triumphantly, and he moved towards the sound as though to a summons. But at one point he turned aside to examine a stone that he liked. It was close to the wall, half hidden in long grass, but it had a better shape than the others and the top of it curved gracefully. There were words on it and his heart warmed as he read them, for he knew that a hand like his own had cut them:

Here Lies

SIMON BENBOW. Ob: 1744.

I know that my Redeemer liveth.

The cock crew again and he went on, through a lych gate into a sleeping village street. There was no food here, but there was a noise which promised food, had al-ways signified food. He knew that, although as yet he made no effort to name the round, smooth, warm shapes which it evoked. This noise had arisen in the same direc-tion in which the cock was crowing: CHOOK! Chook-chook-chook. CHOOK! Chook, chook, chook. . . .

He found a narrow lane leading towards it, between two thatched cottages. Wooden fences railed off gardens.

Beyond them was a meadow full of hen houses. He climbed a gate and found what he wanted in a nesting box behind one of them. They were warm and smooth and brown. He broke the shells and almost laughed with pleasure as they slid down his throat. Five minutes later, feeling much better, he climbed the gate, regained the lane, and wandered back to the street. This was very wide. A strip of grass, planted with pollarded trees, separated the cottages on either side from the road. In the grass he found something that attracted him—two blocks of stone, side by side, one twice the height of the other. He liked their proportions, and sat down upon the lower stone. The climbing sun began to warm his stiff limbs.

Now that his physical discomforts were assuaged the mental blank became a more distressing evil. He wanted to escape from the past, to leave it as far behind him as possible. But he did not know how to advance or where to go. To give a name to anything, even to himself, was to look backwards. He flinched from any name, any word, which was not offered to him *here*.

The village was waking up and with it the sounds of early morning. A dog barked. A pump handle squeaked and whined. Doves cooed on a thatched roof. Some doors were opened and curtains were drawn back from windows. There were, besides, many faint, indefinable sounds—thuds, clanks, humming, far off voices, the whole orchestra of life tuning up. One or two people went down the street and cast looks askance at the queer tramp sitting on the old horse block. But he sat on, motionless, until his ear was greeted by a fresh sound, familiar, reassuring, as much an answer to his needs as the cluck of the hen had been.

Chip . . . chip . . . chip-chip . . . chip . . . chip-chip-chip . . . chip. . . .

He saw the stone, the chisel, the hammer and the hands that held them. He rose and went in search of these things, over the soft wet grass, past the houses. As he went, the sound grew louder: *Chip-chip . . . chip . . . chip. . . .*

The stone, the chisel, the hammer, the hands and the mind, too. A man was thinking. Each pause meant thought, a pondering before the next blow. Ah blessed sound! The earliest, the first sound. He knew now where to go. This was home.

Some way down the street two wooden gates were open upon a yard. A board over the wall announced:

F. TOOMBS. STONEMASON

The yard was full of stone blocks, piled up and leaning against one another. There were several sheds and, at the far end, a dwelling house. In front of the largest shed, close to the gate, sat an old man chipping away at a long smooth stone beam, supported on trestles. The wanderer watched him over the wall. Everything here was familiar; the stones, some rough hewn, some blank, the order amidst confusion, the sheds, the tools, all belonged to a safe world on the far side of that black dream. If only . . . if only he could be inside there, be that man, sitting on that bench, doing that thing. But there was a difficulty about it. A barrier, a danger, kept him outside the wall.

A voice called from the house:
"Frank!"

This, too, was a word of safety. It belonged to the place and had been shouted before in that other yard. *Frank!* he said to himself. *Frank!*

The old man took no notice. He continued to chip, pause, and chip again until a rosy-cheeked young woman came from the house.

"Oh, Dad! Your bacon's getting cold."

Bacon, thought the listener behind the wall.

"In a minute, my girl."

"Mum's creating. She says you didn't ought to work before breakfast, not at your age."

"All very well. I promised Wednesday. Got to be done Wednesday. Not my fault I'm single handed."

The old man put down his tools on the bench beside him, got up, and flexed his arms.

"They're coming for her Wednesday," he said, nodding at the stone. "Be trouble if she ain't done."

The young woman stood beside him and looked at it.

"Looks nice," she commented.

"Not so dusty. Wish they'd left a inch wider space each end though. 'Twould have looked better that way, to my mind. But Mr. Simms, he would know best."

"What's it say? That bit you've done?"

"That's poetry. Says: 'There is no room for death.'"

She sighed and nodded, and then said, "I wish they could have got the licence sooner. So few of the boys remember them now. The boys now were only babies when they went away."

"Boys! Ooagh!" the old man groaned in disgust. "Boys fair give me the sick, these days. Not one of 'em wants to learn a fine decent trade. Why'm I single handed?

66

Who'll do the job when I'm gone? Work with their hands?
Not for Joseph! Clerks! That's what they want to be. . . ."

"Fra-ank!" came the cry from the house.

"All right, Maggie! Coming!"

As the pair moved off down the yard he was saying,
"Though there's premiums offered, premiums mind you,
for any lad that's willing to learn. . . ."

Now the yard was empty. Now the stool was waiting.
Now the hammer and chisels lay idle on the bench.

Inch by inch the watcher crept in until he stood in
front of the stone. He smiled as he read it, for the clear
cutting of the letters delighted him. All was as it should
be, or very nearly. The old man had been right; an inch
more space at either end would have been better. The
stone exclaimed, as though the words were part of it.

This Sports Pavilion has been presented to the boys
of Coombe Bassett by Charles Headley, in memory
of his sons, William Francis and Charles Maurice,
who lost their lives in the Battle of Britain. 1940

Nec morti esse locum, sed viva volare
Sideris in numerum atque alto succedere caelo.

The lettering had been completed as far as *locum*.

The man picked up a chisel and held it in his hand,
staring at it. As yet he had called nothing by name. But a
name now came to him and he whispered it as he fin-
gered the chisel.

"My Redeemer . . ."

At last he sat down upon the stool. For a long while he
looked at the stone. As he considered it he began to whistle. He could not have put words to the tune, but it had

been in the back of his mind ever since he left the churchyard: *I know that my Redeemer liveth. . . .*

Picking up the hammer he began upon the S in *sed.*

Chip . . . chip . . . chip-chip . . . *and He shall stand* . . . chip . . . chip-chip . . . *at the latter day* . . . *chip* . . . *chip* . . . *upon the earth.*

The letter sprang out of the stone. It lived there.

Footsteps passed to and fro outside the yard gates. A car or two drove past. All the village was now wide awake. A wireless loud speaker echoed from an adjoining house with the eight o'clock news. He worked on, concentrated, absorbed, until a furious voice behind him demanded what he was doing. He sprang to his feet and confronted the old man.

"This. . . ." he said, indicating the stone.

Frank Toombs looked at it and whistled. It was, as he saw at once, a very nice bit of work.

"And who might give you leave to do such a thing?" he asked more gently.

There was a long pause. The answer sounded like a question.

"Frank? . . ."

"What d'you mean? I never. . . ."

They stared at each other.

Toombs saw that this man, although he had obviously slept rough, was no tramp. His hands were working hands. His splendid head, the great forehead, the beetling brows and haggard eyes, reminded Toombs of a picture he had seen, some old picture somewhere of a great man. A tramp with a brain box like that would bear signs of drink and degeneration. This man was very pale. He looked ill. But he was no waster.

"Who are you?" demanded Toombs. "What's your name?"

This was the danger point. This was the gulf which had to be crossed. But a bridge now presented itself. The answer was easy. It was given without a moment's hesitation: "Benbow."

PART III

The Friends of the Artist

1

The exertions of Sunday night, the task of keeping the party sweet, of sending it home fuddled but friendly, exhausted Frank Archer. He did not turn up in the Metropole dining room until a quarter to eleven. With one pop of his grey eyes he quenched some suggestion from the waiter that breakfast was off, and ordered kidneys, which were not on the menu. They came. At half past eleven he took a stroll round the town, which he had so far only seen by lightning flashes. It was a small town, and he very soon fetched up in front of its principal attraction, Alan Wetherby's Marine Pavilion.

A long whistle escaped him as he took it in. Turning the corner of the parade and beholding the sea, he had unconsciously expected some cosy little pier with a domed shack at the end of it. There was nothing cosy about this severely functional structure. But they were all exceedingly proud of it. No town in England could boast of anything more up to the minute.

To get inside was no easy task. The engraved glass doors baffled him, as they baffled all visitors, and had baffled the townsfolk during the first week or two. There was a long row of them, immensely tall, through which glimpses could be got of the vestibule within and the shining sea beyond. He tugged and pushed and would have concluded that the place must be shut had he not beheld various strollers inside. Presently two old ladies came up and pushed a knob in the steel frame-work, whereupon a whole door slid silently behind its neighbour, admitted them, and closed after them. He followed their example and got inside, wondering what would happen if the thing shut up again while somebody was standing in the doorway. Upon further investigation, however, he discovered two knobs. One of them held all the doors permanently open, when large crowds were going in and out. The other served scattered entrants on windy days. The whole contrivance prevented unnecessary draughts.

He found himself in a vestibule which ran the whole width of the building. Its northern wall, opposite the doors, was constructed entirely of glass, and looked over the Channel to Wales. Some thirty feet short of this glass wall the vestibule floor fell away into a double staircase, wide shallow steps, leading down to doors which gave on to the sea terrace. The view from the vestibule was thus deprived of all foreground. Air conditioning made the whole building a trifle over-warm. This clement, unstirred ambience struck Archer as unnatural; it provided too violent a contrast to the cold north light, the boisterous spectacle of wind and sea. He found himself perversely wishing for a draught or two, for some indication that Nature was too much for Wetherby. There was none. The outer world, segregated behind mammoth sheets of glass, might be seen but not felt.

On the right was another row of doors, leading into a hall which would seat two thousand people. On the left were various entrances to lounges, libraries and a café.

The floor, a deep azure with a high polish, was made of some material which had obviously been poured upon it and allowed to set. It reflected the scene like a mill pond, but it was not slippery. Age, infirmity and the toddler were safe upon it.

Between the two divisions of the staircase ran a long, low balustrade and, in front of it, was a semicircular space filled with potted plants. Something was needed, he thought, to stick up in the middle of this—some piece of sculpture. East Head would, no doubt, get one in time, as up to the minute as its setting. He next poked his pug nose against the glass doors of the hall, which was dark and shrouded. Posters told him of forthcoming attractions. The East Head Players were shortly offering a performance in aid of the Life Boat Fund.

A name on this announcement caught his eye, Richard Pattison! The local yokel? Could it be that the yokel was playing the part of the convict in *The Bishop's Candlesticks?* It could easily, mused Archer, for this part falls invariably to the pleasantest young fellow in town. This convict, this tough lone wolf, has an irresistible attraction for upright, eupeptic men who pass the offertory bag in church. How wistfully do they portray an ostracism which can never be theirs! *There was a woman . . .* they mutter. *I think she was my wife.* How wonderful not to be quite sure about it! And their undoubted wives, sitting in the front row of the auditorium, look decorously at their laps, hoping that this dangerous line may be got over without exciting giggles among their acquaintance. Archer knew all about small towns and their ways, for he had grown up in one, and it had possessed a dramatic society. He had played a few small parts himself, but looked far too much like a villain to be given the role of the convict. People preferred to laugh at him.

Having now mastered the spell of the doors, he released himself without difficulty onto the lower sea terrace, whence steps led him to the beach. This was unattractive, a vast expanse of mud and slimy rocks. Wetherby's Pavilion towered above it, and prisoners within, on various levels, peered out through glass walls at the sea. They looked small and helpless. In the Channel several coasters were bobbing up and down. The wind had freshened since the storm. The town, behind the Pavilion, sprawled up the twin humps of Bay Hill and Summersdown. Motor coaches, like huge beetles, crept along the coastal road.

The beach was almost deserted save for a few groups of children, playing in the sparse patches of sand. Among them he presently recognised his own, trailing disconsolately over the mud with the three little Swanns. He decided not to accost them, since they did not seem to recognise him. He did not care for children. His own childhood had been so wretched that he flinched from any association which could remind him of it. He had nothing to say to Polly and Mike, save to apologise for begetting them and for having allowed them to be starved at East Head. He sighed, left the beach, and returned to the Metropole for lunch.

By two o'clock he was up at Summersdown. He judged that Elizabeth's hangover would be, by now, sufficiently abated for rational conversation. The house had its customary deserted appearance. He went upstairs and found her moaning upon her bed.

"Is it really you?" she asked, peering at him with bloodshot eyes. "I thought you were there last night. . . . Oh, Christ! My head!"

"I'll get you some coffee," he suggested.

The kitchen looked even dirtier by daylight. He managed to brew some coffee and took it upstairs on a tray. She was now sitting up, a little recovered, haggard, yellow and waspish, but as reasonable as he could ever hope to find her.

"Why are you here?" she asked, as he gave her a cup. "I don't remember a thing, not a damn thing about last night. I was terribly upset. Conrad has left me. Did I tell you?"

"Frequently. Do you think he's gone for good?"

"I wouldn't know. I couldn't care less if he has. It's been all packed up between Conrad and me for some time. It was the way he went that upset me."

This had a familiar ring. No man had ever gone in a way which did not upset her. Presently she added, "But you, Frank? What are you doing here? You've left it rather late, haven't you, if you've come to fetch me home?"

As she spoke, hope flickered in her sad eyes. She longed to hear that he wanted her back.

"I came," he said, "because Conrad wrote and asked me to come. Quite a long letter. The longest I've ever had from him."

"He never! It takes him all day to write a post card."

"He wrote it three weeks ago. But I only got it on Saturday. I've been in the States and my mail was kept for me. I came at once. But before I show you the letter——"

"All about me, I suppose."

76

"Barely a word about you. But before we get on to that, I want to say something about the twins. I've seen them. I think they'd do better in school."

"I daresay they would. But do you mean that Conrad——"

"So I'll fix that, shall I? Find a school and make all the arrangements. And, when I send for them, you'll let them go without kicking up a fuss, see?"

"All right. But you may as well know that what you pay me for their keep is damn all we any of us have to live on."

"I had that idea. It was meant for two children, not five."

"Too right, as you would say. But I never expected that Conrad's children would be dumped on us. It quite spoilt the pattern. What I'll do for money now I don't know, if Conrad has really skipped. He could always raise the wind with the Rawsons. I suppose I'd better go back to the stage."

There was a pause. They both knew that she could not. Her reputation for unreliability outweighed her undoubted talent, and she was most unlikely to get a job. She had fallen behind. She was growing old. Her box-office appeal was as outmoded as her oaths and her slang.

"So that's one thing settled," he said at last. "Now . . . Conrad's letter. You'd better read it."

He proffered her several sheets of expensive note-paper.

"Funny!" she exclaimed, taking them. "I've lived with him for two years, and I don't believe I've ever read a letter of his. He's got nice writing, hasn't he? Beautiful! How odd."

"Not at all. He never has any difficulty in using his

77

hands. It's words that bother him. Who lives at The Moorings?"

He pointed to the address on the notepaper.

"The Rawsons. Why . . . did you think we lived there?"

"No. I supposed he'd pinched some letter paper from rich friends, and I wondered if he has any, except the Rawsons."

Elizabeth began to read the letter. While she did so he wondered how soon he might expect her back at Cheyne Walk. Some pretence at getting a job seemed to be essential to her self-respect. But she would eventually turn to him for shelter, countenance and protection, and he would not refuse it, although he never intended to live with her again. He felt obscurely responsible for her troubles, since he had never loved her as much as he loved Conrad. She read:

Dear Frank:

Can you come to East Head as soon as you can, because I ergently need your opinion. It is the Appollo I have been doing for Gressington. You must no all about that competition. I cannot make up my mind about it. Sometimes I think it is no good and if it is no good I would rather not send it to Gressington. The subject does not interest me but I would like the money. They have given me some books to read about Appollo but the subject does not interest me. Sometimes I think it is all right though. If it is wrong you will see it at once. I shall be gided intirely by you. If you say send it to Gressington it goes, if not

78

not. When I am not sure in my mind I have always relied on your opinion. Though you are generally wrong if we disagree when I am sure in my mind.

I am not happy in my work lately. But this may be because I have indegestion. I never was ill before. I think it is the meals. We have got no cook. We are all rather ill, I think, and it will be a good thing when we can get away from here. There is nothing to do when I am not working except sail a yot which is expensive.

If you feel that you would rather never see me again that is very reasonable. In that case do not bother to anser this letter. If you would like to see the Appollo but do not want to see her, it will be all right if you come early in the morning because she does not get up till the afternoon. You could come to the studio and say what you think and go away again and she would never know that you had been. You could tell me if I am really going out of my mind.

I have read this letter over and see that I have made several very stupid speling mistakes. But I cannot write it again because I have no more paper. I never spell well but these are idiotic. Can you wonder that I wonder about my work? You will see what I mean about going out of my mind. Of course I meant to write urgently, and know, and guided, and answer, and yatch. I repeat: Your decision about Appollo is decisive.

Yours ever,
Conrad

"Well," she said, giving the letter back, "it reads to me as if he's going crackers."

"It struck me that way. Where's he gone, do you think?"

"He's been talking a lot about Mexico."

"Oh, be your age! It'd be a wonder if he had the price of a ticket to Bristol. When did you last see him?"

She screwed up her eyes, trying to remember.

"Oh, God! I don't know. I don't believe I've seen him since Thursday, when he asked me for half a crown."

"Where does he sleep, then?"

"In the studio, more often than not."

"It didn't strike you that he was going out of his mind?"

"God, no!" she cried, startled. "I mean, I've thought he was mad for months. But . . . but . . . you don't really think . . ."

"This letter," he said, striking the pages with a thick forefinger, "frightens me. The spelling mistakes are not normal, even for Conrad. It sounds to me as if he's going cuckoo, though he's making a fight for it. Now he's disappeared. I'm wondering if he mayn't have lost his memory and be wandering about."

"Sweet Jesus! What a mess! But you don't mean really mad. Not delusions. It's a reasonable letter."

"Perhaps I should have said a nervous break-down."

"Nonsense. Conrad is not that type. He's too primitive, too virile."

"Primitive virile types get very bad ones, if they get them at all."

"Oh, no! I've had three myself. They never affected my spelling. I merely got so I couldn't stop crying."

80

"You were taken in time. I mean to start looking for him at once, as discreetly as I can. We don't want a lot of publicity. Can you think of anything to help me. Where would he go?"

"Oh, dear! I've been so miserable myself lately that I've hardly noticed what was happening to anybody else."

"You never do that, even when you aren't miserable."

"You're much fonder of him than you ever were of me."

"If I'd ever been any fonder of you than I once was, Liz, it's I who'd be in the bin by now. You don't deserve more."

She made such a violent gesture of impatience that she nearly upset the coffee tray.

"All my life," she wailed, "I've given love and never had any. Nobody has loved me. Not as I mean it. Look at Conrad! Look at what I gave up for him . . . for this. This! Oh, I can't tell you, I just can't tell you, what it's been. The squalor. The loneliness. Nobody to speak to. Literally nobody. Conrad always working. I don't call those friends of his human beings. I'd have kicked that bitch Martha out of the house months ago if we hadn't depended, absolutely depended, on her for our dinner. Why do these things have to happen to me? Why does nobody love me? It's the last straw, lying here, listening to you going on about your precious Conrad, as if it was all my fault."

"I don't say it was all your fault. I shouldn't have brought him to Cheyne Walk. But I never thought you'd take a fancy to him. He's no oil painting, and you usen't to like him."

Elizabeth cheered up a little, as she recalled a past which had, at least, been dramatic.

"Oh, it was just one of those things," she mused. "It all flared up in a minute. I came in one evening; I'd been to a party . . . such a dull party . . ."

"You told me all about it at the time."

"And of course, Conrad was—is—wonderful in a way. He . . ."

"*Shut up!*"

"At least you can't accuse me of concealing things."

"I don't. But you must agree, now, that running off with him was the worst day's work you ever did in your life."

"For me perhaps," she snapped. "He's all right. I don't seem to have come between you."

He walked up and down, considering the tasks before him.

"First things first," he decided. "Now I'm here I'll see this Apollo. Where is it? Brush up your brains, like a good girl, and tell me."

"I suppose the Apollo must be still in the shed, next to the garage. He put it there for the lorry to come and take it to Gressington. Martha sees to all that."

"His letter gives me authority. If I don't think it does him credit, it shan't go."

"Please yourself. I couldn't care . . ."

"Then I'll find a school for the twins. I'll send for them. It mayn't be for a week or two, though, as I have to go to Rome on Wednesday. Meanwhile . . . you'll want something to carry on with, I imagine."

He took out his wallet and extracted a thick wad of notes.

"If I thought you cared a bean for me," she said, "I'd throw it back in your face. But this is all part of looking after Conrad, isn't it?"

She gave him one of her rare smiles, sweet and candid. As always, he was disarmed by it.

"Thank you," she added.

"You'd better count them."

"Why? You can tell me how much it is. I'm sure you know."

"You take the trouble to count them."

Slowly, for the notes stuck together and her fingers were all thumbs this morning, she began to strew her eiderdown with his largesse. Her cheeks flushed slightly with pleasure, at the sight of so much plenty, and her hair swung forward, hiding hollows and shadows. It was not the bright soft hair that it had once been, and it needed washing. But there was, for a moment, a look upon her which recalled the lovely, gifted, hapless creature whom he had married fourteen years ago.

She must be all of thirty-five, he thought, and she looks fifty. She's gone a long way down hill in two years. Could I ever have done anything . . . ?

He knew that he never could, although he might have done better for himself had he divorced and forgotten her thirteen years before. Her egotism was not a normal or curable failing; it was a disease which must eventually destroy her. If he blamed himself for anything it was for his self-deception during a middle period, when he had tried to believe that they were settling down at last. He had been fool enough to accept her theory that she needed a child, and obliged her with two, which was one too many, since she regarded twins as a very bad joke.

They should never have been born and the time was at hand when he ought to take them away from her.

"That's better than a poke in the eye," she said as she joyfully bundled up the notes. "You can afford it, I suppose?"

"Yes. I can afford it."

"How are you getting along these days? You've got a nice girl friend I hope?"

"Kind of you. I get along all right."

"I never can understand why you don't divorce me."

"Oh, I don't know. Girl friends get swelled heads if a man is free."

She laughed.

"Some sense in that. Nobody can drag you to the altar. Frank! It may be a dream . . . but I've a dim recollection that you said something last night about selling Cheyne Walk."

"I did. But I won't, if you'd rather I didn't. The Grays are there, caretaking."

She looked thoughtful. After a while she said slowly, "Then, if you're not there, and I wanted to come up and see about getting a job . . ."

"Go there by all means. The Grays will look after you."

"Oh, dear! It would have been so nice for me and Conrad . . ."

"No," he said firmly. "Not for you and Conrad. That I shouldn't have allowed. Now I'm off. Goodbye."

He had got as far as the door when she called him back.

"Just why," she demanded fiercely, "are you so demented about Conrad? What is it all about? I've never been able to understand it. Good heavens! If I didn't

84

know you both so well I'd have thought you must be queer."

"Queerer than you can possibly think."

Elizabeth, he well knew, was as likely to master the calculus as to grasp the idea of a disinterested attachment.

"We've been friends for a very long time," he suggested.

"Oh, I know. Ever since your boyhoods, out back in Boogie Woogie, or wherever it was you came from. But you weren't born that way? Or were you? When did it start?"

"I suppose it was because he liked me. Very few people do you know."

"Oh, Frank!"

But her protest was perfunctory. He had spoken the truth. Very few people did like him.

"It's because you expect them not to," she said. "You mind too much about your face."

"I daresay. It's stupid. But I began so young I can't get out of the habit. I was a revoltingly hideous child and I lived among people who made no bones about telling me so. I only had to poke my little mug round the door to send everybody into stitches. And I had these teeth. Stuck straight out of my face like a shelf. At least I got that fixed as soon as I had some cash."

"Why . . . you must have been worse than our twins!"

"Much worse. You did your bit to tone them down. I was a monster. And I minded."

"I suppose you did. You're damned sensitive really."

"Conrad liked my looks. Positively liked them! When we were about twelve he made a putty head of me, an excellent likeness, eyes, teeth, everything, yet extremely agreeable somehow. Was I grateful? I felt I could bear my face. It was one of the first heads he did; he'd begun by doing animals. I thought him a genius, naturally. I pushed him into thinking he wanted to go to Europe. They told us that a genius always starves. So we got it all worked out. He was to make heads. I was to make a lot of money and buy them."

She sighed and gave him another of her smiles.

"I'm glad you've come across with that," she said, "after all these years. Poor little you! And the teeth, too. I could cry. But funny, because it all worked out. I suppose you'd never have been an art dealer if it hadn't been for Conrad."

"Never. I'd have made a packet some other way, I suppose. An ugly man can sell anything to anybody. But it's Conrad's doing that I don't think Giorgione must be some kind of cheese."

She laughed and waved him a friendly farewell.

We are more intimate now, he thought, as he went out to the shed, than we ever were. I couldn't have told her that when I loved her. Heaven knows what I'll tell her when she's in the bin and I go to see her—how I'll bare my soul, during her lucid intervals. Truth among the ruins . . .

2

On Monday evening *The Bishop's Candlesticks* was to be rehearsed at the Pattisons' house. Dickie and Christina had supper early; it was the first solid meal that he had been able to eat that day, for his hangover had been severe and he had not been able to go to the office.

The town was ringing with accounts of the party, which outshone the storm as a topic for discussion. Neighbours in Summersdown had been awakened at three o'clock in the morning by people shouting and singing in the road. Various stories were going about. Loyalty to Conrad was somewhat relaxed among his adherents and not all of them observed Martha's ban upon gossip. They had been promised the Apollo and had been given, instead, headaches of varying severity. But their recollections were hazy. All agreed that a terrific orgy had taken place and that Elizabeth's husband was responsible for it. Some said that he had forced his way into the house and thrown out Conrad. Others asserted that Conrad had run away for fear of a horsewhipping. Those who had left before the end were quite positive that they had not seen the Apollo. One or two, among the more persistent revellers, believed that they had, but could give no clear account of it. Nobody knew for certain whether it had been Martha who made all that noise in the road, but everybody hoped that it might have been.

On any other day in the week Christina would have heard all this in the morning over a cup of coffee in the Pavilion. But Monday was her washing day and she heard no news until the afternoon when her friend, Allie Newman, ran in for a few minutes. Allie was the wife of Dr. Browning's partner and the sister of Timmy Hughes, that furtive frequenter of the Cellar Bar. Her parents had been very intimate with Christina's mother; the two girls had been "best friends" from their cradles. Nothing had disturbed their alliance until Dickie returned to East Head. Nor were they much divided during the years when they sighed for him in vain. A good many other girls were in the same boat and they could all suffer together without any sense of rivalry. But then Christina got him. Despite his obvious determination to remain a free man, he began to listen to her when she laughed. Allie observed it, and immediately married young Dr. Newman, of whom she was reasonably fond, because she could not endure the idea of walking up the aisle as Christina's bridesmaid. Christina was very well aware of this, and walked up the aisle as Allie's bridesmaid with perfect complacency. They still believed themselves to be friends. But Allie was the last person from whom Christina wanted to hear details of this horrible party, the last person to whom she liked to confess that Dickie had come home very late—well, yes, as drunk as a lord—that he had a terrible hangover, and had, so far, told her nothing about it.

"Aren't they awful!" said Allie sympathetically. "I get it when Paddy comes home after a Masonic dinner."

Her grimace suggested that all husbands are alike and that Christina had not done so very much better for herself than anybody else. Christina writhed and resolved to take it out of Dickie.

He could not, in any case, have told her much, because he remembered very little. He was desperately ashamed of himself. He had been drunk before, once or twice in his life, but only upon excusable occasions and never since his marriage. It shocked him deeply to think that his wife should have been obliged to put him to bed, that he had left her all alone and frightened for hours while he made a beast of himself. She had, he felt, every right to be furious and he was most anxious to apologise, if allowed an opportunity. He got none. She would not even permit him to say that his conduct had been bestial. Not at all. If he must know what she thought, when she found him lying on the mat, he had better understand that a man in such a condition is generally rather pathetic. No, she was not angry. She was sorry for him. He need say no more about it.

Free and full forgiveness is the good woman's most formidable weapon. Nothing makes a man feel smaller; yet few husbands have the brutality, or the strength of mind, to reject it. Christina was aware of its essential unfairness, but she was really very angry.

By suppertime he had recovered enough to enjoy his food. Throughout the meal they talked warily about a rock garden which they planned to make. It was not until they got to their caramel custard that the passions, raging beneath this calm domesticity, got out of hand.

A pebble, dislodged, set off an avalanche. Dickie had no interest whatever in the queer behaviour of Sam

Dale's sister-in-law. She was a very dull woman, but she came from London, and did strange things. Now, according to Allie Newman, she was sending her husband and children to a guest house, for three weeks, while she went into a nursing home for a minor operation.

"Why not?" asked Dickie. "If they have no maid. The children are too young to cook, and all that sort of thing."

"She could manage!' cried Christina. "Neighbours would help. Why! When Bobbins was born you never had to go out to a single meal. I had everything arranged beforehand."

Dickie remembered. His home, when Bobbins was born, had been invaded by relays of neighbours who hid his razors, mixed up his books, and were forever offering him cups of tea. He would much rather have eaten out.

"We'd have all gone in and helped," said Christina. "She could have worked it out."

"But why should she put you to such unnecessary trouble?" objected Dickie. "You're all very busy women. In an emergency you'd help, of course. But how much simpler just to go to a guest house and not make these demands on friends."

"Dickie! Think of the expense!"

"Oh, I expect they can afford it. Ted Dale is doing very well. And anyway, that's their business."

"It isn't only the money. It looks so queer. Any other woman would be ashamed to do it. As if she couldn't manage. . . . You don't understand. Men don't."

"Perhaps not."

"I suppose it's what they do in London. It looks very funny to us. We don't do it. It's never been done here."

90

For all Dickie cared, Mrs. Ted Dale might throw her family into the sea. He was so little prepared to lose his temper that his habitual guard was relaxed. The words popped out before he knew what he had said.

"Must we be so provincial?"

"What?"

Christina looked bewildered.

Now he had done it. After months of self-control, fully aware that such a question would be futile and dangerous, he had asked it.

"What do you mean? Provincial?" she asked, flushing.

"Oh . . . forget it! Sorry! I daresay you're quite right. Hadn't we better clear? We've got to move the furniture in the . . . er . . . sitting room."

He had hesitated because she preferred to call this room the lounge. At happier moments they had argued, joked about it; they had compromised by calling it the front room, the best room, or the parlour, when they were in a merry mood. Just now he wished to placate her, but he did not really like *lounge,* and could not bring himself to say it.

"I don't want to be anything but what I am," stated Christina. "I live in the provinces. I was born in the provinces. I don't want to pretend otherwise. I see nothing to be ashamed of."

"So I'm answered," said Dickie. "I said must you? You say you must."

"You said must *we!* You're just as provincial but you're ashamed of it for some reason."

Dickie stacked the dishes in silence and carried them into the kitchen. He could say nothing to get them out of this quandary; any attempt to define the dreadful word would be dangerous. He must just wait until the storm blew over.

The Pattison kitchen so little resembled the Swann kitchen as to deserve a different name altogether. It was a pleasant, orderly place. Christina had stamped herself upon it, for it was the scene of her adventures and her triumphs. The pots and pans were cherished; they were her private and prized implements. Her cookery books did not toss about untidily in the dresser drawer. They were arranged upon a little shelf and, with them, were several notebooks into which she had copied recipes in her neat, immature handwriting. There was a smell of herbs and spices and the subtle memory of many excellent meals.

He put the tray down and glanced at a magazine which lay beside her knitting, open at the headline: WHAT THE STARS FORETELL FOR YOU THIS WEEK.

How can she? he wondered, and lost no time in looking to see what the stars foretold for him that week. What nonsense! He would have consulted the stars for Bobbins had she not come in, whereupon he moved hastily away and turned on the sink tap.

Her eyes were blazing. She had been looking up "provincial" in the dictionary.

"I know I'm rustic and narrow," she said, "but I don't like to see a man washing up. I think it's a woman's work. I daresay it's different in London. Will you go and clear the lounge, if I may be allowed to call it that?"

He shrugged his shoulders and obeyed her. Presently a great bumping of furniture was to be heard in that nameless room. A space approximate to the size of the stage had to be cleared.

Christina whipped an apron over her dress and set swiftly to work on the washing up. Never in her life had anything so insulting been said to her.

(1) Appertaining to the provinces. (2) Rustic, countrified, narrow, illiberal. (3) Something religious which could not possibly apply.

Illiberal! When she had been an angel of patience all day. Narrow! What other woman in East Head would have put up with his behaviour last night? Rustic! Countrified! He had a hangover, he was in a filthy temper, and so he took it out on her. He was ashamed of being provincial, was he? So he made all this fuss about lounges, and *in the circumstances,* and listening to the Third Programme, and mooning round art galleries, and going to get drunk with Martha Rawson! It was one thing to try to be a companion to him, but quite another to abet him in this kind of conceited nonsense.

When she went into the hall the bumping had ceased. A voice in the lounge was dramatically snarling something about *"the hell of Deveel's Island!"* Dickie was rehearsing his part.

She tidied some letters on the hall table and hoped that he would not make too many faces. It always embarrassed her to watch him act because he made such unnatural faces. Everybody said he was a splendid actor but, to her, it was only Dickie making faces and pretending to be somebody else. She sometimes wondered if the wives of real actors felt like this. But real actors did not make faces or seem to be pretending.

Dickie himself was quite certain that he could not act at all. He was only taking this part because nobody else was available, and the Life Boat Fund was a good cause. And that, she reflected, was a nice thing about Dickie. He might have these exasperating ideas, but he was always obliging, and ready to take part in things, and very pleasant to everybody. Nobody could call him stuck up in his manners. Also he was unselfish. He had not wanted to act, and had hoped that they would let him look after the lighting. The switch-board in the Pavilion hall fascinated him. He would have loved to spend a whole evening manipulating the floats, the battens, the ambers, the blues and the spots.

Ah, men! she thought, softened. Just babies really! He didn't mean it. He was in a paddy. I'll forgive him. But he'll have to apologise quite a lot before I do.

The front door bell chimed and Dickie bounced out of the lounge. Upon the doorstep were assembled four people: Allie Newman, Mrs. Hughes, who had come to prompt, Mrs. Selby, the wife of the bank manager, and Mr. Prescott, the editor of the East Head *Gazette*. They all went chattering into the lounge. Something, said Mr. Prescott, had been struck after all. A tree up at Summersdown. The news had just come in.

"Not that old tree in the field behind Swann's?" exclaimed Christina.

Nobody seemed to know. She hoped not, for the poor little Swann children would miss it dreadfully. They had been so touching, with their ladder and that wobbly old chair. She was just upon the point of wondering what might have happened to the chair, when the tree was struck, but Mrs. Hughes expressed a wish to go up and look at Bobbins, and the question was never posed.

Dickie wandered round the room, offering cigarettes and smiling as hard as he could. He knew that they would

94

not begin to rehearse for another twenty minutes. There was always this ritual of punctuality followed by an interval of aimless dawdling. Some mysterious canon of good manners imposed it. To be too prompt and businesslike would have been considered unsociable. It would be midnight, at this rate, before they all went away, and he wanted to make it up with Christina as soon as possible.

He had thought about this while he was moving the furniture. There was nothing to be said, but possibly something to be done. As soon as he had got her to himself he would make love to her so manfully that she would be obliged to forget all about it. He had, perhaps, been careless lately. Last night he had left her to await him in vain, after promising an early return. That was enough to infuriate any woman. But he would make up for it. As soon as the door was shut upon the last of these bores, he would give her ample reassurance. Nor would she find him pathetic at all. He was looking forward to it. In fact he hardly knew how to wait.

Now, at last, Mrs. Selby had actually mentioned the play and was complaining about a line in her part.

"Do I say my little dot or my little doe? I'm supposed to be French, but they might think I was talking about an animal."

"Or pie crust," said Allie.

"Not many people here will know what it means," said Mrs. Selby. "Couldn't I alter it and say my little dowry?"

Mr. Prescott looked solemn.

"When I produce," he said, "I never allow the text to be altered. I think you'll find it quite easy, Mrs. Selby, when you've got into the skin of the part."

Getting into the skin of a part was Mr. Prescott's hobby horse. He was fanatically attached to the Drama. He began now to lay down the law about it and Dickie heard these well-known maxims with relief, since they heralded the end of the social overture. They were still going on when a ring at the door took him out into the hall, to admit a late arrival.

This was Mr. White, a newcomer to the town, a clerk at the gas-works. He was very much pleased to be acting in the play because he was anxious to know more people. He was already apologising when Dickie opened the door: "I hope I'm not frightfully late. The Johndarm doesn't come in till the end, so I thought they could begin, without waiting for me. My landlady wouldn't give me an early supper."

He gazed with humble admiration at Dickie, who was so important a person in East Head. Dickie smiled his nice smile and explained that they had not begun yet.

"You're with Ma Cox in Exton Street, aren't you? She's a terror. Everybody has to go to her at first, till better digs turn up. You won't be there long."

White's anxiety was allayed. Going to awful Mrs. Cox had not, after all, been so very stupid. Everybody had done it. He was treading the appointed path in this new community, and he was pleased to hear Mr. Pattison call her Ma Cox. Not every man in his position would have done so, or talked the language of smaller fry as though he might have been through it all himself. No wonder everybody liked him!

After showing the Johndarm into the lounge Dickie stood in the hall for a moment, fighting off depression. *Ma Cox!* I don't generally call her that. I said it on purpose to cheer poor White up. What a good fellow I am! Saying the right thing to everybody. Mexico. . . .

A door opened upstairs. Christina and Mrs. Hughes were returning from their inspection of Bobbins.

"I shouldn't have allowed it," Christina was saying. "But I shan't let it happen again."

"It doesn't do," said Mrs. Hughes, "to try to order them about too much, you know, dear."

"Oh, I've been very tactful. Very nice about it. That strengthens my position. But I won't have Dickie getting in with people like that. . . ."

Dickie, aware that he was eavesdropping, bolted back into the lounge. He took his part and retired with it into a corner, pretending to learn it. Not tonight, not just yet, could he make it up with Christina. *I shouldn't have allowed it. . . . That strengthens my position. . . .* His ardour had completely evaporated.

"What awful faces Dickie is making," whispered Mrs. Hughes to Christina, who sat beside her in the window seat. "Look how he's scowling!"

"He always does in a play," replied Christina, and added with a giggle, "He's getting into the skin of his part."

3

Wetherby's Pavilion had put sixpence on the rates, and all citizens of substance had therefore a strong motive for regarding it as an amenity. To patronise the Pavilion Café, especially during the morning, had become a matter of principle.

In the old days the morning rendezvous had been the Mandalay in Market Street. There a dark and stuffy labyrinth of small, low-ceilinged rooms, smelling strongly of coffee, and lit by rose-coloured lamps, had provided a background for the natural pattern of local society. Friends foregathered, lovers trysted, news was exchanged and plans were hatched, in twenty secluded corners. Much went on, and not all of it was laid bare immediately. The first news of pregnancies was whispered over these coffee tables, and so, in oblique murmurs, was the truth about fatal diseases. It was to the Mandalay that invalids and the bereaved first ventured on the return of health or spirits. To be seen there, to be welcomed, was a signal of recovery.

In that narcotic atmosphere there were more reconciliations than quarrels. Scandals were doubtless born and circulated, but, at certain tables where the kindest hearts presided, spiteful rumours were frequently contradicted, denounced and slain. For the Mandalay had its natural rulers, unelected and unappointed, as are the rulers in all truly free communities. What some thought mattered more than what others thought. This was as inevitable as the weather and there was as little appeal against it. Character was recognised and received deference.

The Pavilion Café was less kind to human needs. Nobody could creep into it or hide in a corner. Nothing could be arranged in a whisper. All that went on was instantly revealed. Patrons seemed to lose identity and stature as soon as they came into that large, light place. Sitting uneasily round the steel tables, their shopping bags beside them, they looked disconcertingly like the women in a sketch which Wetherby had submitted, when the plans for the Pavilion were first under discussion. They had enjoyed a good laugh over this sketch, which substituted blank pink eggs for faces; but it had proved prophetic. The eager eyes, the sharp noses, the pugnacious chins, which had clustered round the Mandalay lamps, were all fused into a featureless uniformity by Wetherby's great north window.

Here there were no leaders. Everybody was as much reduced, diminished, dwarfed, drained of life, as everybody else. Only Martha Rawson, who always had a special table reserved for her, maintained a kind of individuality.

Sunshine and shadow scudded over the dancing waves outside. It was a restless place, too lofty, too bare, too much exposed to distant prospects of sky and water. A perpetual shrill chatter washed through it, mingled with faint sea music, and the cries of gulls. The steel chairs were not as comfortable as the Mandalay wicker, nor was the coffee particularly good. Sometimes they felt a vague sense of loss as they sat there, hooting at one another. But they did not clearly understand what had been done to them.

Alan Wetherby might be a brilliant architect, but he preferred his buildings to be empty. The intrusion of humanity was always, to him, a pity. He could never quite stomach the notion of worshippers in his Cathedrals, audiences in his theatres, or families in his flats. He made no bones about his dislike for the human race; but it had, as yet, occurred to nobody that the designs of a misanthrope might exert a malign influence. Only the older women whispered occasionally that there had been more going on at the old Mandalay. They felt that the tide of life in this wonderful Pavilion of theirs was weak and aimless, compared with the strong, secret currents that they had known. A few heretics there were, who asserted that the Pavilion did no good to the town. Nobody had actually gone so far as to say that it did harm, for nobody had taken Wetherby's faceless citizens seriously.

"There's that man!" said Martha to Don, soon after they had arrived at their table on Tuesday morning.

"Take no notice," he advised. "We don't want him coming over here."

"I should think not!"

"He is coming though."

"Intolerable! Nobody could have been more snubbing than I was when he rang up last night."

"I'm afraid he's the type you can't snub."

Archer's appearance on Sunday night had taken them by surprise at a moment when they were already confused. They had not acted quickly enough. The party seemed to go better after his arrival. Everybody had begun to talk and laugh, at what they could not now remember. They felt that some great disaster had been averted. It was not until Monday morning that the truth dawned upon them. Don had been indisposed all day, and Martha's headache had prevented her from going up to Summersdown for news of Conrad. In the sick, sober light of day they began to ask themselves why Archer had turned up like this and why, in disregard of all decency, he had insisted upon presiding at Conrad's party.

The answer was not hard to discover. He had not come, as they first conjectured, in search of Elizabeth. In spite of what had happened, he meant to reassert his claim on Conrad, and to become once more the sole vendor of Swanns. Two years ago he had doubtless believed himself to be indispensable, and had expected his former friend to collapse without his good offices. The Venice award, and other indications of a waxing reputation, had taught him his mistake. Conrad was a valuable asset. So he had come to oust the Rawsons, to rob them of the fruits of patronage, by some blackmailing measures best known to himself. Conrad's absence must have been a severe blow to him and he should be sent about his business, if possible, before Conrad came back.

They did their best to ignore his approach, but the unsnubbable creature came right up to their table, pulled out a chair, and sat down upon it.

"I thought. . . ." began Martha.

"Sorry to intrude," he said. "But I'm off at mid-day and I must see you before I go. They told me I'd find you here."

101

Martha looked at Don, mutely commanding him to do something. He avoided her eye. He was not a man of action. A waitress hurried up to take Archer's order. The Rawson table always got prompt service.

"This gentleman," stated Martha, "is not at my table."

"That's all right, Gertie," said Archer. "I'll order later."

Don was forced to assert himself. He rapped out, "We have nothing to say to you. Nothing at all."

"Sorry to hear that. However . . . I've something to say to you. This Apollo. It should have gone to Gressington this week. But now he's gone away. . . ."

"We will see that it goes," interrupted Martha. "You needn't trouble yourself about that, Mr. . . . Mr. . . . er . . . er . . ."

"Archer's the name. I think you know all about me. My point is this; it's not going to Gressington. I went up there myself, yesterday afternoon, and had a look at it. It was in the shed, all right . . . and I don't think it should go."

"I fail to see what say you have in the matter," exclaimed Martha.

"I've Swann's authority. He wrote to me. You can read his letter. I think you'll allow it gives me the right to decide."

"I very much doubt it, Mr. Archer. We are Mr. Swann's most intimate friends, and he has complete confidence in us."

"Why do you think it shouldn't go?" asked Don.

Martha frowned. He ought not to have asked that, as though Archer's opinion merited any attention.

"It's no good," muttered Archer gloomily.

102

"That may be a matter of opinion. I don't think that your disapprobation need prevent it from going to Gressington."

"You'd better read his letter to me."

"I think, perhaps, that might be as well."

"In that case, may I have my coffee?"

Martha signalled to the waitress. Archer produced Conrad's letter and blandly offered it to Don, from whom Martha immediately snatched it.

"Oh!" she cried.

This exclamation was wrung from her by the address at the top of the paper. She flushed angrily. Conrad might be a genius but he was no gentleman. She had maintained him, and his wretched family, for two years. She had bullied several people into buying his work. She had pushed him into entering for the Gressington competition. And what did he do? He stole her note-paper and wrote a treacherous letter upon it, a letter which demolished her right to be called his most intimate friend. Her own note-paper, she kept thinking as she read the letter, and not a word about herself from beginning to end!

Archer sipped his coffee, over which he made a face. A good many people were covertly staring at him. Somebody who had been at the party recognised him. The story crept from table to table: this was the husband.

"Conrad wasn't . . . himself when he wrote this," cried Martha, slapping down the letter. "I shall take no notice of it."

"Do I read it?" asked Don plaintively.

She pushed it across the table and continued, "He would never have written it if he had been in his right mind. Therefore I think it gives you no authority. I shall personally see to it that the Apollo does go to Gressington."

"I can't stop that, of course," said Archer. "But, if he doesn't turn up to speak for himself, I shall do my best to see that it's never exhibited over his name. I shall go there, if necessary. I know the people there. I know the adjudicators. I shall show them this letter and explain the circumstances."

"They'll say he was mad when he wrote that letter."

"They'll say that anyway when they see his Apollo. It's got me seriously rattled about his state of mind. It's . . . it's . . . imbecile. That's all you can say about it. I very nearly took it off and dropped it into the sea."

"If you'd done that you could have been prosecuted."

"It's what he'll do himself when he comes to his senses. It will embarrass them very much at Gressington. They'll jump at the chance to write it off. I'm sure they'll have headaches enough, with some of the entries they'll get."

"Mr. Archer! I don't like to have to say this . . . but you must realise that you are the very last person in the world who ought to interfere in Conrad's affairs."

"Why? Because he pinched my wife, you mean? You think that impairs my judgment of his work?"

"I think it invalidates your judgment. If you really mean to fulfil these threats, I shall write to Gressington myself and tell them all the facts."

"What? About Conrad and Elizabeth? Oh, Lord, they know all about that. Everybody knows."

"I never could spell 'yacht' myself," said Don, handing back the letter.

"I shall make a public scandal of it," declared Martha.

"I don't doubt that you are in with these people and can pull strings. But I shall see to it that the facts are widely known. A great work of art shall not be suppressed in this manner."

"Work of art my arse!" exploded Archer, losing his temper. "My dear madam, go and look at it! Go and look at it!"

"I shall form my own opinion. It's Conrad's work, and nothing that Conrad does ought to be treated like this."

Don, who was more shocked at Archer's language than she was, began to get to his feet.

"Do you want to be thrown out of here?" he asked.

"I don't," said Archer. "I've got a train to catch."

His hasty departure was watched with interest throughout the hall.

"And he didn't even pay for his coffee!" cried Don.

"Winston," said Martha. "I shall write to Winston Churchill."

She frequently wrote to people whom she did not know, and commanded their support in her campaigns. Sometimes she actually got it, and the civil refusals, which she extracted from the Great, were not without their uses, for she could talk about them in an impressive way. Boundless impudence can travel far.

"Bichette," said Don, "we'd better face it. He's too much for us. He's in with all those people. They're more likely to listen to him than to us."

"And what is he but a dealer! A complete barbarian who ought to be selling . . . selling television sets."

"It's Conrad's own fault," said Don, a little testily. "He ought to have sent that thing off. He shouldn't have gone away. You worry too much about him."

105

"I'm perfectly certain, now, that he went because he knew that wretch was coming. He must have regretted that letter as soon as he'd posted it, and simply fled."

"Maybe. But I don't think there's anything we can do."

"Posterity," said Martha, "will think that we ought to have done something. Someday it will be asked why Gressington failed to acquire the Apollo. Why didn't Conrad's friends, who were on the spot, do something?"

"Can't you get somebody else to buy it?"

She shook her head despondently. All possible purchasers of Swanns, among her acquaintance, had already been victimised. East Head was hopelessly Philistine. She had been obliged to fight, tooth and nail, to prevent it from commissioning a portrait of the Mayor, to be paid for out of the War Memorial Surplus Fund. On that committee, as she often told Don, she felt herself to be a voice in the wilderness. A portrait of Sam Dale, to hang in the Town Hall, had been the only proposal so far discussed. Her protests had been over-ridden and the iniquity would have been perpetrated had it not been for Dickie Pattison. He, as legal adviser, had quashed the whole project, upon the grounds that a portrait of Sam Dale would not beautify the town within the meaning of the resolution, passed at a General Meeting, which had earmarked the money for that purpose.

Legal advice! she thought, with smouldering indignation. That they would take. They would listen to a country bumpkin of a solicitor, while her own eloquence went unheeded. They thought themselves quite capable of beautifying their own town, these butchers and bakers and candlestick makers. That they should be left to their own devices was outrageous. In a saner world it would not be permitted; they would not be allowed to spend their money without taking the advice of people who *knew!*

Suddenly her eyes brightened. An idea had occurred to her. It was a most daring idea, a more difficult campaign than any upon which she had, as yet, embarked. The obstacles were most inspiring. She loved to triumph in the face of opposition, and it was not an impossible idea.

"I don't see why not!" she exclaimed.

"You've thought of somebody?"

"The War Memorial Committee. And I know where it ought to go too! In the vestibule here. At the top of the stairs."

"My dear Martha! Not this committee."

"I could try. I've got my way before, on committees. I know what I want and they don't. That's everything."

"The town would never accept it. There'd be an uproar."

"In my experience there never is much uproar *after* a purchase has been made," she said. "It's discussion before, that you want to avoid. Every Tom, Dick and Harry then thinks he has the right to an opinion. The whole thing must be very carefully handled. I must sow a lot of good seed, and get to work on as many members of the committee separately, as I can, before I actually bring up the proposal. And then . . . bounce them!"

She could do that, he remembered. She had done it in the case of the Pavilion.

"The most important person is young Pattison," she continued. "They all listen to him. I wish he hadn't been at that wretched party. And I never feel that his little

wife is very . . . if I could get a chance to . . . is she
here I wonder? She generally is, about now. Oh, yes, I
see her. With Mrs. Hughes. *Mrs. Hughes!* She's on the
committee. Why, I cannot think. I'll just stop on my way
out and say a civil word or two, for there really is no time
to be lost."

She got up and handed him her parcels.

"But, Martha. . . ."

"Carry this one carefully. It's got bottles in it."

"Er . . . we haven't seen the Apollo yet, have we?"

This took her by surprise. The omission had slipped
from her memory. She hesitated and then said quickly,
"It's Conrad's work. Possibly not his best work. But anything by Conrad will be more than these people deserve."

Don was inclined to agree with her. He loathed East
Head.

Had Christina, Allie, and Mrs. Hughes perceived their
danger, they would have got away before Martha reached
their table. But she was an expert in getting quite close to
people before they were aware of it, for she had been
practising this art ever since she could crawl. She sailed
down the room, chattering to Don, and was nearly past
their table before appearing to recognise them. Then, with
a start, she whisked round, flashed her teeth, and popped
into the fourth chair, with a laughing apology. She
wanted to tell Mrs. Hughes how much she had enjoyed
the Congregational Sacred Concert. After which there was
no escape from the hosepipe of her affability.

Don, who stood patiently behind her and held her parcels, could not but admire her skill. Babies were enquired
after, and she managed to get from Bobbins to the Apollo
without any apparent change of subject. The modulations

included a reference to Christina's absence on Sunday night, a deprecating allusion to the party, Conrad's absence, apologies for having involved poor Mr. Pattison in so rowdy a fiasco, thanks for his kindness, hope of his forgiveness, and a promise of the Apollo upon some other occasion.

"For it was that he came for," she concluded regretfully. "That he wanted to see. He's such a busy man, and he gave up his time . . . he must have been so disappointed. It distresses me very much. But I give my word that he shall see it, as soon as I can arrange it. Will you tell him?"

"Yes," said Christina. "I'll tell him."

"Is it very beautiful?" asked the innocent Mrs. Hughes.

That, suggested Martha with a smile, depended upon what one meant by beauty.

"In the eye of the beholder, so they say," put in Allie.

She meant to be sarcastic, but was assured that she had uttered a profound truth. We cannot recognise beauty, said Martha, until we have learnt how to look for it.

Christina sat with her elbows on the table, her chin cupped in her hands, and wondered what was behind all this. Martha was up to her tricks. Christina had suspected as much when the invitation to the party was given. Now she was sure of it. Dickie was to be drawn into something. She knew Martha, if he did not. Some advantage was going to be taken of his affection for Swann. His anxiety to know more about art and culture was, in some fashion, to be exploited.

She had, in the past, despised and derided Martha. Now she was growing actively hostile. She would not have it. Nobody was going to bully Dickie except herself.

109

She began to follow the conversation more attentively than she would otherwise have done. She wanted to contradict this woman, to catch her out in some untenable statement. Nobody ever contradicted Martha. That was the trouble. They might laugh at her behind her back, but nobody knew enough to prove her wrong.

An experimental handful of good seed was being sown. Martha thought the opportunity favourable, since Mrs. Hughes was also on the Selection Committee. The first step must be to break down an inevitable resistance to the unfamiliar. These destined purchasers would certainly dislike the Apollo; of that much she was sure, although she had not seen it herself. Very simply, in terms which the meanest intellect could grasp, she explained to them that many acknowledged masterpieces have been, in their day, derided as ridiculous and ugly. Only the elect can appreciate original and progressive art. By the masses it has always been greeted with shouts of protest.

"Oh, no!" exclaimed Christina suddenly.

Martha pulled up and gaped at her. Mrs. Hughes and Allie, emerging from a lethargy of inattention, gaped too.

The word *shout* had suddenly reminded Christina of Dickie in the British Museum. Somewhere behind him towered vast knees and flowing draperies. Dickie's face, and Dickie's voice, came back very clearly. He was telling her something. *They shouted,* he said.

"I mean," she explained, flushing a little, "they don't always shout *against,* do they? Sometimes they shout *for.* I mean . . . I heard . . . somebody told me . . . when they finished that great temple they have in Athens . . . the . . . the . . ."

110

The wretched name eluded her. Not the Pantheon. What was it? She began to repent of her boldness.

"The Parthenon?" suggested Martha kindly.

"That's it. The Parthenon. Well, when it was finished, last of all they put up those statues, the ones they have in the British Museum now. They're all broken, but you can see they were wonderful. And they were quite a new kind of statue, at that time. Nobody in Athens had ever seen anything like it before. But, when the people saw them, they all started shouting and cheering, even the slaves who had built the temple. Even the slaves saw at once that they were marvellous. I mean, it may be difficult for ordinary people now to admire new art. But it hasn't always been like that, has it?"

For a moment or two Martha had nothing to say. To be pulled up by anybody, on such a point, was an unusual experience for her; to be pulled up by little Mrs. Pattison was outrageous.

"Oh, well . . . the Greeks," she said at last, "they were different, weren't they?"

There was a murmur of assent from the other two. The Greeks could have nothing to do with it. They wore no trousers, spoke a foreign language, and had been dead a long time. It was strange of Christina to bring them up.

Christina, beaten in the first round, found herself wishing, almost for the first time in her life, that she knew more. Generally speaking she believed that she knew all that was necessary to get along very well in the world. From the ante-natal attitude to the Incarnation, she had all the facts and ideas, essential to her credit and comfort, neatly filed in their respective pigeon holes. Some com-

111

partments were almost empty, no doubt; there were a great many subjects about which she did not need to know. But now, disconcertingly, she felt that she was ill-equipped. Martha must surely be talking nonsense, but there was no stopping her, unless she could be met and challenged upon her own ground.

I don't believe the Greeks were so very different from us, mused Christina. They were people. I don't believe people alter so much. Only they had better artists, so it was nicer for them. If I knew more, I'm sure I could think of some people later than the Greeks, just ordinary people, who didn't need to be lectured by Martha before they could see that a statue was beautiful. And now she's telling us that we're so awful, we want art to be just like a photograph, and show us exactly what we see; it's only people like her who can appreciate being shown what they don't see. So what about that picture? That picture we saw once that I loved so much, Dickie tried to get a copy for me? The Virgin Mary and the Baby in front, and, behind, that darling little tiny town, and the river, and all the ships, and the little people, so clear! "It's like a fairy tale," I said. And Dickie said that was the exact truth about it, because it was a magic picture, it gave us a magic long sight, which we haven't really got, because our real eyes wouldn't see all that, so far away, it would just be blobs. He'd painted them as clear as if they were near, only tiny. Which made it like a fairy story. Well, he was painting something we don't see, and we liked it. And it wasn't new or modern. It was a famous Old Master. If only I could remember his name I'd . . . Van . . . Van . . . was it Van Dyck? I don't think so. He painted nothing but Charles the First. If I get it wrong, she'll score off

112

me again, as she did over the Parthenon. Van . . . Van
. . . I must ask Dickie. I will ask Dickie, when we've
made it up. *Provincial!* And he hasn't apologised.

Mrs. Hughes and Allie were not listening at all. They
had no particular reason for wishing to contradict Martha.
Mrs. Hughes thought what a pity it was that Martha's
mother had not put braces on her teeth. It was just like
the Skippertons to have neglected such a detail. They
idolised their child and allowed her to grow up looking
like a ferret. Allie was thinking that she must get some
wire for mending fuses. Something that Martha had said
about the technique of Reg Butler reminded her of it.
She would get it on her way home.

Nobody had anything to say when the little lecture
came to an end. Martha rose, declaring that she was talking too much. They must forgive her. After all, it was
such a privilege to have Conrad Swann living in their
town.

"What rot she talks!" exclaimed Allie, as soon as the
Rawsons were out of earshot.

"Why didn't you say so?" snapped Christina.

"That would have been rude."

"I think somebody ought to stand up to her sometimes."

"Oh, you were marvellous. All about the Parthenon!
She looked as if she'd sat on a pin."

"Why didn't you back me up?"

"My dear! I couldn't know less about the Parthenon."

"I don't believe Martha knows much," said Christina.
"I believe some really educated person could sew her up
in no time. We just let her walk over us. Oh . . . Van
Eyck!"

"Van how much?"

"Just a name I was trying to remember. I'd have argued with her, if only I'd remembered it in time."

"What's the point of arguing with her? I didn't bother to listen. Just a lot of blather."

Mrs. Hughes had been pursuing her own train of thought. Some part of Martha's homily had made an impression upon her.

"It's true," she said suddenly.

"What's true?" asked Allie.

"Some of what she said is true. Look how great artists have always starved. Well . . . often have. Just because they weren't appreciated till too late. I always remember that picture, that famous picture, of the poor young artist, starved to death. Stretched on the couch, with his white face, only a boy really, and the candle flickering out, and the day breaking through the window. Death of . . . death of . . . and all his poems torn up, poor fellow. Yes, he was a poet really, not an artist. But it's the same thing. Starving! Just for want of a little encouragement. It made a great impression on me. Because he was a real man. I'd remember who he was, if I could remember his name. And he did turn out to be a great poet, I believe. I don't know if I've read any of his, because I can't remember his name. Death of . . . death of . . . I can only think of Chatterly and I'm sure that's not it."

"Oh, Mummie," said Allie, "that man died of consumption, not starvation. You're thinking of that book Daddy wouldn't have in the house. He wrote poetry too, I think."

"No. He was quite modern. This poor young fellow lived a long time ago. In the picture he had knee breeches."

"Well, I don't see what all this is in aid of anyway," said Allie. "Who is starving now?"

"Conrad Swann," said Christina. "At least, he's dog poor. If you ask me, Martha wants to raise money for him. Have an exhibition, perhaps, and make us all go."

"Well, I'll go," said Mrs. Hughes. "And if I can manage to appreciate it I will. It's a shame if an artist never gets appreciated till he's dead."

Some of the good seed was already germinating.

4

Early on Tuesday morning a man came to turn off the water at Conrad Swann's house, because the water rate had not been paid, and the final notice had been ignored. He gave Dinah a paper which she could not read; she put it with a heap of unopened bills on the hall table. After that no water came out of the taps. The children accepted this as they accepted other deprivations. They had, luckily, a pump outside the kitchen door which still worked.

They were all listless and depressed. Their few toys and treasures had been destroyed with their tree, so that they had no resources, and did not know what to do with themselves. On Monday they had gone down to the beach, but it was a long walk, and nobody felt inclined to repeat the entertainment. They hung about the house and garden and at last drifted into a sort of game: they caught snails and imprisoned them in match-boxes.

This was perfectly satisfying to the younger children. They would have been content with it for weeks, for it made few physical or mental demands upon them. They had merely to find names for their captives, peer at them in their match-box houses, and issue reports on their progress. But it was not enough for Serafina, who needed some

116

livelier protection from boredom. She had nothing to do, nothing to read, and no company. The apathy, which protected the others, was impossible to her. Some nourishment for the mind she must have, and she preserved herself on a diet of fantasy. Without it, the facts by which she was surrounded would have been too much for her.

Eventually she broke up the snail game with the announcement that a siege was going on. The whole house was surrounded by the Enemy, who had assembled in full force to release their comrade in the shed. The man who had turned off the water might have looked like a human, but he was really an Artefact in disguise and he had been sent by the Traitor.

This was their name for Martha Rawson, with whom Serafina had a long standing feud. From the very first their hostility had been declared and open. Martha had made no attempt to conceal her dismay when the little Swanns were presented to her. To take Conrad and his lady under her wing had been an attractive responsibility. The addition of Polly and Mike had not been so welcome. When, three months later, Serafina, Dinah and Joe had been returned to their father, because he had failed to pay for their board elsewhere, her comments had been bitter. These comments had been made in French, but Serafina had lived in France for much of her life and understood enough to resent them. Collecting what French she could remember, she had fired off her comments on Martha, which were abusive rather than apt.

"*Et pourtant elle pu fortement!*" she had shrieked, before being dragged from the room.

Conrad and Elizabeth had laughed about it afterwards. They did sometimes laugh, there were a few cheerful

117

moments, in those early days at Summersdown. It was only gradually that life had fallen into complete disintegration. Elizabeth had, at first, been rather kind to Serafina, never treating her as a child, but addressing her as an equal in misfortune. A sort of companionship had sprung up for a while. Elizabeth had interesting things to tell about the world, and life on the stage; she even gave Serafina a few lessons in elocution. But now she was always fuddled, and Conrad had been living, for months, so secluded a life in the studio that his final vanishing made very little difference to anybody.

They were both, for some mysterious reason, in the power of the Traitor, who came and went at will, gave orders to everybody, and took a sinister interest in the Artefacts. She was always trying to get into the studio, unless Conrad locked her out. He had, so Elizabeth once said, to sing to her for his supper, although the children had never heard him do it. He never sang at all at Summersdown. In the old lost life, when everybody was happy and quite different, he used to sing beautifully. Now he did not even whistle. He had become increasingly silent, as the siege grew more grievous.

This notion of a siege had been present in Serafina's mind for some months. It was not, alas, something which she had invented; she knew that it was real, but to describe it in these terms made it dramatic and therefore bearable. They had all been shut up in this house against their will, and there was no comprehensible reason for it. Elizabeth was as much a victim as anybody else. She hated being there. Once, when Serafina asked why she had been obliged to come, she had explained it all, very drearily, with a plenitude of physical detail. Everybody had to do it, she said, and she wished to God that it were otherwise, because doing it with Conrad had forced her to sacrifice everything else in life; but people could not help themselves, as Serafina would find out for herself some day. Serafina was sorry for them and glad that children did not have to do it. She felt that grown-up people were more to be pitied than children.

They were all, however, afflicted by a growing solitude, by gathering shadows. Laughter ebbed and disappeared. They were on a little island which kept growing smaller; the compass and scope of life continually diminished. With the loss of the tree, and the departure of Conrad, they seemed to be completely cut off. He, at least, had constituted a slender bridge between the past and the present. He had been there, and now he was here—the only surviving possession that they had, greatly changed, as they all were changed, but a symbol of continuity. In the past he had talked and laughed and played games with them. Here he was haggard, silent and generally invisible. But he still had the same kind voice. When, in extremity, she appealed to him he never refused what help he could give, although it was often pitifully inadequate. His sad eyes, meeting hers, apologised for their common helplessness.

Something like a siege was certainly going on and it was getting worse. She commanded that sentries should be posted all round the house, to ward off further invasions. The others objected to this interruption of the snail game but were easily over-ruled. Serafina patrolled the fortress and received reports.

Nobody else came during the morning except Lobster Charlie. She ran up to Elizabeth for instructions, since

119

Charlie expected cash down and they were generally obliged to send him away, although they all liked lobsters. Today, however, the omens were favourable. Elizabeth was actually up and dressed. She did not ask how the hell she was to pay for lobsters. She told Serafina to buy two, and she took a great deal of money, pounds and pounds, fastened with a rubber ring, out of her hand-bag. One note was extracted. As she gave it to Serafina she said:

"If you want any more for anything, you'll find it in this little drawer in my dressing table. I'll leave some there. Are you looking? This little drawer. I'll put some money into it."

Serafina stared. This was a change. Elizabeth seldom had any money, and it was usually impossible to get so much as sixpence out of her.

Changes, in Serafina's experience, were not for the better. She looked anxiously round the room, which was littered with clothes. A half-filled suitcase caught her eye.

"Are you going away?" she demanded.

Elizabeth started and hesitated before she said, "God no! What put that into your head."

"You're packing."

"No I'm not. I'm only looking over my things. Get along and buy the lobsters. You can keep the change for sweets if you like."

But she is going, thought Serafina, as she ran downstairs. Who will come then? Who will come to take us away?

She had little trust in grown-up people but she still retained some crumbs of faith in certain natural laws. Children, so she believed, were never left alone, quite alone, in a house. She had never heard of that happening. There was always some older person, of very little use perhaps, but a symbol of responsibility. Orphans were put into orphanages because it was impossible that children should be in a house alone. Conrad had gone. Elizabeth was going. Somebody, therefore, was bound to come. Her spirits rose. Perhaps the siege was over.

For a fraction of a second she glanced at the thought that it might all have been a mistake. They might be going right back, to home, to . . . but she winced away from it. No fantasy, no daydream, could include that possibility. She could pretend many things, but not that. *Dead!* There was nothing to be done with that word, except forget it, and forget a morning long ago, when the house had been full of people saying it. *Dead, dead, dead!* And at Mrs. Parker's, to whom they were then taken, people kept saying it too: Poor little things! Their mother is *dead, dead, dead!* It sounded what it was, a sickening final thud.

She bought the lobsters and they all had a lovely but indigestible dinner. The siege really seemed to be less oppressive until Joe discovered that he had been sitting on his favourite snail. He bawled so loudly that Elizabeth came down, complaining that she could not hear herself think, and asking why the hell they could not go off and play in their tree?

There was a shocked silence. They felt embarrassed, as though she had asked some indecent question. Before anybody could think of an answer her attention was diverted: "Look out! That child is going to be sick!"

Joe, between grief and lobster, which never agreed with him, had begun to retch. Everybody dispersed hastily, lest the spectacle should make them sick too. He was left to his fate, in the kitchen. But Serafina went afterwards to help him, since he was too small to clear up the mess adequately. She filled the scrub bucket at the pump and, holding her nose, she mopped the kitchen floor, while Joe hiccupped sadly over the snail, squashed so flat in his little match-box house.

"Do you think it hurt him, Serafina?"

"Horribly," snapped Serafina.

"Has he gone to Heaven?"

"No. To Purgatory, for ten thousand million years."

Joe howled in despair, and her conscience smote her. It was very cruel to torment him because she was wretched herself. She went to the cupboard and found a small mustard tin, emptied the contents into a saucer, rinsed it, and gave it to him.

"Here's a lovely house that won't squash," she said, "and you can put quite a big snail in it. You can keep guard down by the shed, if you like; there are lots of big snails there."

Joe immediately cheered up and decided to call the big snail Harold.

The other sentries were dismissed to their posts and Serafina patrolled the path in the front garden. The Enemy was certainly on the move; there was the smell of danger in the air. She was not in the least surprised to see the Traitor coming up the path.

They glared at one another but did not speak. The Traitor marched into the house, where she had some kind of altercation with Elizabeth. Their angry voices were audible, even out in the garden.

122

Serafina amused herself by doing a smart sentry-go between the front door and the gate.

Suddenly, within a matter of seconds, she became weary of the Artefact game, outgrew it, and discarded it for ever.

It was no help and it was not true. Those things were merely *things;* they could supply no more drama. Yet, without drama, she felt totally unprotected. It was as though she had been thrust out of some refuge which, with considerable valour, she had constructed for herself. The door had been locked behind her. The Traitor was a menace, not because she was leagued with imaginary bogies, but for some much worse, much more mysterious, reason. There was a siege, but children doing sentry-go could not hope to raise it. These evils were real; they were as dreadful and final as her mother's death had been, and there was as little to be done about it.

Desolate, at the end of her resources, she wandered away from the house and up into the meadow. She lay down in the long grass, not far from the blasted stump of their tree. She had thought that she might be going to cry, but no tears came. She wished that she could be nothing; not dead, but just nothing at all. Eternal life was the last thing to be desired.

Presently Joe came into the field. Since she had abandoned the game she did not ask for any report of his observations by the shed. He was carrying on a long conversation with Harold, now established in the mustard tin house. As she watched him she remembered him suddenly as a baby, in a high chair, opening his mouth like a bird for the spoonfuls which their mother put into it.

She saw her mother too, more clearly than usual—the dark hair in a smooth bun on the back of her neck, and an absent-minded expression on her face. She had been feeding Joe and thinking of something else.

Serafina writhed and rolled and drummed her heels on the ground. The ache at her heart was intolerable; it was physical agony. If she could not appease it she would die. She called to Joe and, when he came, pulled him down beside her. She hugged him and covered him with kisses.

"You're cuggling me!" observed Joe in dispassionate surprise.

Caresses were no part of Serafina's technique as a little mother. She had given and received very few since she came to Summersdown. Joe liked it. He submitted himself to these unaccustomed endearments with a pleased sensuous smile.

"Mrs. Pattison cuggles Bobbins," he remembered.

"Yes."

"After his barf. Tell about Bobbins."

He had seen all these wonders himself but he liked to hear them described.

"He has a little basket, lined with blue," said Serafina. "And a brush and a powder puff, with little blue birds on them."

"I sawn it, din't I?"

"You had a basket like that too, when you were a baby."

"I bemember. So I did."

"Oh, no, you couldn't remember. You were only a tiny, tiny little baby."

"I do bemember. I were sick in it."

"You were not sick. Nobody was sick in our home."

124

"I so were sick."

"Don't contradict, or I shall thump you."

Joe rolled away from her and had a peep at Harold who had also, he declared, been sick.

Eased by this little conversation, but strangely exhausted, Serafina fell asleep. She did not wake for a long time. The sun crept across the pale afternoon sky, and the shadows in the meadow lengthened. She lay in the grass, safe from her sorrows.

While she slept, Elizabeth deserted them, slipping quietly out of the house with a suitcase, to catch the four-o'clock train to London. Nobody saw her go except Polly, whom she encountered on the stairs.

"She said," reported Polly, "that she is going to Korea, and somebody is coming to take us away to a lovely place. And there's some money in the little drawer in her dressing table. She said to remind you."

For the rest of the day they were constantly looking out for this person to come. The sun set. Night fell. At last they straggled up to bed. Nobody had come.

"They'll come tomorrow," prophesied Serafina confidently.

Fear had begun to flutter inside her, but she was not going to let the others know that. If nobody came tomorrow she decided that she would take some of that money and buy peaches and cream and tinned chicken. This alluring prospect had power to hold fear at bay for a little while. She was even able to hope that nobody would come until she had spent all that lovely money. Not yet would she investigate the possibility that nobody would ever come, that they had been betrayed and abandoned, that everybody in the world had forgotten about them.

125

5

The river Dare flows into the Bristol Channel on the west side of the town. Here are quays and jetties; here the sand is dotted with boats at low tide. Buoys mark a clear channel of deep water which runs, at one point, close under a long spit of land.

This was the site chosen by old Tom Skipperton for The Moorings. It looked like the yachtsman's paradise which he had intended it to be, and Martha found it difficult to improve. She would have pulled it down, had she been able to bully Alan Wetherby into designing her a new house for nothing. But he was obstinate and ungrateful, and so she had to put up with her father's gables and half timbering.

Inside she had torn down a great deal of pitch-pine panelling; she had abolished the main staircase and thrown several rooms into one. This was called the music room. It had a Bechstein on a dais, a totem pole, and some furniture which felt more comfortable than it looked. A spiral steel staircase, somewhat resembling a helter-skelter at a fair, rose from this room to the upper floors.

The whole effect never satisfied her. She was always changing the position of the totem pole, which persisted in looking as though it had just arrived and was waiting to be put into its proper place. Wetherby unkindly told her

126

that she had not got a room at all, merely four walls containing so many cubic feet of space.

She had, in addition, her own study, known as the book room. To Don she had given the old boat house, now converted into a studio, since sailing made her seasick. He was supposed to work there and was despatched to it every day, immediately after lunch.

Sometimes he did do a little work. More often he read detective novels. Had his etchings ever meant very much to him he would not have married Martha. They had failed to support him and he liked comfort. He had all the whiskey he wanted in the boat-house cupboard, and a plentiful supply of Whodunnits.

Upon this Tuesday afternoon, however, he felt restless, distracted by that inward eye which now so seldom blessed his solitude. Little seemed to catch it at East Head, although he had made numerous studies of boats lying on the sand. Today it had been caught, had been opened, and would not shut again. This had befallen him just as they were leaving the Pavilion. Martha had darted off to discuss something with Mr. Beccles, the manager. Don, while waiting for her, had strolled down onto the sea terrace. While there, he had noticed a particular arrangement of people, reflections and shadows, on the beach. Somehow they were dramatically disposed. But this pattern occurred in a void. There was nothing to contain it. Sky, sea and beach stretched endlessly in all directions. To do anything with it he must . . .

He thought about it for the greater part of the afternoon, and drank a good deal of whiskey while he was thinking. Just as a solution occurred to him Martha's bell, shrilling suddenly, recalled him to the house. It connected

127

The Moorings with the studio, but she never rang it without good cause, for she took his work very seriously.

He swore, and wondered why she should invariably hit upon the few occasions when he was really working. As he walked up the garden path he was aware that he had, in his preoccupation, put down rather a lot of whiskey. The tide was high and washed against the garden wall. The wind blew in soft, short gusts. He felt mournful.

A door led from the garden into the music room, which was empty. All the fluorescent tubes under the ceiling had been turned on, although it was still full daylight. A table stood ready with drinks and glasses. Somebody must be coming for a cocktail and that was why he had been summoned. There were three glasses. He had better begin to mix some Martinis.

As he crossed to the table he caught sight of something unpleasant out of the tail of his eye, and turned to look.

It was on the piano dais—a mean, thin contrivance of rusty-looking metal, shapeless and jagged, yet oddly menacing, as though it might be about to hop down and attack him. The sight of it gave him quite a turn. What a bugger! he thought. She must have brought it this afternoon. She was up at Summersdown. Good God! The Apollo?

He approached it reluctantly, violently repelled, for it had shattered the last fragment of his own private preoccupation. This was not a moment at which he could wish to look at anything by Conrad. He did not much like Conrad's work, although he was fond of the man.

Closer inspection robbed the thing of its formidability. Seen from behind, from either side, it looked like nothing at all. It was not even repulsive; it was merely silly.

"Well?"

128

He looked up. Martha was leaning over the smooth steel wall of the staircase. She must have been standing up there, watching him, for some minutes.

"What do you think of it?" she asked.

"It's Conrad's Apollo?"

"Yes."

She came down the stairs, disappearing and reappearing round the central column, until she reached the floor.

She had put on her cocktail clothes: skimpy black trousers fastened tightly round the ankles with a band of gold, and a short wide coolie coat of black and gold brocade. This exotic finery could not save her from looking like a conscientious governess. She asked him again what he thought of the Apollo. She seemed really anxious to know, which was not always the case when she demanded his opinion. Frequently she merely sought an endorsement of her own. Now, however, she had not quite made up her mind.

"I don't like it," he ventured.

"But it's very powerful, isn't it? Didn't it make you jump when you first saw it?"

"Ye-es. But so would a turnip lantern."

"I'm not quite, quite sure what I think," she allowed. "It knocked me over at first sight. But then I'm inclined to be suspicious of things which knock me over at first sight."

She might well be, he reflected, remembering some incautious enthusiasms from which she had subsequently been obliged to retreat.

"Why did you bring it?" he asked.

"Well," she said, sinking into a chair, "I went up to Summersdown this afternoon."

"Any news of Conrad?"

"I don't gather so. But Elizabeth is quite intolerable. I'm not going to that house again. Conrad must come here, if he wants to see us, and come without her. Why should we put up with her insolence? I shall pass the word round; I think we'd much better, all of us, keep away from Summersdown. She's made it pretty plain that she doesn't want to see any of us."

"What did she say particularly?"

"Oh, she was just incoherent and abusive. She accused me of expecting everybody to sing for their supper! Such ingratitude considering . . . I didn't say anything. I just left her and went off to find the Apollo. It was in the shed."

She turned in her chair to have another look at it.

"I must say," she added, "I find it . . . impressive. You know Don, it is really Apollo. It has such ruthlessness, such non-humanity. . . . And then the thought crossed my mind that it might be in safer keeping. I'm not too sure that Elizabeth hasn't got some understanding with that awful man. One doesn't know what they'd do with it. So I put it in the car and brought it down here. Why don't you like it?"

"It just . . . says nothing to me."

"But his work is so different from yours."

"I know. But this isn't like his work, somehow. You don't get that impact of Conrad's mind . . . his intellect. . . ."

"I'm most anxious to hear what Alan says."

"Oh? He's coming, is he?"

"Yes. He's looking in for a drink on his way back to Bristol. He's been over at Ilfracombe, about a job there."

130

So that was the trouble. She did not want absolutely to commit herself until Wetherby had given judgement.

"He'll crab it," prophesied Don.

"Why should he?"

"He invariably crabs Conrad. You must have noticed that. He won't want a Swann in his Pavilion. He'll be furious."

"I shan't tell him about that. I shall let him think I mean to buy it myself, and ask him for his honest opinion."

"His honest opinion! When has he ever praised anybody?"

The door bell rang.

"There he is," she said. "Mix the Martinis, will you?"

She rose and wandered about the room, examining the Apollo from various angles, her small ferret's head a little on one side. They heard Ahmed, their houseman, going to the door. Presently Wetherby appeared. He could not have failed to see the Apollo as soon as he got into the room, but he took no notice of it. He advanced upon them, rubbing his hands, and exclaimed in solemn tones, "Have you heard the news?"

"No?" cried Martha, looking startled.

"East Head," he told them, "is to have a new Public Convenience."

They smiled uneasily.

"On the parade, beside the car park. It's to be a most striking affair. Your friend, the Mayor, has got the contracts and, if you'll take a tip from me, you'll keep an eye on his estimates, or he'll do you down. I've worked with him. But what a town you are! Always on the move! Always up to something. Thanks, Don."

131

He sipped his Martini and stared blandly round the room, at everything except the Apollo.

"I thought you'd had news of Conrad," said Martha.

"News of Conrad? Why should I? Hasn't he turned up yet?"

"No. We've no idea where he is."

"Ah, well! *Never question a man too closely when he tells you he must go.* Martha, you're a cultivated woman, but I bet you sixpence you don't know who wrote that. Do you?"

"No."

"I knew you didn't. Ella Wheeler Wilcox! Wonderful woman. Said what nobody else dares say. It wouldn't be a bad inscription to put up over your new amenity. Well, Don? Very busy?"

"No," said Don, wondering, not for the first time, why anybody ever let Wetherby into the house.

Martha could no longer control her impatience.

"Alan," she said, with a gesture at the dais, "I want you to look at this."

He gave a dramatic start, went up to it, examined it carefully, and commented, "Very fetching. But what is it, exactly?"

"Conrad's Apollo."

"*What?*"

Sheer amazement, for an instant, ruffled his composure. "You say . . . Swann . . . did this?" he exclaimed.

"Yes."

"You're sure?"

"Quite sure. I've just brought it from Summersdown. It was in the shed, where he put it on Thursday."

132

"If you say so. . . . But what about Gressington?"

Don had been wondering how she would explain that, but she did not seem to find the question embarrassing.

"It's not going," she said, "unless Conrad comes back and insists on sending it. In his absence, we've decided not to."

"No? Really? Why?"

"Some rather disquieting information has come to my ears. . . . I had a talk today with Mr. Archer . . . you know whom I mean?"

"I should say I do, considering what he did to us on Sunday night. It's my opinion he put vodka in that brew. Conrad's dealer, isn't he?"

"Not at all," said Martha crossly. "He doesn't handle Conrad's affairs any more. But he dropped a few hints about Gressington. Of course he knows all the people there. He didn't exactly say so, but I gather the prize is a foregone conclusion. All this business of an open competition is mere publicity. So, if there is no chance that Conrad could win the prize, I don't think he should consent merely to be exhibited along with all the other entries. A good deal of second-rate work will probably be sent in; a lot of headaches for the adjudicators, as Mr. Archer put it. Since I'm in charge of Conrad's concerns, I think I shan't send this in. I wouldn't have urged him to compete, if I'd known as much as I do now about Gressington."

Wetherby nodded. He might be swallowing all this. He might not. His accustomed sly inscrutability had returned to him.

"So now tell me frankly," she finished. "What do you think of it?"

"I?" He looked startled. "Oh . . . I'm only an engineer, though I call myself an architect. What I think can't matter."

"Of course it matters. I . . . I rather thought it might look well in this room. But I'm not quite sure . . . you don't get the . . . the impact of Conrad's intellect . . . do you?"

Wetherby had a sudden attack of coughing.

"Personally," began Don, "I . . ."

Martha silenced him with a peremptory look. They watched Wetherby, who was again scrutinising the Apollo. He went up to it, pulled it unceremoniously towards him, and ran a finger along one of its spikes. Then he turned and gave judgement: "I didn't know he had it in him."

"You like it?" cried Martha.

"A terrific power went to the making of it. You must buy it, Martha. You really must. Just what this room needs! And, if you give a penny less than two hundred pounds for it, you'll be doing poor old Conrad dirt."

"You do think it's wonderful?" she urged.

"I'm stunned. It's a miracle. I can't think how he did it. I've never encouraged you to buy anything before, have I? But I do now. Thanks, Don!"

Wetherby took his second cocktail and grinned at them.

"Exactly what I think," said Martha, in great satisfaction.

"And Don? What does Don think?"

"Oh, he's a little bit frightened of it, aren't you, Don?"

"He'd better get over that, hadn't he?"

Don put down a bottle hastily. He had nearly thrown it at Wetherby's head.

134

"It so defiantly gets away from the grocer's idea of Apollo," suggested Martha.

"Which grocer?" asked Wetherby.

"Oh . . . you know! Clive Bell's grocer."

"I know nothing about Clive Bell's grocer. Why should I? My grocer lives in Bristol, but I don't expect anybody knows about him."

"Oh, Alan, don't be tiresome. You know perfectly well what I mean. 'Art and what the Grocer thinks he sees are two quite different things.'"

"I never met a grocer who thought he'd seen Apollo."

"All grocerdom will shriek at this, thank goodness."

"Very likely. Which reminds me; there was some grocerdom at the party on Sunday. Our Mr. Pattison in a natty lounge suit, looking rather puzzled. Why was he there?"

"Conrad asked him."

"Is that so? You seemed to be oiling him in a marked way."

"I think it's time that the town began to realise something of Conrad's importance."

"I see. They won't dare shriek, as soon as they've got it into their heads that Conrad is a Good Thing. That's the trouble with grocers. They can't even shriek honestly. Anybody can bully them. They haven't even the guts to stand up for what they think they see."

"They're beginning to acquiesce," allowed Martha.

"Then they get what they deserve."

"Quite. I mean, look at your Pavilion! Think of all the opposition there was at first. Now they're getting used to it."

"Just like them," said Wetherby, looking at his watch. "Well, I must be off!"

He took another long stare at the Apollo.

"If only it had gone to Gressington," he sighed. "I really think you ought, you know."

"I don't believe Conrad despises grocers," exclaimed Don suddenly. "I don't believe he despises anybody."

"Man! Where's his integrity if he doesn't? Must go. Goodbye, Martha. Thanks for the drinks. Don't bother to come to the door with me, Don. A little grocerish, that. I'll find my way out."

He strode from the room and shut the door smartly behind him.

"You heard?" exulted Martha. "He thinks it's a masterpiece. And he's given me a figure, too. I shall keep two hundred in mind, when I get to work on our grocers."

"If they're honest grocers they won't give you tuppence."

"Now Don! I must please count on your support. It's everything that I can quote Alan. They have got it into their thick heads that he knows what he's talking about. I might bring half a dozen famous critics down here, to praise the Apollo, without making anything like the same impression."

Don wondered if any famous critic would have come to East Head at Martha's bidding. But he held his peace. It was not worth a squabble. And yet . . . He looked again at the Apollo.

"You're quite sure," he said slowly, "that Conrad . . . that it is . . . that he really did it?"

"Why! My dear Don! Who else could have done it?"

6

"A slight chill and *anno domini,* that's all," said Dr. Browning over the telephone. "This changeable weather tells on old men. Nothing to worry about. I've sent him to bed for a day or two. Your wife was round there this morning arranging things with his housekeeper."

Dickie had just returned from Weston and had an afternoon appointment at Brinstock, but he drove round at once to see his father. He found the old man somewhat petulant at being kept in bed, where he had nothing to do, while a great deal was waiting to be done in his garden. Christina had brought him some books to read, but he never read books in the day-time, except occasionally on wet Sundays. All this coddling was nonsense.

He cheered up at the sight of Dickie, however, and listened with eagerness to all the latest news. The most surprising item concerned Mr. Pethwick, who had decided suddenly to leave East Head and end his days with a married daughter in the Argentine. The sale of Brinstock house was to be put into Dickie's hands; he was going over that afternoon to discuss it, since Pethwick was immobilised with lumbago.

"I wonder Christina didn't tell me about that," said Mr. Pattison. "She might have known I'd be interested. You say he rang you up yesterday? I wonder she said nothing."

"I don't think I happened to mention it," said Dickie. This was an extraordinary statement, and he knew it. Pethwick's departure should have been the main conversational dish at supper last night. He had meant to tell her, but had suddenly, in a fit of irritation, decided to keep the news to himself. He had told her about Sir Gregory's objections to the sewage-disposal scheme, and she had said that it was just like Sir Gregory to object. He had told her about Prescott's tenant, and she had said that it was just like Mr. Prescott not to mend the roof. It seemed to him that he could not bear to hear her say that it was just like Mr. Pethwick to go to the Argentine. This phrase, so frequently upon the lips of Christina and her friends, had always annoyed him. It was the inevitable comment, whatever anybody did, good or bad, wise or foolish. The pattern of events must never be disturbed by conduct which might be called unexpected or unusual. People in East Head were always found to be just like themselves. To be told so, much oftener, was more than Dickie could stand.

His father was looking at him, sharp old eyes peering out of a strangely wasted face. He's aged, thought Dickie. Aged since I saw him last. He's ill.

"Is the doctor coming again tomorrow?" he asked.

"I believe so. I didn't think Christina was looking quite her usual self, by the way. Is she all right?"

"Quite all right. She's very well."

"Not another . . . ?"

"Oh, no. Not yet."

"Nothing wrong at all?"

"Why, no, Dad. What could there be?"

"I don't know. I just got the impression . . ."

138

Mr. Pattison sighed and turned his head wearily upon the pillow. He looked towards the window, where a slow white cloud was sailing behind the branches of a copper beech. A mournful remoteness fell about him as he gazed, as though he could no longer see these things as he once had. He might already have taken farewell of them.

He is going to die, thought Dickie, and remembered that it was only a chill. Browning had said that there was no need to worry. But a whisper of uneasiness remained.

"I can remember my father planting that tree," said Mr. Pattison, "when I was a lad. It's twice your age. Fancy that now!"

He mused for a while and then he said, "Women! It doesn't do to criticise them. They get ideas. They start thinking you don't love them any more."

"Did you never criticise Mother?"

"Not I! Once I got to understand her. They take a bit of understanding, don't you find?"

"I suppose so," said Dickie, without conviction.

"I don't mean I wouldn't speak up, if she did anything I didn't like. If she fed me prunes and tapioca too often I'd say so. But . . . well . . . you can't change them. If they think you want them to be different, then they start thinking you'd rather have married another woman. Then there's trouble."

"Honestly, Dad, there's no trouble between Tina and me."

"I'm glad to hear it. I just wondered. There's a way a woman goes round smiling, when she's got a grievance. . . . If you want your own way about anything, don't start trying to convince her that it's the right way. That only makes them stubborn. She'll take a lot of trouble to please you, yes, and give in to you, because she loves you, not because she thinks you're right."

"I've been married nearly two years," Dickie observed.

"I took longer than that to find out what I mustn't say to your mother. I've been through it all, remember."

Dickie made no reply to this save that he must be getting along to Brinstock.

He left the house in a rebellious mood. The assurance that his father had been through it all before him was depressing. He was only too conscious of treading a well-worn path; older people were always claiming to have preceded him upon it and insisting that nothing done, felt, thought, or said, by him could be in any way original. They knew every inch of the road, and could foresee everything that lay before him until he finished the journey in his coffin.

In vain did he tell himself that he was a lucky man, that many would envy him, and that he led, upon the whole, a pleasant life. He felt like one who strolls across some urban common, and strives to believe it larger than it is. The prospect is very pretty, very rural, if the real countryside can be forgotten. There are houses, miles upon miles of houses, on every side; but it is possible, by an adroit choice of paths, to saunter for twenty minutes without seeing one. There are not so very many other people about, and only a curmudgeon would object to the sight of them. The couples lying in the grass are quiet enough. The troops of hooting boys, wheeling bicycles through the birch spinneys, have a perfect right to be there. Nor are the wider views entirely ignoble; space, distance, can bestow charm of a sort upon gasometers and chimneys and a smoky horizon. But there comes a moment when the cheated soul rebels. Every bush has a rubbed, worn look. Every path has been trodden too often. There are no secrets in such a place; there is nothing to be discovered and cherished as a private memory. Better a corner in the dullest field, so it is far away and solitary. A hedgerow, a haystack, the green shoulder of a down, may be remembered forever, recalled at will. But this! This is merely an exercise ground for prisoners. It is pleasant. It is pretty. And the waves, the waves are breaking on some far, deserted beach, where nobody ever goes. Ah, to be there!

To get out of East Head for the afternoon was at any rate agreeable. Dickie liked driving over the hills and he looked forward to an hour with Pethwick, whom he admired. In their few meetings they had discussed little save business, yet he always got the impression that they had touched upon something larger. There was a spacious energy about the old engineer which stimulated him. Pethwick had been all over the world. He had constructed railways over mountains and through jungle swamps; he had contended with floods, fires, earthquakes, strikes and epidemics. He had carried out great projects in the teeth of enormous difficulties, had ruled armies of lawless men, and must have known how to be tough upon occasion. Yet he gave a strong impression of kindness and geniality.

That this charm of manner had always been Pethwick's most telling asset was an explanation which did not occur to Dickie. Petulant surveyors and rebellious coolies had, in their time, succumbed to it. As an engineer he might not have been exceptionally brilliant, but his projects were carried through successfully because the people working with, and for, him were always in good tempers.

141

Dickie's own temper improved as soon as he found himself in the library at Brinstock. He addressed himself to the business in hand with more gusto than he had felt for any of his work just lately. There was, after all, nobody else in the district who could give Pethwick sounder advice or look after this sale better than he. He would have been sorry to let it appear that East Head was ill served in such matters. His eye brightened and he talked briskly.

Some excellent sherry was brought to them when they had finished their business. They relaxed and chatted a little. Pethwick displayed and explained some of his treasures, a haphazard collection of objects which had caught his fancy in various parts of the world. They were attractive in themselves but not very tastefully disposed. Most of the things in the library came from central Africa, where Pethwick had spent several years among the Dandawa, for whom he had a great affection.

"They're such sensible people," he said. "On the whole they had more sense than any people I've ever met, but nobody gave them credit for having any. When I was there, a tremendous howdydo was going on about a sacred fish they had; a row among the whites, I mean, not the Dandawa. Nobody had seen it; they kept it hidden away somewhere. But it was said to be a carved stone fish that they'd had for a very long time, and it had all sorts of magic powers. *They* said that they had brought it with them over the mountains and that it had originally flown down from the sky. Well this started no end of a rumpus among the archaeologists and ethnologists. It's probable that the Dandawa did originally come from over the mountains, and there are remains of temples over there, at least four thousand years old, in which carvings of this fish constantly keep cropping up. I've got some photographs in the other room; I'll show you. You see, it was the wrong fish. The kind of fish nobody thereabouts could have seen; a sort of dolphin. Who made it? Why a dolphin in central Africa? The whole ethnological set-up seemed to be tottering. Such controversies! You didn't know whom to believe. Nobody, of course, thought of believing the Dandawa, who went on saying that it had come out of the sky. And how right they were! A geologist turned up and managed to have a look at it. He was coal black himself; otherwise he'd never have had a chance. He said it was a small meteorite. And not so very like a fish either. It had got stylised in those carvings. The Dandawa, of course, had never said it was a fish."

"If we got a meteorite in East Head," said Dickie, "there would be no mystery about it. We shouldn't worship it. We should be told exactly what it was, in a very dull way, and then it would be put into our local museum, where children would be brought to see it against their will."

Pethwick laughed and struggled out of his chair.

"That's what I mean about the Dandawa," he said. "They get the best of both worlds. Come and see the things in the other room."

He led the way to a large room on the western side of the house, explaining that it had been a drawing room but that he used it for a dumping room.

"I don't like living among a great clutter of things," he said. "So I bring two or three at a time out of here into the library, where I can look at them, and change them every month or so."

Dickie followed him into the room and was immediately struck by something which stood in the window. A fan of fire seemed to be bursting from a shattered rock. It stood upon a pedestal of green marble, but the split rock was black, and the quivering light, which sprang from it, shifted and changed as they came into the room.

"What's that?" he exclaimed.

"That? Oh, that's Conrad Swann. I wanted to show you that, too. Funny thing! I bought it a month or so before he came to live in East Head. I saw it in an exhibition and took a fancy to it."

Dickie went close to it and discovered that the light came from whorls of clear glass.

"My housekeeper loathes it," continued Pethwick. "She has to dust it, and wipe it over with medical spirit, to keep the glass perfectly clear. Those curves always catch the light in some way, and it's always different, according to where you stand, and what kind of light there is, and where it comes from. Sometimes it's quite a blaze, when the afternoon sun gets it. I like it best when it's just a faint shimmer."

"It has such a lot of power and force," said Dickie.

He retreated to a far corner of the room, so that he could see another arrangement of this darting radiance, this conquest of the airy, the impalpable.

"What I like," said Pethwick, "is the dynamics of the thing. That's what attracted me. It looks right, and it actually is right; it's exactly what would happen. Those lumps of rock would, I think, go spinning off in this orbit. I asked Swann about it, when I met him once, but he's no hand at explaining himself. I couldn't gather that he cared much about dynamics. He admitted he'd watched a

144

lot of blasting. He said he'd lived near some quarries once, and watched a lot of it, whenever he got a chance to get where he could see it. So I told him that he'd got it right. And he said, yes, he thought he had. Meaning he'd got what he meant to get. He may have heard of gravity but I don't believe he'd lost much sleep over it. Getting it right evidently meant something quite different to him."

"It's not exactly like an explosion though," said Dickie. "It's not just crude violence. It seems to be . . . governed by a law. . . ."

"Of course it would be," said Pethwick. "Everything is governed by a law."

Dickie made a sound of agreement, but he was not sure that they meant the same thing. This law, he felt, had something to do with music. There was so much going on, in this creation of Swann's, that it seemed to burst into a kind of music as he looked at it. He had received the same impression before, generally from pictures. But he did not venture upon any explanation, and merely asked what Swann called it.

"Nothing. But he told me that he had watched the blast explosions because he was very much interested, at that time, in the resurrection of the dead! So I call it the Resurrection when I tell Mrs. Soames to dust it. I can't just call it 'that thing.'"

"Is it thought to be good?" asked Dickie.

"Good? Oh, I see what you mean. How does it rate? I don't know. I'm not up in these things. I'd never heard of Swann when I bought it, but he seems to be coming to the front. I just bought it because I liked it."

"You . . . er . . . didn't get advice?"

This question tickled Pethwick. He laughed and asked

145

how anybody could have advised him upon such a point.
"Nobody else can tell me what I like, can they?"

Dickie scarcely knew what to make of such independence. He had always understood that the man who knows
what he likes, and says so, is the lowest kind of barbarian.
He hoped to buy some pictures, or something of that sort,
when he had rather more money, but he had very little
faith in his own judgement. He was by nature modest,
and had contracted an almost pathological humility from
hearing so often that Art and what the Grocer thinks he
sees are two quite different things. He had heard a good
deal of contemporary criticism and had digested this famous precept as thoroughly as even Martha could have
wished. He believed himself to be a grocer and therefore
assumed that what he thought he saw was of little consequence. Anything agreeable, anything immediately attractive, in a work of art, must be suspect until he got
permission to like it from somebody who was not a grocer.

"I've never been able to care for anything of Swann's
that I've seen before," he exclaimed. "I was sorry I
couldn't because I like him, personally, so much. But this
. . . I envy you!"

Pethwick, watching him, was also a little envious at the
spectacle of so much pleasure. He had never enjoyed it
as much as Dickie obviously did; perhaps he had never
possessed the same capacity for enjoyment. But this young
man, he remembered, went in for that sort of thing. He
had been to Italy for his honeymoon. He and his wife
were in with the Rawson set; they had been invited to
that party.

A pity, thought Pethwick, and then reproved himself

146

for thinking it a pity. He had wondered a little why a man of such ability should have been content to settle down in East Head, where the services of a first-rate lawyer could seldom be needed. Most of the work must be sheer routine and very little of it could set any serious problems. In some large and important firm he might have found more use for his brains; here he had got as far as he would ever go and would remain exactly where he was for the rest of his life. He had, apparently, no ambition.

Cultural interests, Pethwick remembered, are a handicap to an ambitious man, since they enhance the value of leisure. A fellow who is determined to get on in the world cannot afford to indulge them beyond a certain point. Dickie, in East Head, could undoubtedly command a great deal more leisure than he could ever hope to enjoy should he find work commensurate with his abilities. If he preferred leisure to success he was probably quite right to choose as he had, especially since his wife shared these tastes. Such companionship must be very delightful, and Pethwick was almost envious of it, although he had lived so very different a life himself. But then his own wife, although lovable, had been an exceptionally stupid woman; the prospect of leisure, spent in her company, had seldom lured him from his work. Upon the whole he believed that a man is more likely to get on in the world if his wife bores him, although he had known some very brilliant men who had died of it, who had worked themselves to death rather than endure domestic relaxation. The ambitious man should work in the evening for five nights in the week, and the conversation of his wife should not, therefore, be too great a temptation. But if, rather than talk to her, he works on seven nights, the consequences are sometimes fatal.

Dickie Pattison would not die in his prime. He would follow in his father's footsteps, live to a fine old age, do the minimum of work, and enjoy himself very much. He might, moreover, preserve certain virtues, an unworldliness, a fresh enthusiasm, which ambition would have destroyed. How wrong to consider such a choice deplorable! Specialists of all kinds are needed in the world, and specialists in appreciation are rare.

"I'm wondering what to do with it, now I'm going to the Argentine," said Pethwick. "I'm sure my daughter won't cotton to it. I'm getting rid of a lot of things. Would . . . would you care to have this?"

"Sir?"

"If you would, I should very much like to give it to you. I'm leaving a troublesome job on your hands. It's a relief to me to be so sure it will be well done. I'd meant to ask you if you wouldn't choose something, by way of a parting gift."

"Sir!" Dickie was incoherent with thanks. "I couldn't tell you how grateful . . . it's too good of you . . . to be able to look at it often. . . ."

Pethwick had a pleasant vision of the cultured young Pattisons, sitting at their fireside, complacently admiring their Swann. He was not to know that this was a most improbable picture. He had not spoken above half a dozen words to Christina in his life, but he had always heard that they were an exceptionally happy couple. He had never seen their lounge. That Christina would be most

148

unlikely to admire any Swann, and that they would have nowhere to put such an acquisition, save on the table where she kept her sewing machine, did not for a moment occur to him.

Dickie continued to walk round his new possession, gazing at it in ecstasy. He knew that he ought to be going, but it was almost impossible to tear himself away. At length he did so, took his leave, and drove home, transported, exultant, as though some new, and much more agreeable, phase in his life was about to begin. Having learnt to like one Swann, he might make other discoveries. He remembered with pleasure Martha's message about the Apollo, which he had not, hitherto, particularly wished to see. Now he was most anxious to see it. Now a new planet had swum into his ken. Now, like stout Cortez, he had got a glimpse of the Pacific.

Since he was alone, he gave way to an impulse which always assailed him when he was happy. He sang. All the way home he sang at the top of his voice, a thing which he never did normally save in his bath. He was a member of the Choral Society but he did not sing very loud there, for fear of making mistakes. The music which he had been hearing for the last half hour burst from him; it took shape and words from a chorus which the Society had sung at the Easter Sacred Concert:

> "The grave will not forever hold me in!
> But when God, my Redeemer, calls. . . ."

He changed gear and charged the top of Brinstock hill. He swung over it. His eagle eye fell upon East Head, extended below him, and the Channel, and the far, blue Welsh mountains. How glorious a sight! He was himself the flame bursting from the rock:

> "Then haste I forth, then haste I GLORIFIED!
> The God of Heaven to meet."

PART IV

Benbow

1

Frank Toombs and Benbow had gone down to the sports field to see the inscribed stone hoisted into place. In their absence the yard seemed empty and silent. No sound of work or voices disturbed Mrs. Toombs and Ivy as they sat in the kitchen; this circumstance loosened the elder woman's tongue. She had, so far, merely hinted at her dissatisfaction. Now she gave full rein to it.

"It isn't that I dislike the poor soul. I don't. There's no harm in him and it halves the work for your father, having somebody in the yard that really understands it. These boys, these apprentices, are more trouble than they're worth. They spoil half they do, while they're learning. But I'd just as soon not have Benbow in the house with us. After all, a tramp's a tramp."

"Oh, Mum, he's not a tramp. Anybody can see he isn't, now he's washed and tidy."

"If he's not a tramp, who is a tramp, I'd like to know? No money. No clothes. Won't say where he comes from. I keep thinking what if he's been in trouble?"

"What if he has? Though I don't think it's that; not the sort of trouble you mean."

"But there's something, or why does he act so queer?"

"I don't think he can help it."

"You mean he's not quite right here?" Mrs. Toombs tapped her forehead. "I've thought that, too, and I don't like it any better. You don't want a person like that with sharp tools in their hand. They may be ever so quiet and then break out all of a sudden."

"I think he's had a terrible shock," said Ivy. "But if he stops here quietly, perhaps it will pass off."

"You think he's lost his memory or something?"

"Well, he can't answer questions."

"Can't or won't."

"I think it's can't. He's happy here and doing a job he likes. That must be good for him. You can't say he gives much extra trouble. He does every little thing he can for you."

"Yes. I give him that."

"Where else could he go? Any other place there'd be a lot of questions asked, and I believe that might set him right back. He's already looking so much better. And we don't want a lot of talk in the village about how we came to take him. People would think Dad is crackers."

"They would, because he is. I never knew him to do such a thing before. Usually he's so careful who he takes on. You could have knocked me down with a feather when he came into the kitchen and said: 'This is Benbow. Give him some bacon.'"

"It's turned out lucky, Mum. We couldn't have a better man for work. Dad says so."

"Thanks. If I hadn't heard him say so I'd be deaf. He isn't generally so easily satisfied. But he's soft about this Benbow, and so are you, if you ask me."

Mrs. Toombs threw an irritated glance at the sock which

Ivy was darning. It was one of an old pair which they had given to Benbow, together with a spare shirt.

"Taken him properly under your wing," scoffed the mother. "I never knew such a girl for wanting to look after people!"

"I'm not a girl any more," said Ivy quietly. "I'm thirty-three, and I've got nobody much to look after, what with Dad so spry and you so bossy."

Ivy was a widow. Her husband had been killed at Arnhem. She had come back to Coombe Bassett with her little girl. Now the child was dead, too, killed on the road by a truck as she bicycled to school. Ivy lived on with her parents, sometimes going out as a temporary cook to houses in the district. Her fame as a cook was widespread and she could afford to pick and choose among ladies all over the county.

"He's not a gentleman," she said thoughtfully. "But I shouldn't wonder if he's lived with gentry, and not as a servant, either."

"He's not rough or awkward," agreed her mother. "But . . . good gracious! Supposing if he's lost his memory, like you say, there might be people seeking him."

"I've thought of that."

"You have? You seem to have been thinking a lot, my girl."

"I believe he's been married and lost his wife."

"Why ever do you think that?"

"I just do. It's just a feeling I've got. I think that might be at the bottom of the trouble. So he ought to have friends beside him when he gets his memory back."

"But has he said anything to make you think . . . ?"

154

"Nothing much. But this morning, when I took in his tea . . ."

"You never take him tea in the morning!"

"I bring tea to you and Dad when I'm home. Why shouldn't Benbow get a cup?"

"Tea? In his room? What next? A workman like him!"

"He's a Christian, I suppose."

"That remains to be seen," said Mrs. Toombs, pursing her lips. "But go on! What happened this morning?"

"He was asleep. I put the tea on his chair and said, 'Wake up, Benbow!'"

"I wonder you didn't offer to dress and shave him, while you were at it."

"So he muttered something . . . it sounded like *Maddy*. I think his poor wife must have been called that."

"Oh, you make a lot out of a little. How do you know it wasn't 'Daddy'?"

"A man doesn't say 'Daddy' when he wakes up in the morning. He says a woman's name, if he says anything."

"Still, that's not to say this Maddy was his wife. My goodness! Is his name really Benbow, do you suppose?"

"No, I don't. And I'm sure he knows it's not."

"For two pins I'd go to the police."

Ivy smiled. She took two pins from the work basket beside her and pushed them across the table to her mother.

"Funny, aren't you?" said Mrs. Toombs, pushing them back.

Nobody in Coombe went to the police if they could help it, for the policeman's mother was the nosiest woman alive. Any appeal in that quarter would ensure the widest

publicity for Frank's strange conduct in engaging a nameless tramp after ten minutes' conversation. The Toombs
family, who had always kept themselves to themselves,
would have detested this.

"Dad'll create if you upset Benbow before they get all
those orders done," said Ivy.

Her mother nodded.

"Perhaps you're right. No harm in waiting a bit. After
all, we don't know, do we?"

"That's them coming back," said Ivy.

Footsteps and voices were heard in the yard. Ivy rose,
put away her sewing, and began to lay the table
for supper. Presently her father came in, looking very
much pleased with himself.

"Mr. Headley was in the field," he reported. "And he
said what I say. There should have been a inch extra,
each side of the lettering. We won't say so to Mr. Simms,
he said, but you were quite right, Mr. Toombs, he said. It
looks a treat now it's up."

"Anybody else there?" asked Mrs. Toombs.

"Mr. Saunders. He's still a bit sore, I fancy, that it
wasn't a library."

"That wouldn't have been the same thing," said Ivy.
"Those two poor boys, Mr. Bill and Mr. Maurice, they
were all for games, not books. Where's Benbow?"

"He stopped in the shed. He'll come in when supper's
ready, if we give him a call."

There was a short pause. Benbow's position as a lodger
was scarcely settled yet. He ate with them but he had
nowhere to sit. He spent all his leisure hours in the sheds.

"He's welcome to sit here evenings," said Mrs. Toombs,
taking a fish pie out of the oven.

156

Her husband gave her a grateful glance. He had not
liked to be the first to suggest it.

"I'll tell him," he said. "But I really think he likes
pottering about in the sheds. He's no talker."

"He can listen to the radio," said Mrs. Toombs.

They all laughed. Frank was old-fashioned about the
radio. He did not like to have it turned on all day, as their
neighbours did. He complained of the row it made, and
would only turn it on for the purpose of listening to it.

"He might like *The Archers*," said Ivy.

He looked at his watch. He was as much interested in
the adventures of the Archers as were his women.

"Plenty of time for supper first," he said. "They don't
come on till a quarter of seven."

"I'll go and fetch Benbow," said Ivy.

"You've no call . . ." began her mother.

But she had gone.

"All this fussing over Benbow!" complained Mrs.
Toombs.

"She's a good-hearted girl, is Ivy," said Frank.

"Yes, but we don't want . . ."

She stopped. To put into words what they did not want
would be to bring it nearer. She did want, more than
anything in the world, for poor Ivy's aching heart to be
filled again. She had prayed for some nice chap to come
along. But Benbow! She thrust the idea from her without
naming it. That's Ivy's way, she told herself. Always running after lame dogs.

Ivy found him chipping away in the big shed. He rose
and smiled at her as she came in.

"Always at it!" she scolded gently. "Too much is as
bad as too little. You should take your proper time off.

157

Now it's supper, and after that you're not to come rushing out here again. You're going to stop with us and listen to the radio."

"Thank you," he said. "I'd like to."

"It's the Archers. They . . ."

She was pulled up by the expression on his face, the spasm of doubt and fear. He knew that name. It meant something to him, something which had no connection with the radio. Could it be his name? She did not think so.

"That family," she said. "You know. On the radio."

He shook his head and picked up a chisel. She had noticed his habit of doing that, his liking to hold some tool in his hand, as though it gave him confidence.

"I don't remember," he said, in a low voice.

Yes, but he could though, she thought. He could remember a lot, but he doesn't want to.

That name was a clue. She would try it again. She was sure that, by her own methods, she would get at the truth sooner or later.

"Don't worry," she said. "You'll remember by and by."

At that he gave her a puzzled smile. "By and by? That's a song, isn't it?"

"Yes. 'In the Sweet By and By,' it's called."

"No. Not that. There was another one we used to sing."

"You're fond of singing?"

Her mother would rebuke them for dawdling, but she was not going to miss this chance of getting him to remember something.

"I used to be."

"You haven't forgotten all your songs?"

He shook his head, turning the chisel in his hand. Then he sang:

158

"Not the labours of my hands
Can fulfil Thy law's demands;
Could my zeal no respite know,
Could my tears forever flow,
All for sin could not atone,
Thou must save and Thou alone."

"You ought to sing in the choir," said Ivy. "You've got a nice voice and we've got no good bass. Did you never sing in a choir?"

"Yes. At home. When I was a boy."

"You had a yard, like ours at home, didn't you?"

"My father had."

"Where was that? Up in the Shires?"

"In New South Wales."

She felt that this was disconcertingly far off. Instinct forbade her to ask any more. He was beginning to look hunted.

"Well, you don't need to listen to the radio if you don't like it," she said. "All I mean is, it's not expected you should work, evenings."

"I thought I'd like to finish this," he explained.

He picked up a lump of stone. She recognised it: they used it as a doorstop to the wash house, but she had not seen it since Monday, when they washed the sheets.

"I thought it looked so like a cat," he said, showing it to her.

It looked much more like a cat now, although he had not done a very great deal to it. Ivy gave a gasp. "Why! It's our Flo!"

"I thought you wouldn't mind."

"I should think not! Well, I do think that's clever of

159

you, Benbow. Really I do. So that's what you've been doing, evenings? How could you get it so like?"

"You can still use it for the door."

"I must show it to Mum and Dad. They'll laugh."

"It's not finished yet."

"Never mind. You can finish it afterwards."

She hurried back to the house, followed by Benbow, who looked rather worried. Mrs. Toombs stopped short, in the middle of a tirade against their unpunctuality, when she saw what had happened to her door stopper.

"Flo to the life!" she exclaimed. "If you'd smooth it down a bit."

"He hasn't finished it yet," said Ivy.

"I'll put it back for your door on Monday," he promised.

"Oh, it's too good for a door stopper now," decided Mrs. Toombs. "If you finish it nicely I'll put it . . ."

She was upon the point of saying that she would put it in the front room. But this would be going too far.

"I'll put it somewhere in the house where we can look at it. Really, it's a lovely likeness, isn't it, Frank?"

Toombs, who had been considering it solemnly, now spoke for the first time. "It's more than a likeness. It's a heffigy."

PART V

The Honest Grocer

1

"Mrs. Hughes, what do people mean, exactly, when they call anyone provincial?"

Mrs. Hughes could not immediately answer, for her mouth was full of pins. She and Christina were revolving round the Pattison dining-room table, pinning a paper pattern to some material.

"They say it in such a sneering sort of way," continued Christina. "What right have they to?"

"They're silly," said Mrs. Hughes, taking the last pin out of her mouth.

This sort of conversation, this kind of enquiry into the exact meaning of a word, did not appeal to her. Nor, generally, did it appeal to Christina. One knew what one meant oneself, and one seldom said anything so unusual that other people were likely to be puzzled. Arguments are not polite, and sensible people take care to say things with which everybody can agree.

"Look out, Christina! You're pinning two left sleeves!"

"No! . . . I am though!"

This, also, was unlike Christina, who seldom made stupid mistakes. She began to pull the pins out angrily, tearing the paper pattern. Mrs. Hughes perceived that she was really provoked by sneers against provincialism.

162

Not for a moment could it be supposed that she wished to discuss the topic by way of entertainment. There was some personal implication. The puzzled matron put down her scissors and tried to consider it.

"Provincial? Well . . . you know how tiresome some people can be about their own town. They can't talk about anything else; they aren't interested. They only read the local paper and get it sent to them if they go away."

"There are some like that," agreed Christina.

"My sister-in-law, the one who lives in the North," continued Mrs. Hughes, "she's like that. We all had a holiday in Paris once, and really! Everything she saw reminded her of Yarnborough, or else they had it better in Yarnborough. And she puts on an accent and says things like: 'Ah do like ma tea hot, sitha! I suppose it's because Ah coom from Yarnbro!' As if anyone, anywhere, doesn't like their tea hot. She got on my nerves so much I just couldn't help telling her that I thought the people in Yarnborough were very rough and inconsiderate, the time I was there. Getting onto the trams they pushed like a herd of cows. Even then she was quite well satisfied. 'Oh, that's our way in Yarnbro! You must take us as you find us.'"

Christina followed this with an intent frown. Then she burst out, "Still, I don't get this idea that people in London are so much better than we are. How are they better? I've been in London. I've stayed with my cousins in Bayswater. They hardly ever see any shows. They've never been to the British Museum, which I have. Of course the shops in Bond Street are wonderful. But they don't shop in Bond Street. They shop in the same chain stores we do. They hardly ever go anywhere."

"I suppose there's more going on in London," said Mrs. Hughes, who could not make head or tail of this tirade.

"If there is, nobody in London seems to know about it. They don't know the names of their neighbours, or the girls in the shops, or the people in church! I think they lead very narrow lives, compared to us. We know so many more people. When Mummie died, everyone was sorry. Wherever I went, they all looked at me so kindly, in the shops and the post office, and the policeman, even. They knew I'd lost my mother, and they knew Bobbins was on the way and she'd never see him, and they were sorry. People in London aren't human."

Christina made a wide indignant gesture and upset a box of pins upon the floor. She knelt down to collect them and added, "I'm not ashamed of loving my own town. *I* was glad, when I married, that I didn't have to go away from all my friends."

Light broke upon Mrs. Hughes. Dickie was at the bottom of all this. There had been some dispute. Instinctively she took Dickie's side. Christina was a dear girl and would have been wholly admirable had she not admired herself so naïvely. Her self-complacency often irritated her friends; that it should have provoked Dickie was not very wonderful.

"It doesn't do to be too thin skinned," she advised. "A little criticism sometimes is good for all of us."

"I've no ambition to be different from my friends," asserted Christina.

"I daresay, dear. But perhaps not all of your friends are quite so pleased with themselves as you are."

"*What?*"

164

Christina sat up, looking dumbfounded. It was not 'just like' Mrs. Hughes to say anything so sharp.

"You think I'm too pleased with myself?"

A little plain speaking, thought Mrs. Hughes, might be a kindness in the end. She had feared lately that something was amiss in the Pattison household. Now she was sure of it. If she did not speak to Christina like a mother, nobody else would. Not that Christina's own mother would ever have administered a dressing down. That doting woman's uncritical adulation had been responsible for most of the trouble.

"Well, you've got a tremendously good opinion of yourself, haven't you? And you make no secret of it. It's not to be wondered at. You've never been checked or criticised. You've always lived among people who praised and petted you. I'm not saying you don't deserve praise. You've always been successful; head girl at the high school and quite the belle of East Head till you married. But you seem to think you're perfect, and it annoys people."

"Just what have I said or done, Mrs. Hughes, that you take me up like this?"

"I suppose it was Dickie who upset you by calling you provincial?"

Christina flushed and said nothing. She crawled about, collecting pins.

"I don't say it was kind of him. Perhaps he shouldn't have said it. But you ought to ask yourself what provocation you gave him."

He had none, thought Christina. Only a hangover.

"I've known you both since you were babies and I'm very fond of you. I was delighted when you married. But I did just wonder if Dickie had done as well for himself as he deserved. You seemed to think the luck was all on his side. Most girls improve a lot, after they marry. I wondered if you'd think there was any room for improvement."

You think he'd have done better to marry Allie, thought Christina. But she did not say so. The knowledge that she had refrained from making so catty a remark did much to restore her composure. It was funny really! Her mulish expression exasperated Mrs. Hughes into more acerbity than was quite prudent. When gentle people brace themselves to scold they often go too far.

"You never seem to grow up. You're still the same complacent little thing you were in high school. It quite shocks me to hear the way you order Dickie about. No wonder he snaps! I don't want to be disagreeable. But I do think you're making a terrible mistake. When people marry they . . . they both change a little, and grow up together, and help each other to face life. But they must be ready to alter their points of view to suit each other. A married couple . . . they aren't just two people. They can be one person, in a sort of way; a kinder, wiser person than either of them could have been alone, because two people's experience has been put into it. They help each other not to make mistakes. But if one of them won't change, and thinks they're perfect already, then it isn't as happy a marriage as it might have been. You don't know what problems mayn't come to Dickie that you could help him to solve if you are truly at one with him. A woman is sometimes much shrewder than a man."

Christina had now collected all the pins and was standing, icily patient, on the other side of the table. She had made up her mind what to say and said it, as soon as Mrs. Hughes came to a pause.

"Thank you, Mrs. Hughes. If you've quite finished, shall we get on with our cutting out?"

"Oh, I've finished. You needn't think I like preaching sermons, Christina. But I can't bear to see you making a big mistake which you'll regret later on."

Since Christina made no reply to this they continued their work in silence.

So Allie feeds her husband out of a tin from Monday to Saturday, thought Christina, and Timmie is always in and out of the Cellar Bar, so Mrs. Hughes takes it out on me. She must be very worried over her own children, poor thing, to burst out like this. I shan't let it annoy me. She has always been very kind and we must bear with people when they are upset. Thank goodness I'm not the sort of person to bear a grudge and fly out over little things.

The soothing sense of her own tolerance enabled her, after a while, to make some pleasant remark. Her friend eagerly responded. Their work continued in apparent amity until half past four, when they broke off for tea.

They brought Bobbins in from his perambulator outside the window and put him in his play-pen. Just as they began to clear the table there were sounds in the hall; Dickie had come in and was talking to someone. Christina ran out to see who it was. Quite a commotion seemed to be going on; they all went chattering into the lounge. Mrs. Hughes, who was chirruping to Bobbins, thought she could distinguish Martha Rawson's voice, fluting, monotonous and inescapable. Presently Christina re-appeared.

"Is that Martha Rawson?"

"Yes. And know what? Dickie's asked her to tea! It's lucky I made a cake."

Christina dived into her sideboard and extracted a number of green baize bags containing her silver tea service. It was, of course, brilliantly polished, but she began rubbing each of the pieces over with a bit of chamois leather.

"In that case," said Mrs. Hughes, "I'll slip off."

"No, Mrs. Hughes. I asked you to tea and I didn't ask her. It seems she blew into the office to tell Dickie how much she admired him in *The Bishop's Candlesticks*. And then she asks if he thinks I'll give her my recipe for Polish borsch. It seems the Idens told her I can make it, and she's gushing about it like a geyser. So Dickie falls for all this and brings her along, since he's coming home to tea himself."

"Cooking!" marvelled Mrs. Hughes. "That's new. I wonder if that's to be her latest craze."

"Let's hope not!' said Christina. "Poor Us, if Martha starts on cooking. She'll want to get laws passed to stop us eating what we like."

"Bobbins needs changing. Shall I . . ."

"Oh, if you would! I have to cut cucumber sandwiches. All this would happen on my busy day."

Christina took the silver into the kitchen, set a tray with her best china, found a lace tea cloth, and went into the lounge. Martha and Dickie were hard at it. They scarcely noticed her as she got out the tea table and put up the flaps. Dickie was looking crestfallen.

"I don't see how an abstract can be sentimental," he protested.

"Oh, but Mr. Pethwick's Artefact isn't exactly an abstract, is it? It has definite associations. It represents something: an explosion."

"Yes. But how can an explosion be sentimental?"

"All Conrad's work, in that period, had just the least taint of sentimentality. Just a little too deliberately agreeable somehow. It's a tendency he's quite thrown off now."

"I suppose I haven't seen enough to judge."

"No," agreed Martha. "But the central truth about an explosion is its terror. If Conrad were to do anything of that sort now, it would frighten you. You'd want to run from it. Now his Apollo . . ."

Christina returned to the kitchen. Mrs. Hughes, having changed Bobbins and put on the kettle, was now cutting cucumber sandwiches.

"Poor Dickie!" reported Christina, with callous glee. "He's made a mistake. That statue Mr. Pethwick gave him, the one that Mr. Swann did, well, he thought it was *good*. But it's turned out to be *bad*. He's looking so apologetic."

"Where is it?" asked Mrs. Hughes. "Have you got it here?"

"No. It's in a packing case down at Dale's Warehouse. And perhaps it can stay there, now it's turned out to be bad. Martha says what's wrong is that it doesn't make everybody run away."

The kettle boiled and they took the rest of this elaborate tea into the lounge. Martha was so much absorbed in her subject that she barely greeted Mrs. Hughes. She turned again to Dickie and said, "So we decided not to send it to Gressington after all. It's rather a wonderful colour, by the way. I don't know how to describe it. Like . . . like dried blood. . . ."

169

"Quite my favourite colour," murmured Christina, as she poured out the tea.

It was said so softly that Martha did not catch it. The other two did, and Dickie flushed angrily.

Mrs. Hughes wished that she had not upset Christina by that little scolding. She would not have done so, had she known that this trial to Christina's patience was about to occur. Only a saint could put up with Martha, who was behaving very rudely herself, talking only to Dickie, and refusing, in a superior manner, to eat anything. Christina was beginning to look so aggressive that Mrs. Hughes intervened hastily with enquiries after old Mr. Pattison, who was still in bed.

They were safe while they kept to this topic, but neither Dickie nor Mrs. Hughes could spin it out for very long, since there was nothing much the matter with the old man. Martha fidgeted and awaited an opportunity to sidle back onto her hobby horse. At the first pause she turned to Christina and congratulated her upon the acquisition of a Swann. It must, she said, have been a wonderful surprise.

"Yes," agreed Christina. "We never expected it. But Mr. Pethwick is a very keyhotic man, don't you think?"

Neither Martha nor Mrs. Hughes could make anything of this queer word. Dickie averted speculation by plunging into an incoherent account of the difficulties he was having in the sale of Brinstock. From there he proceeded to the housing situation in general. Mrs. Hughes supported him, for it was plain that Christina and Martha must not be allowed to converse. Together they shook their heads over subsidised rents and agreed that the

170

new Council building estate was too far from the shops.

Martha became increasingly impatient and showed it by making a little noise which was characteristic of her when she was thwarted. It sounded like *Heh! Heh!* and implied that she was joining in this conversation but had something much more important to say, as soon as she was allowed to take the floor.

Christina calmly presided at her tea table and watched them all. She knew that Dickie and Mrs. Hughes were on tenterhooks and she was not sorry, because she was furious with them both.

"Heh! Heh!" put in Martha, at last. "And when are you all coming to *my* house? I've got something to show you."

"Whenever you ask us," said Dickie, who was anxious, by marked cordiality, to atone for Christina's rudeness.

"Sunday evening? Sixish?" suggested Martha, smiling. "A few people are coming in for sherry and I've got a little surprise for you all. Mrs. Hughes? Can you and Mr. Hughes come?"

Mrs. Hughes was not sorry to be able to say that Sunday evening was impossible for a minister's family. Christina said nothing until Dickie had accepted for both of them; she then reminded him that she would be putting Bobbins to bed. She made no attempt to thank Martha or to express regret. Her open hostility to her guest could no longer be ignored.

Martha, however, was used to hostility. She countered it by an enquiry about the borsch. It was so wonderful of Christina to have got the recipe. The cook at The Moorings, quite a good cook in her way, Provençal, had, alas, certain limitations. She refused to believe in any dish outside her own repertoire. This stupid Annette had denied the existence of Polish borsch. Could Christina find it in her heart to disclose the secret?

Christina curtly named a fourpenny women's weekly magazine of which Martha had never heard. There was, she said, no secret not shared by thousands of house-wives.

"But it isn't real borsch," she added. "Not Russian borsch." She made a vague circular gesture and shook her head. "*Il n'a pas assez de ça!*"

She was a clever mimic. They all recognised Don Rawson's phrase and gesture when finding fault with a picture.

"I don't think," said Dickie, "that you quite know what you are talking about, Christina."

She opened her eyes innocently.

"Oh, but I do. It hasn't got what really makes Russian borsch. Wild duck stock. Polish borsch is a cheap sort, you know. Just for the masses."

"Suppose you go and get the recipe?"

He gave her a look which sent her scuttling into the kitchen. Mrs. Hughes, following with the tea tray, found her standing there, obviously upon the defensive.

"Well she deserved it," began Christina at once, although her friend had made no comment.

"I'm off," said Mrs. Hughes, putting down the tray. "Thank you very much for an excellent tea."

"Now you're annoyed with me, I suppose."

"I'm distressed, because I'm fond of you. All that fuss about the cake and the silver and the sandwiches, and you haven't the self-control to be polite to your guest. It was ugly, that's what it was."

172

"I suppose it's provincial to eat anything for tea."

"I was thankful I was the only person to see it. A good many people in this town, Christina, would have rushed off and made a great tale of it. And you needn't think they'd have admired you. They'd have laughed at you, for making such an exhibition of yourself. I shan't tell anybody. Goodbye."

Mrs. Hughes took her departure, not without dignity. She kept her word and said nothing about the incident, not even to Mr. Hughes. But she prayed long and earnestly for Dickie and Christina before she went to bed that night.

Dickie, left alone with Martha, felt obliged to attempt some sort of apology for his wife's behaviour. It was received very graciously. Christina's imitation of Don had been brilliant, declared Martha. But brilliant! She must remember to tell him; he would be very much amused. And then, before Dickie could collect his wits, she confided to him her little plan for the Apollo. She had not meant to do this quite so soon, but her intuition told her that the moment was favourable; she would never get him more completely at a disadvantage. In strictest confidence, what would be his attitude, if she put this proposal before the committee? What was his opinion of the legal position?

Dickie was so sure that the committee would be hostile that he doubted whether the legal position would be of importance. But he was anxious to be as pleasant to Martha as he could, since she had been so grossly insulted in his house, so he refrained from throwing cold water on the scheme. She would find out for herself, soon enough, that it would never go through.

173

"The resolution specified a work of art for the town," he said, "without mentioning any particular site. I don't see that that rules out the Pavilion. Of course, the Pavilion trustees wouldn't own anything bought with the War Memorial money. But I don't see why the town shouldn't lend . . ."

"Supposing all that could be arranged," said Martha, "you wouldn't object to the purchase, as you did to the portrait of Mr. Dale?"

"Why, no!" said Dickie. "I objected to that because I didn't consider it would be a work of art, within the terms of the resolution. Swann's Apollo isn't in the same category. . . ."

At this point Christina appeared and offered to Martha, with a subdued demeanour, a copy which she had made of the recipe. The guest was shown off the premises. The door was shut behind her.

"All right," said Christina, getting in the first word. "Blow me up. It was mean to pinch your crack about keyhotic."

"I've no intention of blowing you up," said Dickie, quite incorrectly. "If you aren't sorry, it's no use to discuss it. If you are, you must be as anxious to forget it as I am."

"Martha Rawson gets in my hair. She . . ."

"You made that perfectly plain. Believe me, Christina, I never have the slightest difficulty in knowing what you think about anybody or anything. I'm told. Repeatedly. Nobody who has to live with you can be in any doubt about your opinions. Your idea of conversation is to make them known. I know what you think of Martha Rawson. I know what you think of Martha Rawson. *I know what you think of Martha Rawson.* I know everything you're

174

going to say before you say it. So that's why I'm a little agitated just now. You see, you've surprised me. Yes! You've actually taken me by surprise, when I thought you never could. I thought I knew you, through and through. I'd have sworn you were incapable of it. If I hadn't seen it, I wouldn't have believed it. You, who talk so severely about other people's filthy manners . . . flouncing about like some cheap little . . ."

Dickie was by now addressing the hall clock. Christina had rushed upstairs.

2

Upon the thirteenth day of the great siege the Swann household hauled down its flag. Nobody had come and the money which Elizabeth had left was spent, squandered, during the first week, upon all kinds of unusual delicacies.

After this week of feasting came a few days of fast. Meals grew scantier and less satisfying. They began to look out, with sharpened anxiety, for their promised deliverer, and even left the door open when they went to bed, in case the person should arrive during the night. But nobody ever came near them except Lobster Charlie, from whom they could no longer afford to buy, and a supercilious school-child with a paper parcel from Miss Byrne. This contained a horrid little hat and a message that Serafina was in future to wear it at Mass. Serafina flung it away in disgust, but, as hopes of deliverance sank, she took to wearing it. She did not quite believe Miss Byrne's statement that Our Lady had sent it, but she felt that she could not afford to offend anybody.

On Sunday morning, having breakfasted on milkless tea and stale bread scraped with anchovy paste, they had reached the end of their resources. There was nothing for

176

it save an appeal to the Traitor, who had, as they all knew, provided food in the past. So much at least was clear to Serafina although she still maintained a brave face before the others. She would, she said, go and fetch supplies from the town if nobody had come by suppertime, but she did not tell them where she meant to go. Such a course was abhorrent to her, but she could think of no other. Conrad and Elizabeth had obviously suffered much in consequence of their dependence on the Traitor. There was no knowing what she might demand, what new bonds might be forged, by this appeal. It would have been far better to keep away from her, but they could not starve.

They spent the weary day creeping about after snails and running to the gate, every few minutes, to see if anybody was coming. Joe greeted the appearance of every casual stroller with howls of joy and often brought them out of the house on a false report. By six o'clock they were all so hungry that Serafina decided to wait no longer and went in search of her holy hat.

This had been a school-girl's round straw hat, but it was now limp with age. The crown ran into a peak and the brim hung down all round. It was what Serafina called a "repenitance" to wear. She crammed it down on her head and looked for a basket in which to bring home supplies. The only basket in the house turned out to have a broken handle; the scrub bucket would hold more and be easier to carry. She rinsed it out under the pump.

None of the children had ever been inside The Moorings but they knew where it was. The distance was not great. Had she felt less languid and giddy she could have got there in half an hour. There was every reason to hurry, but she could not do so. She crept along, stopping every

177

now and then to pant a little. The bucket was un-
expectedly heavy and bumped against her legs.

Bells were ringing everywhere for evening services. The
people in the streets looked gay and relaxed. They wore
their best clothes and their holiday faces. Serafina, clank-
ing through the town with her squalid bucket, felt as solitary as though she had still been up at Summersdown,
peering down the road for somebody who never came.
Those who noticed her thought that she must be a gypsy's
child; the peaked hat, with its drooping brim, was like the
hats gypsy women wear when they come selling clothes
pegs and sprigs of lucky heather through the streets.

At the corner of Market Street she encountered an
acquaintance, a child in her class at school, called Sheila
Tooley. They were not friends. Sheila was one of those
who shouted rude remarks after the Swanns, because
"things" had been found on Dinah's head. But she now
ran up to ask why Serafina had stopped coming to school.

"School's been open a week," she said. "You'll catch it."

"Some people," said Serafina, "can't mind their own
business."

"Some people have dirty heads."

Serafina searched her mind for a taunt which could be
flung at the invulnerable Sheila.

"Some people's brother is so stupid he can't get to be
an altar boy."

She stalked on, but Sheila got in the last word.
"Oh, hat!" she shouted.

In River Road a drum thumped. There was a bray of
brass, and voices were raised in a hymn. The Salvation
Army was holding a street service, standing in a ring on
the jetty. The singers looked thick and red in their serge

178

uniforms. Serafina envied the women their bonnets, which looked much holier than her hat. They had cheerful faces, but they were singing something very sad. *Till the storm of life is past,* they sang. She hurried to get away from it and took the road to The Moorings. The music grew fainter behind her, but she could still hear it when she reached the house. A long line of cars were drawn up opposite, against the river wall; she had never seen so many cars outside the Traitor's house before.

She rang the bell and nerved herself to confront the enemy. A heathen person in a turban opened the door. She had not expected this, and stood dumbly staring, until he asked what she wanted. It was reassuring to find that he could speak English, but there was something alarming about his intonation. It was soft and sinister, not the speech of a fellow creature.

"I want to see Mrs. Rawson," she managed to say.

"She is engaged."

This puzzled Serafina, who had thought that the Traitor was married. Then she understood. "I'll wait till she comes out."

"She can't see you. She is busy."

"It's very important. What is she doing?"

"You want . . . ?"

"I want some food," said Serafina, indicating her bucket.

He looked at it and a queer spark flashed for a moment in his black eyes. He's cruel, thought Serafina. He's a murderer.

"Mrs. Rawson," he said, "gives nothing to beggars." The door was slammed in her face.

A strain of persistency in Serafina had probably ensured the survival of the Swann children. She never thought of retreat. After a few minutes she rang the bell again. The door opened. "I want to see Mrs. . . ."

It slammed again. Further assaults upon the bell were ignored.

There was, however, a knocker, an elaborate affair in wrought iron. Nobody ever used it, since the bells at The Moorings were never out of order. It was there for ornament but it was capable of producing a tremendous racket. A dozen bangs on it brought a sound of voices arguing on the other side of the door. Serafina did not intend to be shut out this time. As soon as the door opened she darted into the house. The heathen caught her and tried to thrust her out, but was checked by the Traitor's husband, who said, "No, Ahmed! Wait a minute." And then, to Serafina: "What is all this? If you go on making this noise we shall have to send for the police."

"I want to see Mrs. Rawson."

"You've been told. You can't see her. In any case, she never gives to people at the door."

"I couldn't help being at the door, when he kept on keeping me outside it."

The heathen was pinching her and she turned to say, "If you make any bruises on me I shall tell the Society for the Promotion of Cruelty to Children."

Her voice and manner startled Don Rawson. He had not recognised her, in that hat, but he realised now that she could not be a tramp. He told Ahmed not to be so rough with her, and asked her who she was.

"I'm Serafina Swann. I've come for our supper."

"Your supper? Did my wife invite you . . ."

"No," interrupted Serafina impatiently. "Not here. But

she always gives us our supper. I've brought a bucket to take it back in. It's outside on the step."

"What sort of supper?" asked Don, bewildered.

"Food. F.O.O.D! What you put in your mouth and swallow."

Serafina yelled this in exasperation, maddened by a smell of cooking, which hung faintly about the hall.

Don looked at Ahmed and asked if any orders had been given.

Ahmed shook his head. "It's not true," he murmured. "Nobody come here for food."

"I really don't think . . ." began Don.

He was quite at a loss, and unwilling to disturb Martha by referring the matter to her. She had sent him out to deal with it, when the din on the knocker began, since she had quite enough on her hands, doing the honours of the Apollo to forty people.

"Come back later on," he suggested.

"I want it now. We're hungry."

"Did Elizabeth send you?"

"No. She's not there. I came of my own accord. Children have to eat, too, don't they?"

"My dear child, this is nonsense. If your father or your . . . or Elizabeth want anything, they let us know. We can't have you children coming down here like this."

"You mean you'll give it to them and not to us!" cried Serafina, in horror. "But what are we to do then? If you want me to sing for it, I'll sing. I can sing."

In a high sobbing voice she began to sing *Annie Laurie*, which was the first tune that occurred to her.

Martha burst out of the music room in a towering rage.

"It's Serafina Swann," said Don helplessly.

181

"Food! Food! Food!" screamed Serafina. "I want some food. I won't go away till I've got some food. I've sung for it. You expect people to sing for their supper, don't you? But I did sing. And I'll sing and sing and sing until . . ."

Martha seized her far more roughly than Ahmed had done, and shook her till she was giddy. This invasion was the last straw and it sounded like a deliberate piece of insolence on the part of Elizabeth.

"Get out!" she commanded. "Go away! I'm not doing a thing more for any of you. Understand? I've had enough of you."

The door was still open. She flung Serafina out of it and slammed it. A terrific hammering immediately began on the knocker.

"Don't take any further notice," she said to Don and Ahmed. "Let her get tired of it and go away."

Serafina thumped until her arms ached. She then sat down beside her bucket to rest a little. Get in she would. She was not going back to the others without food.

They would never open the door. To get in by stealth was the only alternative. The windows on the road side of the house were high up, but there was some wisteria which might give a foothold. She put down her bucket and began to scramble up towards a small window which opened on a tilting slant. As she got near to it a great clamour reached her ears. A lot of people were talking and screaming and shouting in there.

At last she was level with the window sill. Clutching the wisteria trunk with one arm, and bracing her feet against it, she leaned sideways to look. Inside, below her, she could see clouds of cigarette smoke and a lot of heads.

182

The noise was terrific. Then her eyes fell upon a sort of platform; upon it stood . . . THE THING!

In the utmost terror and confusion she slithered to the ground again, picked up her bucket, and fled. Panic so overpowered her that she was running past the band on the jetty before she knew where she must go, and remembered the one person, in this terrible town, who had been kind to her.

3

The party at Summersdown had been a nightmare, but Frank Archer's brew provided a powerful anodyne. Martha's sherry, at The Moorings, did nothing of the sort. After ten minutes of it Dickie escaped from the music room into the garden. Courtesy demanded that he should hang about for a little longer before getting away, but he had seen quite enough of the Apollo. He could never like it. Things of that sort were above his head and he had been a fool to expect otherwise. No wistful staring, no elucidations from Martha, no intrinsic faith in Conrad, could exalt what he thought he saw.

The clamour of forty enthusiasts, shouting in the music room, sank to a raucous murmur as he strode down the garden. Even in the distance it sounded unpleasant and he commented on this to an imaginary companion, a *Doppelgänger* who filled a social gap in his life, and with whom he frequently had conversations. This friend could be a man or a woman. At the moment she was a woman, because he wanted one and his marriage bed was temporarily strewn with nettles. She strolled beside him and laughed at his jokes. What reason, he asked her, have we for supposing that John Milton would have agreed with us about Martha's party? Oh, said she, taking it up at

184

once, Oh! Milton? When does Milton talk about Apollo? Oh, I know! *Apollo from his shrine, Can no more divine. . . .* No, darling. Think of the three lines just before: *The oracles are dumb. No voice or hideous hum Rings through the archéd roof in words deceiving!*

Hideous hum! That's it exactly. How clever of you, Dickie! But the oracles aren't dumb, surely? Just listen to them! Hard at it explaining what the Apollo means.

The garden was shaped like a very long triangle. At its base stood The Moorings. Little grass grew there and no trees. The greater part of it consisted of crazy paving, intersected by pergolas. Rockeries rose, here and there, like miniature mountains; the whole effect was hard and stony. There was no reason why any object should be where it was, and little had been done to it since old Tom Skipperton ordered it from a firm in Bristol. The original site had been waste land running by the river, a region of starved, salty soil and rushes. Nothing grew there easily and Martha, who did not care much for nature, had left it as it was.

Dickie wandered along the twisting stone paths, seeking company. Several strangers were sitting upon the river wall. He got a glimpse of Carter, under a pergola, engaged, apparently, in ponderous flirtation with a man in suede shoes. Nell Manders was peering forlornly at some gold-fish in a lead tank, but she hurried away when she saw Dickie. Ever since the Summersdown party she had been wondering what, exactly, she had said to him. Had she really told him that she would like to marry him although he was not a gentleman? If that was the case she had better keep out of his way for the rest of her life.

He strayed on, past the boat-house and down the triangle to its apex, where the garden walls met at a kind of
look-out, a round tower which commanded a view of the
river mouth and the marshes. Here sat a woman whom he
had met before, once or twice. Her name was Dottie Miller and she was married to a literary celebrity who lived
in Ilfracombe. She had fine eyes and a concave face; her
thick sandy fringe and her jutting chin were so prominent
that her nose looked almost flat. He had never thought
her pretty but she managed to be striking, and he was
glad to see her sitting on the stone seat which ran round
the look-out. She wore a dress of black and green harle-
quin lozenges with a wide skirt and very little top; the
black jacket, which she had worn in the music room, lay
on the seat beside her.

"Hullo, Dickie!" she said.

He had not supposed that they were Dickie and Dottie,
but he had no objection. He went up the four steps to the
look-out, bowed, and said, "Dr. Livingstone, I presume!"

She laughed loudly and gave him a look which completely unmarried him. This was refreshing. Most women
nowadays looked at him as though he had no gender at
all. He would have been rather shocked if the women of
East Head had done otherwise, but Dottie came from
Ilfracombe. He returned the look adequately and suggested that parties like this were not very much in their
line.

"I couldn't agree with you more," she said. "But Edgar
would come. Coo!"

He smiled. "Coo" struck him as naïve and charming. It
was not one of Christina's expletives; she would have
thought it common. Sitting down beside her he took a

186

brief glance at her shoulders and then concentrated upon the view.

This was extensive but monotonous. On one side were mud flats, boats and buoys. On the other were ready fields. In front was the line of the sea, but a thick heat haze obscured the distance. There was no horizon, and no coast of Wales, on this heavy afternoon. Behind them, half hidden by the rampart of The Moorings, rose the hills and roofs of the town. It was comparatively quiet. Seagulls occasionally squawked on the mud flats and a distant band blared a hymn.

"Why do we never meet nowadays?" asked Dickie, coming back to Dottie's shoulders.

"I can answer that in two sentences. You never come to Ilfracombe. I never come to East Head."

"I think that's rather sad," he decided.

"Very sad. Life's like that."

A gust from the band echoed her words with sad music:

> Jesu, lover of my soul,
> Let me to Thy bosom fly!

Bosom! thought Dickie, and stared thoughtfully at the gulls on the mud flats. Presently he asked her what she did with herself all the year round in Ilfracombe.

"Me? I look after Edgar and the offspring."

"Not really? Why, that's what all the girls do in East Head. I'd hoped Ilfracombe was different."

"Why?" asked Dottie, after a pause.

"Because I have a hopeful nature."

"What did you hope the girls in Ilfracombe were doing?"

He gave no answer. None was needed. Idly he followed the hymn in his mind. He had sung it so often that he knew it by heart.

> Cover my defenceless head
> With the shadow of Thy wing.

"You can't even make a limerick about Ilfracombe," complained Dottie.

"No," he agreed, after trying. "Whereas East Head . . . just think of all the rhymes! Bred, wed, fed, dead, led, sped. . . ."

"You've forgotten bed."

"No, I haven't. It was the first one which occurred to me. But I thought it a little obvious.

> "Of respectable men in East Head
> There is not very much to be said:
> They are bred, they are wed,
> They are fed, they are dead,
> And they dread to be led from East Head."

Dottie looked glum. She thought it a deplorable limerick and so did he. But he could not bring himself to tell her any dirty ones, although she had given him tacit permission to do so by raising the subject. It had been a hint that he might take liberties, a recognisable step in an adventure which had hitherto proceeded upon the usual lines.

She was dog stupid, thought Dickie, but would meet him more than half way if he chose to start anything.

Anything they might start would soon become a bore.

188

But there was a distinct stimulation in the thought of being a naughty boy with Dottie Miller, and a more attractive woman would not have filled the bill half so well. Dottie would merely be an accomplice. He had to spend a day in Porlock next week; he was certain that she would meet him for lunch there if he asked her. Later there might be other meetings: a brief, vicious, hard-hearted satisfaction, a temporary escape from boredom, which would impose no obligations upon either of them. In some obscure way the need for it was connected with his disappointment in the music room. He had reached a dead end there, and wanted to revenge himself upon those cheating hopes.

"Dottee!"

A voice came bleating down the garden.

"That's Edgar!" she murmured.

Edgar sounded anxious, as if wondering what she was up to. There was still time to mention Porlock. She was waiting. They might settle it in a quick, warm whisper, while the bleating voice drew nearer. He looked at her and saw that her eyes had suddenly filled with tears.

Poor Dottie! he thought. Poor girl!

The impulse died. One must not pity an accomplice. He said nothing.

She seemed to be aware that the moment was over. She turned her defenceless head away and stood up, smoothing her brilliant skirt. She looked childish and forlorn.

Edgar Miller came into view. He supported Dottie and the offspring by writing crime novels under a pseudonym, but his standing with Martha had been earned by his poetry, which did not sell. His appearance was romantic; Dickie had once told Christina that he must have ordered it from the same firm which supplied Tom Skipperton's garden. *Literary Gent, virile, bronzed, complete with pipe, 59/6d.* Christina had laughed and said that he probably got it at half price in a sale. (Christina's laugh! Heard no more.)

A cloud of uncertainty lifted from the bronzed virile face when Miller saw what Dottie was up to. No situation could have been less secluded than the look-out, no company more harmless than that of Dickie Pattison, a model family man, a pillar of society. Such unconcealed relief rather annoyed Dickie. So I don't rate as a billy goat? he thought. Well, I suppose not. Anybody's wife is as safe as houses with me.

"We ought to be going, dear," suggested Miller.

Dottie, shrugging herself into her little black jacket, said that she couldn't agree with him more.

"And how's the Law?" he condescendingly asked Dickie.

"Too little of it," said Dickie. "Everybody has made a will and nobody seems to get into trouble, nowadays."

"Ha! ha! Well . . . we must be getting along."

The Millers departed. Dickie sat down again in the look-out and envied the hard-heartedness of naughty boys. To be sorry for people was a fatal encumbrance. He could feel no triumph in this decision although he could not exactly regret it. Dottie might have been unwilling to let him go, when he had had enough of it. The whole thing would have ended in squalor, misery and self-reproach.

He looked at his watch and saw that he might now quit The Moorings without incivility. But he lingered for a few minutes longer, leaning on the parapet, for it was not unpleasant occasionally to be alone. The tide was rising, and the river channel, meandering through the mud, was fuller. A yacht crept down towards the sea, her sails filling with a light evening breeze. He thought of Conrad, and of their day together, and wondered that he should have built so much upon it.

At last he set off up the garden again. Just beyond the boat-house he met Martha; she was running about like a sheep dog bringing in strays, and she greeted him severely:

"Oh, there you are, Mr. Pattison! Where have you been! I've been looking for you everywhere."

"I was . . ." began Dickie.

"Come into the boat-house. I want a word with you about our little plot."

What plot? wondered Dickie, as she pushed him into the boat-house.

"Here he is!" she announced triumphantly.

Four people were there: Don Rawson, Carter and a couple called Meadowes who were among Martha's most loyal supporters. Meadowes was a retired schoolmaster and served on the Selection Committee, but he had taken no part in the great fight over Sam Dale's portrait because he and his wife had been abroad at the time. They had only just returned to East Head.

"They're all in the know," said Martha to Dickie. "I've told them about it, in strict confidence. We're all such friends of Conrad's that I thought we might take this opportunity to put our heads together."

They were staring at Dickie as though he were some kind of converted cannibal. He had renounced the heresy that he knew what he liked and had received Grace enough to like what he ought. Mrs. Meadowes smiled at him in warm congratulation. She was sure that he would never eat a missionary again. Her husband's expression was less cordial; he could not so easily forget the murky past. Carter's hostile glare suggested that she expected a relapse at any moment. Don looked blank; he balanced on the edge of a table and watched the scene.

"The committee," explained Martha, "will want very adroit handling. We must expect some stubborn opposition. I realise *that*, from some of the comments on the Apollo that I've heard, even from people who should know better. Luckily we have Mr. Meadowes back and I have hopes of Mrs. Hughes. But the others . . ."

She threw out despairing hands.

"Quite," said Dickie, who now realised what was in the wind. "You'll never get them to consider anything so . . . so. . . ." he sought for a word which should not outrage them, "so unconventional."

"Oh, I don't despair. I think, we all think, that it will be so much more acceptable to them if it's your suggestion, if you sponsor the proposal. You have such influence. They'll listen to you. They always do."

"Oh, no! No! I'm not at all the right person," exclaimed Dickie, recoiling.

"You're exactly the right person. Isn't he?"

Martha turned to the others. Their murmur of assent was not very enthusiastic for three of them thought that Mr. Meadowes would be a better sponsor. They overlooked the fact that any proposal from Meadowes was liable to provoke an automatic resistance. He had a chilly, conceited voice, and a way of looking down his nose, which exasperated the mildest auditors. Martha, however, was aware of this. She knew that Dickie's slight West

Country burr would ring more pleasantly in the ears of his fellow townsmen.

"I shouldn't know what to say," began Dickie.

"Of course you would. You'll say that Conrad is a local man, emphasise that, with a considerable reputation. Mention the Venice award. Say that this is his finest work; you can quote Alan Wetherby. And point out that we shall get it for a tenth of what we should have to pay if we waited. They'll all grasp that."

"But they won't like or understand it, and I'm not qualified to tell them why they ought to."

"Mr. Meadowes or I will do that, when supporting you."

"You can tell them," put in Don suddenly, "how much *you* like it, even if you can't tell them why."

No way out of it, thought Dickie. I must tell the truth.

"I'm afraid I don't like it," he said.

There was a general recoil, as though he had spat upon the floor, or perpetrated some other gross indecency. Carter gave a gruff chuckle. Once a cannibal, always a cannibal.

"It's my fault, I dare say," continued Dickie. "I don't pretend to understand these things. I can't see anything in it at all. It strikes me as it will probably strike most of the committee: ugly and senseless. So I'm not the person who should sponsor it."

Don gave an imperceptible nod. The others turned to Martha as if asking what she had to say for her convert now.

"I had no idea of this," she said accusingly. "I thought you admired Conrad's work. Considering how enthusiastic you were, over that very inferior example of it which

. . . Why didn't you tell me this when you saw the Apollo in the music room?"

"I didn't think my opinion was of the slightest importance."

"Not of importance? When you had assured me of your support? I think you might have warned me that you had changed your mind."

Never, thought Dickie. I never assured you of my support. You don't bounce me like this. I may have been a little too encouraging; Tina had flustered me. But . . .

"I think," he said pleasantly, "that I only told you I wouldn't oppose the suggestion upon the grounds that the Apollo is not a work of art."

"I should hope not!" snapped Meadowes. "You know that Wetherby considers it Swann's finest work?"

"Yes. Oh, yes."

In Dickie's mind two convictions were locked in a sort of stranglehold. Wetherby liked the Apollo because he had superior taste. Wetherby must be an ass if he liked the Apollo. Doubt of Wetherby's good faith might have resolved the conflict, but it did not occur to him; he still had a great respect for all the non-grocers.

"I know so little about these things," he repeated.

"Precisely," replied Meadowes. "So why not listen to those who do?"

"I want to listen. I'm anxious to be convinced. But, until I am, I must . . . speak as I find, mustn't I? Especially on this committee, where we are responsible for public money."

"Mr. Pattison!" said Martha solemnly. "Here is a work of complete integrity. It makes no compromise, no concession, to what the public may demand, or think that it

194

likes. To state his secret, private vision is all that concerns Conrad. Can't you understand?"

"That," put in Carter, "is something which you can't expect anybody to understand but us, Martha. The artists are the only honest people."

Dickie smiled at them. The fact that Martha had tried to bounce him, now that it was revealed, did much to restore his composure. He had, at first, been sorry to disappoint her and he was still regretful at having to stand in Swann's way. But he was not to be bullied, and knew how to hold his own with people who tried. Nor was he now in danger of losing his temper. A tussle of this sort rather raised his spirits.

His equanimity daunted them a little, as it had daunted Sir Gregory Manders, in the fight over the sewage-disposal scheme. Martha adopted a more conciliatory tone.

"If only," she said, "you could . . . could . . ."

Don intervened again.

"Assume a virtue if you have it not," he suggested. "You want to admire the thing. You know you ought to. Perhaps you will, eventually. Why not stretch a point?"

Don and Dickie looked at one another.

"And what," Dickie asked them, "about my . . . integrity?"

He did not like to use such a pretentious word about himself, but could not resist the temptation to make them jump.

He did. Carter gave an audible gasp of protest. What could a little provincial solicitor mean by talking about his integrity?

"Perhaps," suggested Martha gently, "we attach rather a special meaning to that word."

"I see," said Dickie. "Let's say common honesty."

"*Common* honesty?" queried Mr. Meadowes, smiling a little, as if he found the expression a contradiction in terms.

"Telling the truth," explained Dickie. "Saying what you mean and meaning what you say. Sticking to your bargains."

"You mean purely moral integrity?" said Martha, impatiently. "There are other loyalties. . . ."

"Swann has his," agreed Dickie. "I think I must be allowed to have mine. I don't think the town had any purchase of this sort in mind, when we were entrusted . . ."

"The town will lynch us later on," interrupted Meadowes, "when it realises what an opportunity we've missed. We shall go down to history as dolts and dunderheads."

"Yes, indeed," said Martha. "I happen to know that the town is far from satisfied with the committee. I often think there is more liberality, more perception, among simple working people, than there is among those who ought to be choosing for them and guiding them. Sometimes, just instinctively, they *know*. Only nobody listens to them."

Like the Dandawa, thought Dickie, and their sacred fish. The poor black boobs said it fell from heaven, and nobody listened.

"I think," she said, "that the town ought to have an opportunity of judging. I've a very good mind to arrange a public exhibition, before we put forward our proposal."

There was a stir of surprise and alarm. It was a dangerous move, and Martha knew it, but Dickie's unexpected obstinacy had destroyed her chances of bouncing the committee. The pressure of public opinion was now her only

196

hope. Few people on the committee would court unpopularity by resisting a widespread demand. It would not, she believed, be impossible to create and stimulate discontent with the committee. The odds were against her but she was inclined to take them.

"I must think about it," she said. "But in that case I must ask you all to treat what's been said here as confidential. I should just want the people to see the Apollo, and judge, before my proposal goes before the committee. Can I rely on your discretion, Mr. Pattison?"

"Oh, yes," said Dickie. "I think a public exhibition would be a very good idea."

It would, he thought, put an end to the whole business.

"But it's too much to hope that you won't crab it though," muttered Carter.

At that his temper began to slip.

"I haven't the slightest desire to crab it, Mrs. Hobhouse. I don't ask that the majority should support Mrs. Rawson. But there ought to be some respectable backing among the people who are, after all, paying for it. If there is, I agree that we should be justified in going ahead of popular taste. But if there is none, I think it is too soon to buy a work like this, however much we may be abused and derided later on."

He pulled up, aware that he had been provoked into saying too much. The less he said, the better he could preserve his liberty of action.

"And are we not respectable?" demanded Carter.

"I should be happier," he said, "if the suggestion was supported by a few people who were not personal friends of Swann. And now . . . really I'm afraid I must . . ."

No effort was made to detain him. He had as good as

cooked a missionary before their eyes. Don, however, escorted him off the premises and unlocked a little door in the garden wall which gave access to the road. Before they parted Dickie suddenly asked him if he liked the Apollo himself.

"No," said Don, who was filled with envy at Dickie's honesty. "I take your view. I think it's ridiculous."

"You don't think there could possibly be a mistake?"

"A mistake?"

"I mean . . . could it be anybody else's work?"

"I'm afraid not. I don't think it could possibly be."

"It doesn't look like Swann, somehow," complained Dickie. "Of course it looks like . . . I've seen a lot of contemporary stuff that looks rather like it . . . I don't know enough to know good from bad. I suppose some is good and some is bad. All I know is that this . . . this doesn't look like Swann."

Don nodded, and checked the impulse to suggest that Swann might have gone mad. Martha would never forgive him if he did that. He said goodbye and hurried back to the boat-house.

Dickie drove disconsolately home. The afternoon had battered him. Martha's behaviour obliged him to think ill of her, and he disliked having to do so. But, the more he thought over her manoeuvres, the more unscrupulous he found them. She had tried to rush him into compliance and she had used very unfair weapons. Not only had she attempted to exploit his goodwill towards Swann, she had taken advantage of his probable reluctance, as her guest, to challenge or criticise her taste. Moreover she had endeavoured to confuse him, by suggesting that he had committed himself, and forcing him to contradict her in public. There was an appearance of premeditation in the whole assault which he did not relish at all. She was a dangerous woman and he wished to have no more dealings with her. He would have liked to talk it over with Christina, but that, at the moment, would not be easy.

Christina was standing at their gate when he got home, and she had somebody with her, a ragged child in floods of tears. They were both carrying heavy baskets of what looked like food. As he got out of the car she was thrusting the child and the baskets into the back. Then, with an indignant glare, she turned on him.

"Your supper," she said, "is in the fridge. Salmon mousse and blackberry fool. There's a salad in the dining room, and some Brie cheese. Coffee is all put ready. Will you lift Bobbins at nine o'clock if I'm not back?"

"But where are you going?" he exclaimed, as she pushed him out of the way and climbed into the driver's seat.

"To see after something that I think is important, although you and Martha Rawson don't."

4

Serafina did not often shed tears, but when she did she outwept Niobe. Having started she could not stop; kindness, promises of help, baskets of food, were of no avail. She felt herself to be beyond the reach of consolation and sobbed steadily during the whole drive up to Summersdown.

Christina also was greatly agitated. Her pity and concern for the children were genuine, but her strongest feeling was one of indignation. She wanted to punish the people who had been responsible for this; she hoped that Elizabeth might be put in prison for it. As for the Rawsons . . . here a certain element of satisfaction tempered emotion which might otherwise have been too painful. She was not sorry to have such a good case against Martha, for her conscience had been troubling her ever since that tea party. Now she could feel that her conduct had been justified. Martha Rawson was a fiend who turned starving children from her door. It was a positive duty to be rude to her.

"Now, Serafina," she said, when they got out of the car at Summersdown, "you must stop crying dear, or you'll upset the others. It's all over, you know. All over. It won't happen again."

Serafina struggled and gulped.

200

"From now on," continued Christina, "everything is going to be all right. I'll see that it is. You'll have nothing more to bear. I promise. You believe me, don't you? I promise."

The look which she got in answer to this was most disturbing. It was almost compassionate, as though Serafina pitied the simplicity which could offer such a promise. That child, she thought, as they walked together up the path, knows too much. She knows more than a child ought to know. She knows more than . . . more than . . . Christina was upon the verge of thinking: *she knows more than I do!* But that was nonsense. How could a child know more than a woman of twenty-five, a wife and a mother? What could she know? What secret lay behind that look? That nothing is safe?

For an instant Christina flinched and hesitated upon the threshold of the house, as if unwilling to enter it. A desolate uncertainty invaded her, even when she thought of her home and Dickie and Bobbins, and of all the security which she had taken as much for granted as the air she breathed. Anything can happen to us, she thought. Anything! And that's what Serafina knows. I promised she should have nothing more to bear. I don't know what I'm going to have to bear myself, yet.

Serafina had run into the house, calling to the others. No answer came.

"They must have gone up the garden," she said. "I'll fetch them."

She ran off, her shouts dying away as she turned the corner of the house. Christina still lingered in the doorway, fighting this inexplicable depression. Five minutes ago she had been perfectly sure of her own future. Now

201

she was sure of nothing. She wanted to rush home and make certain that Dickie and Bobbins were still there. That bright beloved place no longer stood at the centre of the universe, sheltered and unshaken, a stronghold from whence the unfortunate, the culpable and the foolish might be admonished or consoled. It was no more than a solitary shack, surviving on a boundless desert, spared as yet, but spared only by chance. Anything might sweep it away, and send her forth to wander, no better equipped against calamity than anybody else. How could she help the helpless? They knew more about the inclement world than she did.

There was a movement inside the house. Serafina had come in again by the kitchen door, still shouting for the others. Then there was a startled cry and silence.

Anything! Anything! thought Christina, forcing herself to go inside.

"Mrs. Pattison! Oh, Mrs. Pattison!"

Serafina met her in the hall. She was triumphantly waving a piece of paper.

"They've come! The person's come! They've left a letter."

"What person?"

"Oh, I don't know who. But they've left a letter. Look!"

She thrust the paper into Christina's hand. This single promise redeemed meant more to her than any number of new ones. Upon the paper a few words were scrawled:

SERAFINA!

All gone to eat at the Metropole Hotel.
Come along down and join us as soon as
possible.   F.A.

202

"It was on the kitchen table," said Serafina. "They must have put it for me to find. Wasn't it a clever idea?"

"But who on earth can it be?"

"It must be somebody rich. The Metropole is very expensive. Do you think we're going to live there now?"

"Well, thank goodness somebody has turned up. I'll drive you down and find out what's been settled."

"Shall we take the baskets back? We shan't need them if we're going to live with a rich person."

"Put them back in the car. We'll see."

The drama of all this banished Christina's depression. On the drive down to the Metropole she made up her mind that she would interview this belated protector, make sure that everything was now on a satisfactory footing, and rebuke him or her for not having come before.

"You could leave that hat behind in the car, couldn't you?" she suggested, as they arrived at the hotel.

"Thank you," said Serafina, "but I have my reasons for perpetually wearing it. Religious reasons."

Christina could not argue over this, although she did not relish having to enter those magnificent portals in such company, and felt that Serafina might look less conspicuous without the hat. We can but be thrown out, she thought, advancing as boldly as she could towards the dining room, and completely unaware that she was still wearing the flowered plastic apron in which she bathed Bobbins. Ever since Serafina's arrival upon her doorstep she had been agitated and not quite herself. She had been so anxious to get food to those children that she had rushed out of the house, just as she was, as soon as Dickie brought the car home.

Before they reached the dining room a waiter darted

from a side door, as though he had been on the look-out
for them. With a glance at the hat he suggested that
they belonged to Mr. Archer's party, and led them off
down a corridor.

Mr. Archer! thought Christina. The husband! How
stupid of me not to have guessed. Well . . . he's going
to get a good piece of my mind. His own children!
Starving!

They were conducted into a private room where Dinah,
Mike, Polly and Joe, seated round a table, were silently
stuffing themselves with roast chicken. Frank Archer sat
in an armchair by the window. His assurance was equal
to most situations but he had not quite enough of it to
bring these filthy brats into the public dining room. He
was looking out to sea, so as to avoid the spectacle of
their table manners. When the new arrivals appeared he
jumped up.

"Hullo, Serafina!" he said. "Mean of us not to wait
for you but we were all so hungry, and we didn't know
how long you'd be. Siddown. What'll you have to start
with? Soup? Grapefruit? Shrimp cocktail? Hors d'oeu-
vres?"

"Shrimp cocktail," said Serafina, sitting down.

"Shrimp cocktail," he said, to the waiter, "and chicken
to follow."

The prawn's eyes then popped at Christina who drew
herself up haughtily and began on her dressing down.

"I don't wish to intrude," she said, "but I'd like to be
sure that proper arrangements are being made. I understand that all these children have been left alone and
abandoned for nearly a fortnight with nothing to eat. That
seems to me to be a very disgraceful thing, and I'd be

204

glad to know that it won't happen again. I was thinking of
going to the police."

"Quite right, Madam, quite right. Disgraceful is the
word. My name is Archer. I'm the father of Polly and
Mike."

He looked at her enquiringly.

"I'm Mrs. Richard Pattison," she said.

"Oh?"

He searched among his recollections and impressions of
East Head and remembered the local yokel.

"I believe I've had the pleasure of meeting your husband."

Christina looked down her nose and was rewarded by
the sight of her plastic apron. A thaw set in. She blushed
deeply and snatched it off. Archer, enchanted, took it
from her with a courtly bow and draped it over the back
of a chair.

"There's a veranda just outside," he said, "with chairs,
and a nice view of the sunset. It's quite warm still. Perhaps you'll take a glass of sherry with me out there, and
I'll try to set your mind at rest."

A glass of sherry would have been very welcome, but
she refused it, remembering what he had done to the
drinks at Summersdown. But he ordered two glasses all the
same, and when they arrived they looked quite harmless.

"It's very, very good of you," he said, sitting down
beside her, "to be so concerned about my children."

She tried to look as though their paternity was a fact
in their disfavour.

"I should be concerned about any children neglected
like that," she said. "People can be put in prison for it.
They ought to be."

He gave her a glance of respectful admiration. She turned away and contemplated the sunset.

"I hadn't," he said, "the least idea that they'd been abandoned like this. I've been in Italy. I didn't know my wife was back in London till she spoke to me on the telephone this morning. She then seemed to be so vague about arrangements this end that I took the next train down. Cigarette?"

"No, thank you."

"I'm taking them back to London on the nine-o'clock train tonight, as I have an important engagement in Town tomorrow morning. They will sleep tonight at my house in Cheyne Walk. Tomorrow I shall ring up a reliable firm called Fairy Godmothers Ltd., with whom I have already had some dealings. They will provide some good lady who will look after the children for the day and buy them clothes. On Tuesday I shall escort them myself to a school which I've found for them near St. Albans."

"What kind of school?" asked Christina of the sunset.

"Oh . . . just a school, you know. For little children. A few boarders and the rest day scholars."

"Progressive?"

"What's that?"

"One of those places where they don't teach them anything or look after them or make them go to bed. Just neglect them and say it's education."

"Now why should I send them to a school like that?"

"I don't know. I thought you might."

"They're terribly expensive, those schools," he protested. "If I thought neglect was education, it would be much cheaper to leave them here."

206

She looked round quickly to see if he was laughing, but he had a perfectly straight face.

"This school," he explained, "is kept by two elderly women and their young niece. One of the aunts used to be a nanny. The other was a kindergarten teacher. The niece is trained for nursery-school work. The children don't smell. They are taught to read and write and say their prayers, and they go to bed at six o'clock."

"It sounds quite harmless," allowed Christina.

There was a long pause. Nothing had as yet been said about the Swann children. Each waited for the other to begin, Christina in some astonishment, Archer with considerable amusement.

"I hope your mind is at rest?" he said at last. "I do wish you'd drink that sherry."

Christina looked again at the sherry and decided that she would. It was not as easy as she had supposed to scold him for neglecting the Swanns. He might not regard them as his responsibility. She sipped her sherry for a while before she ventured to ask what was to be done for the others.

"The others?" he said. "I've only got the twins."

"I mean . . . the little Swanns. Who is going to look after them?"

This question appeared to surprise him.

"I suppose some of Swann's friends will," he suggested. "He seems to have a devoted band of friends here. What about those people . . . the Rawsons?"

"The Rawsons!"

She gave him an indignant account of the Rawsons' behaviour.

"They can't have understood," he protested. "They can't have known what they were doing."

"People ought to know what they're doing," said Christina. "That's an excuse I never listen to."

"Are you quite warm enough? Wouldn't you like your . . . your little wrap?"

She remembered the apron and became less truculent.

"They threw Serafina out of their house," she said.

"I expect she frightened them. She's a terrible child."

"Excuse me, Mr. Archer, she's a very brave child. I think she's managed wonderfully, considering. I don't know what would have happened to your two without her. They'd be dead by now, probably. You owe her quite a bit, I think."

"So what ought I to do?"

"They mustn't go back to that awful house. No water . . . no food . . . it makes me wild to think of it. They ought to go straight into a nice hot bath and then into good clean beds."

"Yes. Yes. I expect they ought."

"So aren't you going to do anything about it?"

"My dear Mrs. Pattison, why should I?"

"You can't just leave them to starve."

"But I haven't. I've given them a most expensive dinner. You think I ought to do more?"

"Yes. I think you ought to find some nice person who will look after them till their father comes back."

"Oh? I see."

He gave an enquiring look at this nice person who had so obligingly presented herself. Until she turned up, he had been desperate. He had almost decided to take the little Swanns to London, too.

208

"I can't imagine anyone, *anyone,* knowing about it, and not doing all they could," cried Christina.

"Perhaps you're right," he said, feeling in his pocket for a cheque book. "So we'd better get down to it. You find the nice person and I'll find the cash."

"What? Me?"

"You're better equipped than I am. You know this town. And I really must leave by that train."

"I really don't see that it's my business."

He paused in his cheque writing to stare at her.

"I thought you said you couldn't imagine *anyone* . . . You mean you came here merely to lecture me?"

"I . . . I . . ."

He went on writing.

"What would a nice person charge?" he asked.

"I'd have to work that out. They need clothes, too. They haven't a thing, and what they're wearing ought to be burnt."

"Mrs. . . . Mrs. . . . what is your first name?"

"Christina."

He completed the cheque and made an entry on the counterfoil. *Conrad again.* £100.

"You'll let me know immediately, won't you, if there is any news of Swann? Here's a card with my London address. I shall be in England for some months now. And here's a cheque. It will do to go on with for a few weeks. You must write to me if and when you want any more."

"It's plenty for the moment," said Christina, taking the card and the cheque. "Anything that isn't spent can be sent back to you. I shall have to take them to my house tonight. That's what I shall have to do."

Archer, who had been determined that she should do this, gave a convincing start.

"Not really? Dear me! I'm afraid that will give you rather a lot of trouble."

"It will," she said grimly. "But I couldn't find anywhere else, tonight, at this short notice."

He smiled benignly. He could, as he had told Elizabeth, sell anything to anybody, but he had never done a slicker deal than this. To have sold the little Swanns to so excellent a guardian, without moving from his chair, was a master stroke. She would, he was certain, never shirk any responsibility which she had undertaken. She was obviously an admirable woman. Had it not been for that little oversight about the apron, he might have thought her almost oppressively admirable.

"Have you room?" he asked sympathetically.

"Oh, yes. The girls can have the guest room. And Joe . . ."

Suddenly she laughed. Archer sat up. What a delicious laugh! Admirable? This girl was a honey!

"Joe," she said, "can have a bed in . . . in a little room, it's going to be a nursery, but at present it's my husband's dressing room."

A strange light had come into her eyes; it was not, he thought, entirely the light of loving kindness.

"But won't that be a great nuisance for him?"

"He's very *fond* of Mr. Swann."

"I see."

And she'll larn him to be fond of Swann, thought Archer. She well may. People who love Conrad must accept the consequences.

So I can't surprise him, thought Christina. He always

210

knows what I'm going to do next. He's got a big surprise coming to him now, anyway. He'll be furious, but he won't be able to say a thing, not even that I'm not nice to his friends. Mr. Swann's children, who all his other dear friends will do nothing for, because they think ridiculous ugly statues are more important than children. I always did want to get hold of those children and look after them a bit.

She jumped up.

"I'll take them now, if they've finished their supper. The sooner they're in bed the better. Thank you, Mr. Archer!"

"Not at all. Thank *you!*"

They beamed at one another, each with a pleasant sense of triumph. Christina thought that she had twisted him round her little finger; only a very short scolding had been needed to make him see his duty. He was quite easy to manage. Had she been at that stupid party, she would never have allowed him to make everybody drunk.

"You'll let me know if you hear from Swann?" he repeated.

"Yes. Mr. Archer . . . I do appreciate . . . I mean . . . I do see that anybody might think you had no particular cause for . . ."

"Oh. I'm fond of him, you know. Like your husband."

"Are you? Oh, that's . . . I mean, I'm glad. I mean, it's nicer to do things for people if you are fond of them."

"It is, isn't it?" he said, conducting her back to the sitting room.

All the children were sitting in a state of glazed repletion except Joe, who had gone to sleep with his head in a plate of ice cream. Archer picked him up and carried him out to the car. In the lobby Christina remembered her apron, and ran back for it. She found Polly and Mike sitting by themselves at the table, staring sadly in front of them with their pop eyes, waiting for something else to happen. With a pang of compunction she kissed them and told them that they were going to a lovely place where they would be very happy.

"Who will be there?" asked Mike doubtfully.

"Kind people and a lot of nice children to play with. It's all going to be quite different."

For the first time the twins displayed emotion.

"I don't want different," announced Polly.

"People here is kind," gulped Mike. "We get shrimp cocktails. We have too got nice children to play with. Serafina and Dinah and Joe."

"We like it here," wailed Polly. "We have snails."

Tears made them look more hideous than usual. Christina was still trying to comfort them when Archer came back, having stowed all the Swanns away in her car. She shook hands with him and ran off, leaving him to still their mewing sobs as best he could. Her last glimpse of the Archers was so forlorn that she began to feel quite sorry for the man, wandering through the desert with a worthless wife and two ugly little children whom nobody could possibly want except Serafina and Dinah, who began to cry, too, when they realised that the twins had been taken from them.

"People laugh at them," howled Serafina. "People call them little horrors. We don't. We lo-o-ove them."

Joe, waking up, joined in the chorus, bawling lustily.

"Everybody goes away," cried Dinah. "Mummy and Conrad and Elizabeth and Polly and Mike."

212

Their tears were still flowing when they reached Bay Hill. Christina was disappointed. She had looked forward to seeing Dickie's face when they all came trooping in, and he learnt what happened to people who were fond of Swann. But she had pictured Dickie as the only person in the scene who was not smiling and contented; his dismay should have been a contrast to her own motherly common sense and the children's rapture, at the prospect of a hot bath and clean beds. To herd these wailing infants into the house was not quite so satisfactory; she felt that they had taken the wind out of her sails.

5

"I happen to believe Serafina," said Christina. "And I've no time to argue about it on a Monday morning. Will you give me your soiled collars, please?"

Dickie went into the little room where he kept his clothes and was confronted by Joe, majestically enthroned, according to the morning ritual in all well-managed nurseries.

"I'm doin' my business like a good boy," stated Joe.

"I should have thought," said Dickie, hunting for his collars, "that you might have gone next door."

"Dinah's next door."

That's the hell of it, thought Dickie. Dinah had been locked up next door for the last twenty minutes, as he knew to his cost.

"She's constlipated," explained Joe. "We're all constlipated. Aunt Chris says she isn't surprised. She's going to give us something for it that tastes like chocklick. Are you constlipated?"

"I'm going to be," prophesied Dickie.

In the bedroom Christina was swiftly stripping and folding up sheets. He gave her the collars.

"I'm sure Serafina means to speak the truth," he said.

214

"But it's monstrous to accept this story about the Rawsons on her bare word. They're Swann's most intimate friends. She seems to be muddled about a lot of things. She told you that her mother had gone to Korea."

"That woman is not her mother."

"You know perfectly well what I mean."

"It just shows how little you and the Rawsons care about those children. I at least know who their mother was."

"So do I. It was a slip of the tongue and you know it. Wait a minute, Tina! Don't go!"

"It's my washing day. It's Monday. In the provinces . . ."

"I'm going to ring the Rawsons up."

"Do. I can't stop you."

"Until we've got their side of it you are not to go about spreading this ridiculous story."

"I don't see anything *ridiculous* in it."

"Do you hear me? You're to hold your tongue till I've got at the true facts. It may turn out to have been a mistake."

"You think it's a nuisance having the children, so you want to make out that it wasn't necessary."

"You and Archer had no business to settle it like that between you. Why didn't you get in touch with me?"

"I can't see that you'll suffer much. You'll be out all day and I'll have them in bed by the time you're home. I know it's all rather a muddle, this first morning, but I'll get it straightened out."

"I'm not talking about the inconvenience. . . ."

"I'm only pointing out that I settled it with Mr. Archer because I'm the one who'll have to cope. You don't think

I took on three extra children just for fun? If I'm willing . . ."

"I know. I know. It's noble of you."

The generosity and unselfishness of Christina's conduct
were very confusing to Dickie. In any other circumstances
he would have applauded them warmly. But now they
merely made it more difficult to explain that she was in
the wrong. He believed that she knew this perfectly well,
and found it hard to keep his temper. With a great effort
he smiled and said, "Of course, darling, if it turns out that
the cygnets have no other refuge . . ."

"The what?"

"The little Swanns."

"Funny. Tell Martha. She'll roar."

"Oh!" He gave it up. "You're impossible. You understand me quite well and you won't . . . I'm simply telling you this. You are not to say that Martha turned a
starving child from her door."

"I'm to say exactly what you say? How mediaeval!"

"Not at all. I say medieval. If you prefer mediaeval, say
it by all means. It does credit to the high school. . . ."

"I knew quite well, only I wasn't thinking. No need to
start cracks about my education. . . ."

"You hold your tongue about Martha. Understand?"

"And what if I don't?"

He had been walking up and down excitedly, but now
he drew up and looked at her.

What if she did not? One cannot beat one's wife, he
thought. What does one do when she seems to be asking
for it? Would she really prefer to be beaten, or did she
want it both ways? Did she expect the privileges both of
an equal and of an inferior?

216

"I don't know," he said. "It will only be one step nearer, won't it?"

"Nearer? To what?"

He gave her a look, so sad that it frightened her a little.

"Nearer to what, Dickie? What do you mean?"

"Let's not put it into words. I suppose I mean a point from which we can't come back."

Did he mean that all this would not blow over in due course? Why did he have to take everything so seriously?

"All right," she conceded. "I won't say anything to anybody, if you must make all this song and dance about it."

She spoke sullenly but he was satisfied. He knew that she would always keep her word.

Does he think I'm mentally deficient? she wondered. Do I make a habit of telling stories I can't prove? Of course I wouldn't spread this all over the town until I was quite sure; he ought to know that, after being married to me for two years. Fancy taking me seriously, just because I teased him a little.

"Can I go now?" she asked, with provoking meekness.

"What? Oh, yes. That's all I wanted to say."

She went downstairs with her pile of linen. It was just like him to suppose that she would have time, on a Monday, to go rushing round the town with any story at all. He could never get it into his head that washing day was hard work.

Nor had she, as a matter of fact, much wish to meet her friends until she had disarmed all possible criticism by a spectacular transformation of the children. People would think, and say, that she had acted in a very

217

peculiar way. She meant to silence them by securing their applause. She meant to silence her own conscience, which kept on suggesting that she was being very mean to Dickie. A miraculous improvement in the little Swanns was to atone for everything.

Presently she heard the door slam behind him. He was in a hurry to get down to the office and ring up The Moorings. Further dealings with Martha Rawson were not agreeable to him for he had made up his mind to steer clear of her. He saw no alternative, however, and tackled the distasteful task at the earliest possible moment.

He spoke on the telephone, first to Don and then to Martha. Their distress was obviously quite genuine. They were shocked and horrified. All was as he had thought; they knew nothing of the children's plight and had supposed Elizabeth still to be at Summersdown. Serafina's appearance had been, to them, quite inexplicable. They blamed themselves severely for sending her off, and explained that this sudden interruption to their party had flustered and confused them.

Something, declared Martha, must of course be done at once. Something would have been done sooner, had she known sooner. It was exceedingly kind of the Pattisons to have come forward like this, and she was most grateful, but the responsibility must be regarded as hers. Dickie was to thank Christina for all her trouble and assure her that other arrangements would be made immediately. Such a burden must not be imposed upon her for a moment longer than was necessary. There was an excellent progressive school at Brixcombe, over which Martha appeared to have some hold; she was sure that it would receive the little Swanns at the request of so influential a

patron. Mr. Archer's money must be returned. He had
no right to interfere in Conrad's affairs, whatever his pre-
tensions might be. He must be sent about his business,
since there was no knowing what he might attempt to do
next; from disposing of the children he might proceed to
claim some interest in the contents of the studio. It was
therefore imperative that Joe should be removed from
Dickie's dressing room at the earliest possible moment.

Dickie heard all this with relief. He was glad that this
plague of children was not to afflict his house for long;
he was glad that Martha had been able to clear her character to some extent. He put the whole business out of
his mind, plunged into the day's work, and thought no
more of the cygnets until he encountered them in his
front garden when he went home.

Since they were no longer so distressing a problem he
was able, for the first time, to view them with charity.
They were, in any case, easier to view. A great change
had taken place in their appearance. Christina, in spite
of her washing day, had begun upon her miracle. She
had managed to clothe them. They were combed and
washed. Even their complexions had improved; they were
less pasty and Joe's cheeks were quite pink. Christina's
prompt attention to their bowels might account for this.

The group which they made held Dickie's attention.
They had been left in charge of Bobbins for a few minutes. Christina felt no fear in doing this; their gentleness
and care of the baby had struck her ever since she had
known them.

Serafina sat upon a rug on the grass, with Bobbins in
her lap. Her hair had been smoothly brushed back from
her bony forehead, and braided. She wore a blue dress.

219

For once her sharp restless face was calm, as she gazed down at her charge in an ecstatic trance. Dinah, who knelt beside her, reflected the same gravity. For the first time Dickie perceived Dinah's likeness to Conrad; in a girl it was unfortunate and gave her an elderly look. Bobbins, rosy and lively, with the radiant bloom of a well-tended child, might have belonged to some different species, might have been some godling tended by awe-struck mortals.

Amidst all this motionless solemnity a little private game was going on between Bobbins and Joe, who, smiling, held out a nasturtium towards which the baby stretched a dimpled hand. It was Joe's smile which arrested Dickie's attention; an unusual smile, never seen on an adult face. There was in it indulgence towards a younger creature, yet a certain complicity, the tacit understanding of an equal. These two were living in a world apart; they attached their own meaning to a nasturtium.

Pretty! thought Dickie, looking also at the wall of flowers which rose up like a tapestry behind their small heads. Beautiful. I've seen it before. Where? A Memling . . . in several Memlings . . . this group—the grave girl, grave angels, grave saints, and that quiet little game going on between the Child and one of the young-eyed Cherubim. *Young-eyed!* Fantastic, unrealistic pictures, they might be called. But here it is. Here it is, he told his *Doppelgänger*, who, on this occasion, failed to turn up. He was alone and nobody else was looking at it.

He hurried into the house to find Christina before the group broke up. She liked Memling and he was sure that she would like this; looking at it together, they might bury the hatchet. Through the open kitchen door he could see lines of sheets and shirts flapping gently in the breeze. Christina came in with a basket of pegs.

"Tina," he began, "do come. . . ."

But she interrupted him furiously. "So you rang up Martha Rawson?"

"Yes. Has she . . ."

"Did you, or did you not, give her leave to come and take those children away?"

"Why . . . I . . . I . . ."

"Because that's what she seems to think. She telephoned. I had quite a job to convince her that she's going to do nothing of the sort, whatever you and she may have arranged between you."

"Now Tina, she has a far better claim. . . ."

"No, she hasn't. They've been entrusted to me."

"By whom?"

"I've more right than she has, since there's nobody really to say who has the right. I'm prepared to do it myself and do it properly. She means to shove them into one of those awful . . . She'll have to kidnap them, if she wants them. I don't give them up of my own accord."

"Do be reasonable. She's their father's intimate friend. We are only slight acquaintances. Supposing he's deserted them? Supposing he's dead? She's a rich woman. I'm not . . ."

"What kind of a woman are you then?"

"You'll hand those children over when she sends for them. This is my house, remember, and I have some say in what goes on here."

"I won't. She may be rich. But I'd be sorry for a dog, I'd be sorry for a rat, handed over to her. She isn't kind. She doesn't want them because she's sorry for them. I've always been fond of them and taken an interest in them, but she only thinks of her honour and glory. She doesn't want anybody else to butt in over Mr. Swann's affairs, because she thinks he's famous. If anything happened to make him less famous, she'd drop them like a hot potato. I don't trust her a yard, nor do you. If it was Bobbins, which would you give him to? Me or Martha?"

Dickie had no immediate reply. It was quite true that he did not trust Martha a yard.

"You haven't any answer to that," said Christina, "because you know I'm right, and you know you oughtn't to have gone behind my back like that. Are you going to cut the grass before supper? You said you would, if you got home early."

The grass certainly needed cutting. It had better be cut. He took himself off to do it.

The Memling group had broken up and taken itself indoors when he brought the mower to the front lawn. This was very small, and to cut it was a tiresome little job; he was always having to turn the machine round. He set about it after giving a friendly nod over the fence to his next-door neighbour, who had been sent out upon exactly the same errand. Up and down their tiny lawns they went, in opposite directions, passing one another at a laburnum tree which grew half way along the fence

Clankety - clankety - burra - wurra - wurra - wurra - wurra - wurra - Brck!

Turn the thing round. *Clankety-clankety* . . . What is *he* thinking of? He looks resigned enough. Is he thinking of a liner and a gang-plank, and going up it never, never to come back? Is he? *Wurra-wurra-Brck!* Round. . . . Entirely my fault. We don't suit. I shouldn't have married her. Having married her I should have put up with it better. *Brck!* Round. *Clankety-clankety* . . . She'll never forgive me. She may pretend to, but there'll always be this bitterness. This bitterness! *Brck!* Round . . . This bitterness, this continual trying to score off me, I cannot stand. Not forever. When the children go, there'll be something else. *Brck!* Round. . . . She's a good wife. Never looks at another man and feeds me like a Strasbourg goose. I'd rather . . . tinned food . . . a slut . . . *Brck!* Round . . . Anything would be better than this continual sour bickering. She'll never drop it, even if I declare I think she's perfect. I don't mind being bored . . . *Brck!* Round . . . I could stand that, if we could be good-tempered and peaceful. But I won't stand this forever . . . only while Dad is alive. *Brck!* Round . . . Can't break his heart. Idiotic to ruin my life, coming back here to please him and then . . . *Brck!* Round . . . But not forever. One day I'll clear out, and sail across the sea . . . sea . . . sea. . . .

The meek noise of good husbands cutting the grass floated into the house and gratified Christina's ears, as she bustled about putting four children to bed. In Joe's little room, which looked onto the front garden, it was particularly loud. Joe, in all the glory of his new slumber wear, was finishing a glass of milk. Christina took the glass from him and tucked him up for the night.

Clankety-clankety-burra-wurra-wurra. . . .

"Why doesn't Uncle Dickie have a sort of . . . sort of . . . sort of thing he sits on, to do that?"

"Because the lawn is so little."

"There was one in our field. It went round and round and round, and Mr. Hackett sat on it, makin', makin' hay.

We sawn him when we were in our tree. Weren't it sad about our tree?"

"Very sad. You must have missed it."

"Our ole chair did it."

"Did what?"

"Killed our poor tree. The ole chair what we used to climb on. So the Traitor took it away."

"Who's the Traitor?"

"Marfa. She took it away in her car, din't she? Did you know what our chair were called?"

"No. I didn't know it had a name."

"Nor din't I, till she told me. It's called Apollo."

"Apollo? Your chair? Joe! What do you mean?"

Burra-wurra-wurra-Brck!

"Couldn't Uncle Dickie get a very, very tiny small sort of thing to sit on?"

"I don't think they make them as small as that. Why did Martha Rawson take your chair?"

"What for don't they make them so small?"

"I don't know. But when did she take the chair? Where was it? In the field?"

"Oh, no. It were in the shed. We shut it up in prison. Do you think Bobbins would like a nice lickle snail, if I catch one for him tomorrow?"

"Joe! Do try to tell me about the chair. I want so much to know what happened to it."

Joe wriggled impatiently. "I can't bemember," he protested.

"Try to. Try to tell me all you remember and I'll . . . give you a chocolate biscuit."

This bribe was effective. Joe frowned and then said, "We were . . . we were . . . we were in the field, and we

224

sawn it, we sawn it, hoppin' about and shootin' at us, and pretendin' to be an Arfitax. So we—we—we—put it in the shed and we rescued a poor Form what was in the shed, and we put the naughty ole chair in the shed, and then, and then, Marfa, Marfa came and took it away."

"That same day?"

"No. Another day. I . . . I . . . I were on guard. So I chaglenged her and she said, she said it were quite all right. She, she, she wanted to keep it quite safe. And she told me its name. Can I have a biscuit now?"

"Did she say anything else?"

"No-o-o! She said it were very wonderful. She said Conrad made it."

"What day was it?"

"A long time ago. A year ago?" suggested Joe.

There was no more to be got out of him. Christina gave him the promised biscuit and went into the girls' room. Serafina had protested against so early a bed time, but had been packed off with the others because her company at the supper table would have been a nuisance.

"If you don't want to go to sleep just yet," said Christina, sitting on the bed, "I'll bring you a nice book. You can read until Uncle Dickie and I have finished supper, and then I'll come and tuck you up. What sort of book would you like?"

"Any book!" declared Serafina fervently. "I haven't had a book to read for a long time."

"I'll bring you one of the books I had when I was a little girl. Your books were all lost when your poor tree was killed, I suppose?"

There was no doubt about it; both the children froze at the reference.

"What happened," asked Christina carelessly, "to that old chair you used to climb up on?"

This question did not seem to disturb them. They looked vague, and said that they did not know.

"I forgot about it," said Serafina.

"Wasn't it there, when you found your tree was dead?"

"No. It was gone by then."

"Poor chair!" mourned Dinah.

"Was there nothing in the field, then, besides the tree?"

Now they were really scared. They looked at her, looked at one another, and looked at her again.

"No," said Serafina at last.

Christina realised that nothing short of the rack would produce any other reply. She let it go. She was sure that she could, in time, get it all out of them.

Down on the path below there was a rattling and a clatter. Dickie was taking the mower back to the tool shed.

"Hear that?" said Christina. "That's our mower, going to be locked in our shed. You had a shed, didn't you? What did you keep in it?"

Again she was confronted by that frozen stare.

"I don't know," said Serafina.

"I don't know," said Dinah.

"I'll get the book."

Plain as a pikestaff, thought Christina, going downstairs. She was almost sure that she knew exactly what had happened, although there were certain details which she must confirm. It must have been on the Sunday, the day after the tree was struck. The chair must have been so much twisted that they did not recognise it; only Joe seemed to have done so. They had put it into the shed, where that

226

fool Martha had found it. All the muddle at the party had been because the Apollo was supposed to be in the shed So now . . .

So now there would be no more nonsense about progressive schools. Oh, no! If Martha started pushing people about she would hear something which would make her jump. I haven't mentioned it to anyone else *yet,* but I thought perhaps you ought to know. . . . Oh, no, not at all. I've seen a lot of modern statues which looked like thunderstruck garden chairs. I don't wonder at anybody making a mistake about it. What I'd do, in your shoes I'd quietly take it away and bury it somewhere. Nobody need know. And I'm so glad you think I'd better keep the children. I thought you would. . . . Of course I won't say anything. Well, you won't be saying quite so much after this, will you? Not quite so much about knowing better than the masses. I daresay I'll tell my husband, someday, but you can be sure he'll hold his tongue. No, I can't promise not to mention it to him, because he thinks I can't give him a surprise. But not yet a while. Not till I've settled with you, Mrs. Rawson. If I told him now, he might warn you.

Dickie had locked up the mower and was watering the tomato plants. There was the clank of the can and the drumming roar of water from the tap outside the kitchen door. Then silence, when he turned the tap off. His footsteps went away down the back garden to the vegetable beds. He was whistling a sad old song:

> And when will you come home, my dear?
> Home, my love, to me?

This was a moment which she was to remember for the rest of her life; how she stood in the kitchen and heard Dickie's footsteps going away down the path. He went and never came back, although it was long before she could believe it. The lover, the young husband who had had her maidenhead, who had brought her to this house, who had given her Bobbins, with whom she had squabbled and laughed, went away forever down the path that evening.

Even at the time a sudden foreboding seized her, as she hunted among her books. Such a silly old song, she thought impatiently. Why should it be called *Edward! Edward!* Nothing about Edward in it from beginning to end. Yet it always made her sad when Dickie put the record on. It was the tune. Those old tunes had something, that was why they lasted. Two men fought, they never knew why, just about a poor *little briary bush!* And one killed the other and he had to go away in a ship over sea. And she asked him when he would come home and he said never! *That will never be . . . be . . . That will never be!*

I'll hide that record one of these days, thought Christina. It's too sad. There are enough sad things in real life, I say, without making yourself miserable over the gramophone.

6

"*Ça marche!*" said Martha, as she looked through her morning's letters. "The Brixcombe school has climbed down. They will take the little Swanns at reduced terms. I thought they would, considering all the pupils I've sent them."

"Good," said Don.

He was reading the newspaper and answering Martha, an accomplishment which he had mastered pretty well. There was no need to listen to her with close attention. She made four kinds of noise. The first denoted pleasure, the second annoyance, the third was informative and the fourth asked a question. He rang the changes on four answers.

"I must let Mr. Pattison know. I shall avoid further dealings with his wife, after her abominable rudeness to me over the telephone."

"A nuisance!"

"I'm sure he wants to get rid of them, poor man. He's had them a fortnight. I shall simply ask him to bring them all here on Wednesday morning, and then I'll drive them over to Brixcombe. He and his wife can fight it out."

"Good."

There was a short silence while she opened another letter.

"Nigel Meadowes," she said. "Proofs for his article on the Apollo, for Friday's *Gazette*. He wants me to look them over."

"Good."

"By Friday everyone will have seen it. Yesterday I don't count because Monday is washing day, for most of them. Hardly anybody goes to the Pavilion on a Monday."

"Really?"

"You could exhibit the Crown Jewels in the Pavilion vestibule on a Monday and nobody would be much the wiser."

"A nuisance."

"I wasn't surprised when Mr. Beccles told me over the telephone that he didn't think anybody had noticed it much. But, did I tell you, Don? Sir Gregory happened to come in. You can imagine what his reaction was."

"A nuisance."

"Well, I'm not so sure that it was. Controversy is often very stimulating. I'm glad he saw it."

"Good."

"He went off, so Mr. Beccles said, declaring that it was an outrage and threatening to have it removed. How could he have it removed?"

"What do *you* think?"

"Of course he couldn't. Sir Gregory has no say at all in what happens at the Pavilion. But he went off to bully the Mayor about it. He won't get much change out of Mr. Dale. He actually called it obscene."

"Good."

"Well . . . yes . . . I agree with you. In a way we

230

couldn't have a better antagonist than Sir Gregory. He's such a bully and so unpopular. If he says it ought to be taken away a great many people will automatically feel that it ought not. Yes! I want controversy of that sort."

"Good."

"Mr. Dale is surprisingly favourable. Of course his taste is non-existent, but he likes to think he is a live wire—progressive. He likes anything that attracts attention to the town. Attention means custom. I think a good many of the tradesmen may take that view. They feel they are putting East Head on the map. A *succés de scandale,* perhaps, but a *succés.*"

Martha opened a third letter saying, "Alan Wetherby."

"Really?"

The flow of comment ceased. There was such a long silence that Don began to be aware of something unusual. He looked over the top of his newspaper.

She was staring at her letter with a blanched face and a stupefied expression. It seemed to be quite a long letter; there were several sheets covered in Wetherby's minute, angular handwriting.

"What does Alan say?"

"He . . . he . . ."

She gave him a strange, despairing look.

"Martha! Are you all right? Are you quite well?"

"No. . . ."

She picked the letter up and put it down again.

"No," she repeated faintly. "I . . . I don't feel very well. I think I'll go upstairs . . . and lie down for a little. . . ."

"Has Alan . . . is he being tiresome about something?"

"Oh, no. No! It's just that I don't feel well. I'll be quite all right by and by. I'll just lie down quietly for a little."

"Anything I can do?"

"No. Nothing. It will pass off. Just a little faint, that's all. It's nothing."

"You look ghastly. I believe I ought to send for Dr. Browning."

"Oh, no. Please don't. I shall be all right."

She picked up the sheets of her letter and went upstairs to her room, waving him away when he tried to come with her. For nearly an hour she lay upon her bed in the sleepy lassitude which succeeds a tremendous shock. Not immediately could she bring herself to re-read Wetherby's dreadful letter. But a moment came when she had to do so.

Dear Martha,

If you must quote my opinions, please do so correctly. I ran into your friend Carter last night; she's in Bristol for a conference, so she says. I heard from her that you are telling everybody that I *admire* a contraption which I saw in your music room, the last time I was at The Moorings—a piece of scrap metal which you (*not I*) assumed to be Conrad's Apollo.

You have no grounds whatever for making such a statement. When did I say that I admired it? I said I was stunned. I was. At you, for supposing that Conrad could ever have been responsible for such a ludicrous object. I am not, as you know, one of his *claque,* but I should never have done him so great an injustice.

I think I said that Gressington had missed something. I am still sorry that you did not send it there;

232

I should have enjoyed hearing what they made of it.

I also said I wouldn't have thought Conrad had it in him. He might, I agree, have been capable of exposing some metal object to a tremendously powerful electric current, but he could not possibly have known what the exact effect would be, and could not, I think, have handled it during the process without electrocuting himself. He must simply have turned the current on and left it to God.

You will therefore, in future, refrain from saying that I consider it to be Conrad's best work. I am not one of those who confuse Conrad with the Almighty. And, moreover, I don't believe he even turned on the current. I have good reasons for supposing that he never saw or handled the thing in its present shape, and knows nothing whatever about it, for I believe that he had left East Head before this 'Act of God' took place.

Why do I think so?

Well! This 'Apollo' struck me as oddly familiar, when I saw it in your house. I was convinced that I had met it before, in an earlier incarnation. I cast my mind back. I remembered a stroll I took round Conrad's estate one day, when you escorted me there to hear Carter reading poetry. I was much struck by several of his domestic arrangements. My insatiable curiosity even took me up to the meadow behind his garden. Perhaps you have never been there? It had a tree in it—a tree which was struck by lightning, I believe, on the first night of the storm. Conrad, as you have often observed, is a very simple person. Tree climbing appeared to have been one of his hobbies. It

wasn't an easy tree to climb, but he is a man of re-
source, and had pinched one of those steel chairs
which used to be round the band-stand at the end of
the Marine Parade, before the worthy Mr. Dale substituted deck chairs, at double the price. I say pinched,
knowing Conrad, but I may do him an injustice; he
might have bought it, for I believe they were sold in
job lots. Anyway, it gave him a leg up into his tree.

When I recollected Conrad's chair, this tantalising
familiarity was solved; only you'd got the thing upside down. That great flat *foot* was once the back,
and the *head* a molten blob at the end of a chair leg.
And it used to be green. Immediately after leaving
you, that afternoon, I went up to Summersdown to
have a look round, and was lucky enough to fall in
with the farmer who owns the meadow. We inspected
the ruins of the tree. He told me that he had discovered the accident at six thirty A.M. on Sunday and
described the strange transformation of the chair,
which stood, so he said, immediately under it. I then
had a hunt round for *Conrad's* Apollo and found it,
as I believe, hidden in the garage. It must have been
taken from the shed, and God's Apollo substituted, at
some time between six thirty A.M. on Sunday, and
Tuesday afternoon.

God's Apollo, however, is presumably Conrad's
property. I gather that you abstracted it from his
premises, during his absence, and without his leave.
If you want it for your music room I think you
should pay him for it. I suggested what I thought to
be a reasonable sum. Two hundred pounds might,

234

anyway, sweeten Conrad's temper when he comes
back and discovers what you have done.

I said nothing of all this to Carter. I had an idea
you might prefer that I didn't. But I shall say a great
deal, as publicly as possible, if you go on misquoting
me. She told me that you had some plan for an exhibition. I doubt if that is wise. I dare say it's highly unlikely that Farmer Hackett would attend it, but he
just conceivably might. I know that 'what he thinks
he sees' is of no importance, but it would be awkward
if he insisted that he thought he had seen it before.
He might not, however, recognise it—upside down
and all dolled up, as I'm sure it will be. Still, it's not a
risk I'd take myself.

Yours ever,
Alan Wetherby

This second reading brought on a violent spasm of nau-
sea. For the greater part of the morning her physical dis-
comfort was so great as to leave her little leisure for reflection. She had an excellent constitution and did not know
how to be ill. But these unpleasant sensations had one
merit; they induced a salutary blankness of mind. She
could not, she would not, she must not, understand what
had upset her so much. At one point she burnt the letter
without reading it again.

There was an aspect of this calamity which she could
never have understood, however often she read the letter.
Wetherby's spite and malice would always have been incomprehensible to her. She was a pretentious fool, conceited, a bully and an egotist, but she was not cruel and

had never in her life taken pleasure in other people's misfortunes. She had never cold-bloodedly inflicted pain, or felt any temptation to do so. In this respect she was more innocent than many of her betters.

Don came up at lunch-time and again suggested calling the doctor, for he was alarmed by her looks. When she refused all medical advice he brought her a stiff tot of brandy.

This really did her a little good. He had left the bottle, and she took a second tot. After that, a few ideas began to float through her mind. They were disconnected and therefore endurable.

One was in no way responsible for Conrad Swann or for anything that he might have done. One had been very kind to him, but one could not be regarded as his representative. No!

One had arranged this exhibition with the trustees of the Pavilion. That was all.

Dr. Browning was stupid and behind the times. Really she must be quite ill. A London doctor would be better. Get away, to London.

Who could be described as Conrad's representative? Who would naturally act for him? His solicitor? Had he one? Mr. Pattison? He saw to that business when the truck knocked down the wall. *Mr. Pattison!* He had the children.

Since she felt so ill, something should be done about it at once. There was no point at all in delay. Delay might even be dangerous. A London doctor ought to be consulted at once.

What arrangements Conrad might have made with Mr. Pattison one didn't know. One hadn't been told. Mr. Pattison was looking after the children; that was evidence that he acknowledged some kind of responsibility. He had been told about the exhibition, in the boat-house, and he had raised no objection.

Don had looked so worried. It was not fair to worry him. There was no reason why they should not go up to London tomorrow, by the first train.

Perhaps a London doctor might say that she had been doing too much. Travel . . . a long cruise . . . he might suggest something like that. There was nothing to keep her in East Head. If necessary, she could leave it for a very long time. Don had never liked it. He would be happier elsewhere.

One had done one's best, but it was an unrewarding place. One's efforts had not been appreciated. These people would really, so it seemed, prefer to be left to their own devices. If they got themselves into some ridiculous scrape, one had better not be concerned in it. One need never really have to know about it. One could be on the high seas. . . .

Annette! Ahmed! Board wages! Packing!
There were a million things to be done immediately, if one was to get away by an early train tomorrow morning. This brandy was wonderful. It had cured one, for the time being.

She found herself upon her feet again, restored to health and able to think connectedly. She could even address herself to an unpleasant task, which she must undertake before plunging into more welcome activities. By some disclaimer of responsibility she had better make her whole attitude about . . . about the incomprehensible . . . perfectly clear. She must write a letter to Mr. Pattison.

She sat down to it at once. The ease with which it flowed from her pen surprised her. Somebody might almost have been dictating it to her.

Dear Mr. Pattison,

I enclose a letter which I have had from the Brixcombe school. You will see that they are willing to take Conrad Swann's children at reduced terms.

Of course it is for you to decide whether he should take advantage of this offer or not. I thought it no harm to make enquiries and pass this information on to you. I am afraid I can't do anything more in the matter myself, as I have been far from well lately and my husband insists upon taking me up to London to see my doctor there. I may possibly have been overdoing it; a long rest and change of scene may be necessary.

If Mr. Swann does not return, and there is any question of disposing of his property, I had better mention that the piano, in the Summersdown house, is mine. I lent it to him.

Yours sincerely,
Martha Rawson

She addressed this letter to Dickie's office, not his house, because she did not want him to get it until after she had left East Head on Wednesday morning. She ran down herself to post it in the pillar box on the quay.

Upon her return, the household was roused to a whirlwind of activity. It soon became clear that she was preparing for an absence of several months.

Ahmed and Annette were not merely delighted at the prospect of a long period of inactivity on board wages; they were in transports of relief. A private problem of their own was now likely to be solved. Annette was pregnant, a fact which they could not have hoped to conceal from Martha for very much longer. They turned to with a will, and accomplished miracles in the way of rapid packing.

As for Don, he was so much overjoyed to get out of East Head that he found it very hard to regret Martha's timely indisposition. He hoped that it would not hurt her much and would keep them both away for a very long time. Upon the whole it did not greatly perturb him; she had been ill all the morning, but she looked much better now. He had no doubt about the cause; these distressing symptoms had been brought on by Alan Wetherby's letter, the contents of which he was, apparently, never to know. He had no wish to do so. Wetherby was a nasty specimen and his letter unlikely to make anybody feel good. People who cultivated his acquaintance must expect these shocks. Now perhaps it would never be necessary to hand the brute another Martini.

As Don bustled about, bringing his personal possessions from the boat-house, he hoped that he might not see the place again. He might even rebel, if Martha threatened to bring him back. He said to himself, when he slammed and locked the door:

"Were I from Dunsinane away and clear,
Profit again should hardly draw me here."

7

Whatever's that?

On loan it says.

But what on earth is it?

"Apollo. By Conrad Swann. On loan to the Trustees."

Oh, *him!*

Just like him, I should say.

We mustn't laugh, I suppose.

No. I suppose not.

Well . . . I don't know.

I don't know, I'm sure.

I never can remember which is the heavier: fifteen or thirty denier. I say, Muriel! Just look at that!

Oh, I've seen it. I saw it yesterday. But did you know they've got these new fishnet ones in Mason's?

Is that supposed to be its head?

They say Mr. Wetherby says it's marvellous.

My nephew, the one in the B.B.C., explained it to me. . . .

Well! You can't say we aren't up to date!

No, Mrs. Dale. We're modern, anyway.

Oh, Nell? Where's Martha? I thought she'd be down here by now. She said she was coming in this morning.

241

She's ill. I rang up The Moorings. Some kind of indigestion, so Don said.

Fancy Martha! I can't imagine her ill somehow.

Art doesn't have to be beautiful any more, so my nephew says. Because artists can't go on doing the same things over and over again and they've done all the beautiful things already.

Are we allowed to laugh?

Goodness no! My dear!

There's to be a picture and an article in this week's *Gazette*. I shall send it to my sister in California. She loves getting the *Gazette*.

I don't suppose they have them like this in America.

Oh, I expect they do. It's the same all over everywhere, nowadays. Art, I mean.

How can people like us know?

That's what I say. If it looked like anything at all, then we'd know what we thought it was like.

The Americans are more modern than us. So they have it worse, I daresay.

Poor Them, in that case!

It takes a bit of getting used to, certainly.

We needn't look at it, if we don't like.

Monica! What's that thing there? I never noticed it before.

Oh . . . something or other.

Was it here always? I don't seem to remember it.

I wouldn't know. I expect so. Goodness! It's nearly a quarter past! I must fly.

Mum! Mum! I don't like that thing.

Geoffrey says of course he has his tongue in his cheek.

Mr. Swann, I mean. He knows quite well it's rubbish.
But he wants to be in the swim.

Well, it makes me want to laugh.

You'd have thought those things would be beginning
to get old-fashioned by now.

What I always say is they do them because they *can't*
do it properly.

Don't be silly, Terry! It's not alive.

Now, Miss Manders! You're a great friend of Mr.
Swann's, aren't you? Can you explain this to us?

Why, you see, it's like something written in quite a new
language. We can't expect to understand it. I mean . . .
well . . . it's like a page written in Chinese.

But what good is that to us? I mean, if we see a page
of Chinese we wouldn't know what it said; it might only
say that eggs are dearer this week.

Oooh! Stan! Whatever is it?

Statue or something. Mod'n.

Fancy anyone doing that on purpose! I heard about it
yesterday in the Blue Kettle.

It's not impossible to learn Chinese.

Still, we're all busy. Can't we have it in English?

It wasn't exactly meant for *us* to understand, perhaps,
Miss Collier.

No, Rita. Nobody could of done that on purpose.

Why Stan! Somebody must of. It's a statue.

You don't understand. You ask any electrician. There's
been a high voltage discharge used to get it that way.

We can get somebody who understands Chinese, and
they can translate it.

Somebody who says they do. How are we to know?

I often wonder how much Martha Rawson . . .

Mr. Wetherby. He must know.

Hullo, Rhona! How's your mother keeping?

She's all right thanks, Allie. What do you think of . . .

I think it's the dog's dinner, and you can tell Mr. Swann so, with my compliments.

My dear Allie! Conrad couldn't care less.

Ah! Here it is! But . . . I don't . . . I'd heard that Sir Gregory complained it was obscene!

Conrad is not trying to say anything to anybody.

Why Stan! You mean they do all their statues that way now then? Electric? And don't really know how they'll come out?

May do. Looks like it. I'm not interested. Come along, if you want any coffee.

Conrad is just talking to himself. He doesn't care a hoot if we overhear him or not.

Then, I suppose it's all right to laugh.

Obscene? You mean rude? Well, no, you can't call it that can you? Of course, you can't tell really what it's meant to be. What all those sort of spokes are . . . or anything.

Only I wish he wouldn't talk to himself in a public place.

Good morning, Mrs. Dale! I hear that Sir Gregory has been making trouble again. Just like him!

Isn't it, Mrs. Prescott? He and Sam had quite a fussification.

If you want to laugh, Allie, nobody can stop you.

I should hope not. This is still a free country.

He said it was a disgrace to publicly exhibit it.

Well! My goodness! I hope Mr. Dale stood up to him.

After you've looked at it for a bit, I believe you begin to get something.

Get what?

Sam pointed out that this is a free country. There's no law, Sam told him, to say what's good art and what's bad.

Get what, Miss Collier?

I don't know. It gives me a kind of feeling.

There's no law, not yet, to stop people laughing if they want to. Excuse me! There's my mother.

Oh, there you are, Allie! Sorry we're late. I went with Mrs. Selby to the dentist and we were kept.

Good morning, Mrs. Selby. I hope he didn't hurt?

Oh, no, he gave me a local. But my mouth feels a bit stiff. Is this *it*? Well!

Rhona says we may laugh if we like. We have Mr. Swann's kind permission.

Well! I don't know!

Mummie likes it, Mrs. Selby.

Mrs. Hughes! No! You don't? Not really?

It's nothing to do with Sir Gregory what we have, or don't have, in the Pavilion. Chale Park doesn't own this town any more.

I don't pretend to understand these things, Mrs. Selby. But I think we ought to try and be broadminded. They mean something to the younger generation. We've got to accept it that the generations are different.

Every single improvement he's tried to stop. Look at the trouble he's making over the new Convenience! He says we don't need one, with all these motor coaches coming through the town.

Personally I think we are very broadminded to put it

up at all, considering the stories that are going about.

I don't believe all I hear. I'm sure some of those stories are very much exaggerated.

Sam says we actually need something like this in here. Something old-fashioned wouldn't suit.

He and she and the husband used literally to live together. Even she doesn't know which of those children . . .

Sssh! Take care!

What? Oh. . . . Hullo, Christina!

Hullo, everybody.

Brought all your little family I see.

Yes. I promised them choc ices.

Ices? Oh, you lucky little things!

And Bobbins! Hullo, Bobbins? Hullo! Hullo! How's old Mr. Pattison, dear?

He seems a bit better, thank you. But Dr. Browning won't let him get up just yet. His heart isn't too good.

Much wiser just to keep him quiet. Hullo, Bobbins! Well! There's a lovely smile! Peak-oh! Peak-oh!

As Sam says, we must keep up with the times. I say! Are those children *those* children?

Yes. You wouldn't know them, would you? A wonderful difference since Christie took them on.

They still look rather peculiar though. Sort of white and scared. Look at them now; you'd think they'd seen a ghost.

What's your opinion, Christina?

I'm not talking, Mrs. Selby. Little pitchers have long ears.

Oh, yes, quite. And Dickie? What does he think?

Oh, he's cagey. Won't say. I know what he really

thinks, but he's got a thing about all this modern art, in case it turns out that Bobbins thinks it's wizard.

Bobbins!

Peak-oh! Peak-oh! Yes, Christina, that's just the point. The younger generation is going to like all sorts of things we don't.

I dare say, Mrs. Hughes. But that's not to say they're going to like this.

Serafina! I want to whisper. *How did. . . .*

Sssh! Don't talk. Don't say anything. It's dangerous.

I mean why should we surround ourselves with things we think are awful because Bobbins may be going to like something we can't understand? Whatever we have, he'll probably call it old-fashioned and throw it out. So we might as well please ourselves. We'll be laughed at when we're dead, anyway.

Serafina! That did be our ole chair, din't it?
Sssh!

It's the insecurity. It's natural the children should see things differently. They've had such a different background . . . growing up in the raids. . . .

You're getting the generations mixed up, Mummie. Bobbins never heard a bomb in his life.

But it did!

Yes, Mrs. Hughes. Being in a raid might have upset Mr. Swann so much he had to get it out of his system this way. But, by the time Bobbins is grown up, he'll either be dead or safer than we are, if you know what I mean. So this is just what he won't cotton to.

AAAH! AAA-OOOO! Serafina pinced me!

Serafina! How can you?

Ahoo! Ahoo! Ahoo!

Ha! ha! Ha! ha! Ha!

He! he! He! he!

Ahoo! Ahoo! Ahoo!

Just hark at those people laughing!

Oh, they're just trippers, off a motor coach. They wouldn't appreciate . . .

Ahoo! Ahoo!

Stop it, Joe! You aren't all that much hurt. Come along and have your choc ice. You can wheel Bobbins, if you're careful.

Let me! Let me!

No, Serafina. It's Joe's turn. Gently now.

Can I wheel him genkly right into the caffy?

Yes. Bye bye, Mrs. Hughes. Bye bye, Mrs. Selby. Be seeing you, Allie. A great blessing not having any steps in here, isn't it? For the prams, I mean. That's one thing they did manage to think of. No, Joe! Not so fast!

Poor Christina! She's got her work cut out!

She's wonderful to take it on.

Just like her. When isn't she wonderful?

Don't be catty, Allie.

Saucer of milk for Mrs. Newman. All right. But none of *us* could have done it half so well, could we? Hullo, Mrs. Browning! We don't see you in here often.

Hullo, Allie! Good morning Mrs. Hughes. I just came to see . . . Oh! My goodness!

First Aid for Mrs. Browning! Help! Ho!

I'd heard rumours. Well!

Lovely, isn't it?

I must say . . . I can't see . . . I'd heard rumours that it was . . . well . . . *you know?*

It was Sir Gregory said that.

248

Well . . . I'm disappointed. . . .

Ha! Ha! ha!

Allie!

Allie, you are dreadful. I didn't mean . . . what is it exactly?

Nobody knows. Everybody says all sorts of things.

It's mad.

It's revolting.

Mr. Wetherby says it's good.

We mustn't laugh.

We're old-fashioned.

It's a hoax.

I don't know, I'm sure.

We ought to like it, I suppose.

Who is Sir Gregory to lay down the law to us?

Mr. Swann is a local man.

The younger generation is different.

But what *is* it?

I don't know.

PART VI

Swann

1

"Birds flying!" said Ivy. "That's early. Means a hard winter, so they say."

Lying on her back she could see nothing save bracken fronds over her head, a hazy blue sky, and a wedge-shaped flight of birds, travelling southwards.

Benbow lifted his head from her breast to look at them, too. Then he scrambled to his feet in order to watch them better.

"What birds are they?" he asked.

"I don't know. Some kind of geese, I should think. They fly high, don't they? Every year they come, a little later than this though, generally, and fly away over the sea. I've never seen them except hereabouts."

She sat up herself and shook some dried bracken from her hair.

Now she could see the world below, the steep fall of the hill, the flat floor of harvest fields, the distant sea. It was a hot day and not very clear. The sea and sky merged in a pale shimmer. Between the fields and the coast there was a long narrow strip of inland water and, beyond it, a rampart of pebbled beach where nobody ever went and where nothing grew except sea poppies.

Benbow watched the birds eagerly until he could see them no longer. Then he too looked downwards and asked if she had ever been on that beach.

"On Hodden? No. There's nothing to see there, only stones. You can't bathe; the sea sucks you down, even in a dead calm. You could wander for miles there and not see a soul. Coast guard, he goes. Nobody else."

"I should like to go, sometime."

"Well, you could, if you take the bus we came by today, and go on to Friar's Barton, just down below there. Then you could walk over the fields. But I don't know how you'd get across Hodden Water."

"We'll go and find out, shall we?"

He sat down again beside her, picked a harebell, and began to examine it as though he had never seen one before. But that was his way, she had noticed. He looked at things more than most people did.

"Depends," she said.

If he did not ask what she meant she would leave it alone. The time might not have come. He scrutinised the harebell and stuck it in his buttonhole.

"It depends?" he repeated.

"It's not so easy," said Ivy. "My mother, she thinks I'm shopping in Beremouth."

"And you don't like to deceive her?"

"No. Nor upset her either, by telling her the truth. Unless it's for an important reason."

"But you have an important reason, haven't you?"

"That's what I don't know yet. If I knew how important it is to you, then I'd know if it was important to me."

There was a slight quiver in her voice. She had risked so much for him and she was not quite sure of the issue.

But he answered at once: "It's very important to me. I want to marry you. Surely you know that?"

"I suppose I do," said Ivy quietly.

He took her brown, capable hand and held it for a moment against his cheek. Then he kissed it and began to twist her wedding ring round her finger.

With a pang of dismay she realised that she would have to take this ring off, if she married Benbow. She still called him Benbow, even in her thoughts, although she had got him to tell her his former name. She was sure that she could never marry anybody else, but not even for him could she take off poor Bill's ring, and put it away as though something had been wiped off a slate. To do so seemed like a sort of treason; it was a denial that there had ever been such a person as Bill. Death had dissolved her vows, but it had not quenched her love for him, although she now loved Benbow, too, without feeling herself unfaithful to the dead. But what did widows do with their rings when they remarried? Didn't they kill a man all over again, when they took his ring off?

The problem was solved for her by Benbow, who said, "It doesn't seem quite right that you should ever take this off, even if you do marry me. You don't want to, do you?"

"No."

"Then don't. I'll get one; I believe we have to have one for the ceremony. You must take this off, just for that day, and let me give you mine. Afterwards you can wear this again and put mine away in some little box."

This was just like Benbow. He gave everyone their place, she thought, even the dead. Any other man would have been jealous of that first love, would have wanted her

254

to obliterate all that she could not share with him. She had refused several offers, for that very reason, and had expected never to marry again. She could not possibly forget Bill. But Benbow was the least possessive creature she had ever encountered; he accepted her grief as part of herself and would never ask her to dismiss those memories of young love and lost happiness. She could live with him at ease, and perfectly herself.

"I'll make you a little box," he added. "I'll get some gold from somewhere and make it myself."

"Aren't you going on a bit fast?" enquired Ivy. "I haven't said yet that I'll marry you."

"You've not made up your mind?"

"You and your boxes! You needn't start getting gold from anywhere, until you've answered three questions."

"Questions?" said he, frowning.

"First, about the children. I'm willing to look after them. I'd like to. But where are they?"

He would not give a direct answer to this. He merely said, "I'll get hold of them and bring them here. I must think of some way to get them here."

His evasion assured her that the children must be in that place from which he had run away when he came to Coombe Bassett. Had they been anywhere else he would have told her so by now. But of that place he was determined never to think or speak. It must, she thought, have upset him in his nerves very badly. She had got everything fairly straight up to Maddy's death; after that came a two years' gap concerning which he was mute.

"You remember all about it now, dear, don't you?" she asked, more gently.

"I can't quite remember how I got here. All the rest

. . . it's like something packed away. I could think of it. But I don't want to."

"Still, I don't see how we can get much further till you've thought a bit. I've done more for you than I ought, perhaps. I wanted to help you. But that's no use if you won't help yourself. Married or not, you owe it to yourself to get quite all right. Quite like other people, I mean."

"I am helping myself. I'm quite all right if I don't think about anything except just what I'm doing at the moment."

"That's all very well, till you start thinking ahead, which you're bound to do, if you want to get married. Once you think ahead, you must think back. I know it's hard. You've had trouble. So have I. When they brought my Pam home to me, that day . . . oh, that day! . . . I kept thinking I shall never forget this. Never! But I wouldn't want to forget it really. It's life."

He nodded in agreement, and after a while continued, "You see, I got quite wrong somehow. Like a train derailed. I couldn't go on without an accident. My work . . . I couldn't see people any more. So I went right back and started again."

This she understood very well. In her father's yard he had returned to a point which took him out of his difficulties by ante-dating them. He had sought an earlier time and place—his own boyhood and a stone mason's yard in the Antipodes. In future he meant to call himself Benbow. That might have been possible, she believed, had he come to Europe alone. He might erase that disastrous excursion and start afresh, were it not for the other, who had come with him.

Yet she hesitated before asking her second question. She knew it to be the most dangerous of all.

"And what happened to Frank?" she demanded.

"*Ivy!*"

He leapt to his feet and looked as though he was going to run away.

"Becaue he always mattered most to you, didn't he?"

More than Maddy did, she thought. More than I shall. But that's natural, sometimes, when two men are great friends. Like David and Jonathan.

"He's not dead?" she pursued.

"No."

"You quarrelled?"

He looked puzzled, as though genuinely uncertain of the answer to that. After a while he said, "I wrote him a letter. He didn't answer."

"Probably got lost in the post," said Ivy.

"No. I don't think so. Anyway . . . I shall never see him again. Don't talk about it, Ivy."

"All right, I won't. But it's something you've got to get over, isn't it? You can't do that by all this Benbow business, and pretending that half your life, almost, never happened at all."

He nodded, turned away, and set off walking very fast along the ridge of the hill. She made no attempt to go after him. This dangerous moment had not gone off too badly. He might refuse to think. He might prefer to remain but half a man for the rest of his life. In that case she would still marry him, but she must face the fact that she was marrying a kind of cripple. To look after him would be better than nothing, since she loved him, and

257

half a loaf is better than no bread. She still hoped, however, for a nobler fate than that.

She must wait. She sat on the hill and watched a
threshing machine at work in a field below. The whirring
noise of it came up to her on the still air, and faint shouts
from the men who tended it.

Plans for the future occupied her mind. She owned
a cottage in the village which was let furnished; she had
lived there until the death of her child, after which she
had gone to her parents for the sake of company. This
little house would do nicely for herself and Benbow. Her
tenant, a retired school-teacher, was leaving anyway in
the New Year and would probably be ready to turn out
at Michaelmas, if it suited Ivy better. Those children
must be brought to Coombe Bassett. Benbow could go
on working for her father, who would welcome the prospect of keeping so good a man. There would be some
trouble at home; her mother would violently oppose the
project, but the storm would blow over if everybody was
sensible.

They would be a little short of money. She would
lose her widow's pension if she re-married, and she could
no longer earn large wages by going out, at intervals,
to resident posts. But she had a nice little sum laid by
and would be getting allowances for the two younger
children. Daily work in the village might be possible; there
were several ladies who would be glad to employ her.
Serafina and Dinah would be in school and off her hands
for most of the day, but, if Joe was only four, she must
leave him with her mother when she went out to work.
A lot of fuss her mother would make, but she would take

him all right, and spoil him, probably, to a shocking degree.

They would get along perfectly well. Many a family of five had less to live on than the wages Benbow was getting. Moreover, if he took it into his head to turn any more door stops into cats, there might be some profit in it. He had, she gathered, sold such things before, or, rather, the lost Frank had sold them for him. She would not go on at him to do any more unless he felt like it; if he did, she might show them to Mr. Headley and ask his advice about selling them. Mr. Headley knew about such things and valued good work; he would know what sort of shop would be likely to buy them.

But, if he gets quite all right again, she thought . . . and realised that all these plans were made for a Benbow who was not quite all right. Should that other return, that whole man whom she was so anxious to recall, she must pay for it by some measure of uncertainty as to the future. For that man's needs she could not prepare so confidently nor could she foresee the life which they might lead. She only knew that she would be ready to follow him anywhere, and would rather do so, to the ends of the earth, than make a home in Coombe Bassett for Benbow who dared not face the past.

He had gone quite far away, to the end of the ridge. Now he was striding back in a great hurry. She thought that he must have decided to tell her everything, but, when he got nearer, she saw that she had been wrong. There was no resolution in his face. He was excited and harassed; he must have looked like that before he ran away. She had never see him in such agitation. He flung himself down on the grass beside her, gave her a wild look, and exclaimed, "I must tell you something. I've never spoken of it to anybody. I'll tell you, Ivy. I'll tell what was driving me . . . driving me . . ."

He looked round suspiciously, as if afraid that they might be overheard. Then he confided, almost in a whisper, "Something very horrible and dangerous is happening. We have enemies. Hidden enemies. Nobody knows about it. Nobody is going to notice in time."

Oh, dear! she thought. I oughtn't to have stirred him up. It was too soon.

"We are all being persuaded to despair," he continued, in the same low, shaken voice. "We are being convinced that we are worthless. It's being done very cleverly. People don't see how clever it is. They think it's an improvement. Have you noticed?"

"Can't say I have," she replied, placidly. "Nobody's tried to convince me I'm worthless. I'd like to see them do it."

"They don't say it openly. But it's going on, everywhere, all the time. I began to notice it before Maddy died. Maddy dying, and everything that has happened since, have nothing to do with it really. I didn't understand what was happening, though, till one day, when I was in a great dark place full of voices. I had felt it before, you understand? I had begun to feel anxious. I had stopped being able to see people; I couldn't be sure what they were. As if a curtain had come down. I used to think: How can I get out of this? I used to go up to the quarries, and watch the blasting, and think: How can we escape from this? Have you ever felt like that?"

"I get in the dumps sometimes."

"No, it's not like that. After a while I realised that we are all gradually being brought to think less of ourselves. It's not merely being attempted. It's succeeding."

"Honestly, Benbow, I think you're wrong. People don't believe they're worthless. Not the people I know, anyway. What's wrong with most of them is they think they're worth a lot more than they are."

He considered this with frowning attention.

"A protection," he said, nodding. "A natural protection. But will it last?"

"Oh, yes. People don't alter."

"They're being undermined, though. That's it. Undermined. Very crafty. Very crafty. Very crafty. . . ."

It was of no use to argue. She decided to dispute nothing, and listened to him. He maintained this mysterious manner as though he were revealing some dangerous secret. Between each sentence was a pause, while he sought for words.

"It's done cheerfully. It's encouraging and reassuring, so that people are ready to believe it. But all the while this terrible idea is being planted in our minds. This idea of ourselves as very small and weak and stupid. This idea that we don't know what we are doing, and can't know, and can't help it. And the bait is this: that we don't have to be sorry for what we do. We don't have to think that there are any wicked people. Nobody is strong enough, or clever enough, to be wicked. So there is to be no remorse. No remorse. No guilt. They offer to rid us of our guilt."

"But who are they then?" exclaimed Ivy.

It was nonsense. She knew that it was nonsense. But he spoke with so much conviction that she was shaken.

"I don't know. They hide. You never see them. But they must be there, or all this wouldn't be happening. I felt it coming on, for years. But I knew it, I knew it, in that fearful place."

"The place you ran away from, when you came here?"

"No. Before that. About a year before Maddy died."

He was silent, collecting his thoughts. After a while he resumed:

"They attack our sadness. Although it is natural for people to be sad. They have been, always. You can see that if you read history books. And that is a very clever thing to do: to suggest that we can't bear sadness. Sorrow and guilt. We listen to people who offer to take those away from us, because we think we want to be rid of them. But, when we have given up sorrow, we have given up all our greatness. Sorrow is our right. There can be no joy without it. Don't you think so?"

"It says in the Bible: Blessed are they that mourn," agreed Ivy with a sigh. "But then it says: For they shall be comforted. I sometimes wonder what that means."

She thought again of her own unwillingness to forget grief, and his acceptance of it. Their relationship, which had in it so much of comfort, seemed to have sprung from sorrow.

"No joy," he said. "Only pleasure, perhaps, which is something quite different. Joy and sorrow could not live in that place, but there was a great deal of pleasure, I suppose. Did you go there?"

"I don't quite know what place you mean, dear."

"Oh, it was a horrible place. Horrible! Maddy and I went because I wanted to see the glass. I was interested in working glass. We didn't know what it was going to be like. They had a lot of little paper windmills every-where."

He shuddered, pulled a piece of bracken, and began tearing it to pieces.

"In the middle of it," he said, "there was a huge dark place, full of voices. *Not human voices.* We had to creep along and see what was shown, and hear what was told. The first thing we saw was an enormous telescope. It was a cheat. Nothing could be seen through it. If they had wanted us to see more, they might have given us a smaller one, through which we could have looked at the stars. But they didn't want us to see more. They didn't mean us to ask for more."

This telescope explained everything. Ivy realised that he was talking about the Twentieth Century Exhibition, held in Gressington some three years earlier. She and her parents had gone to see it, in a motor-coach, because everybody seemed to be going. It was reputed to be painlessly educational and designed to cheer people up, since it only exhibited the more hopeful aspects of Twen-tieth Century Civilisation.

Although it was but a small affair it had attracted a good deal of attention. The largest public park in Gress-ington had been decorated with sculpture, attractive cardboard cut-outs, kiosks, milk bars, and side shows of various kinds. In the centre stood a vast globular con-struction, a round world, designed by Alan Wetherby, and entitled the Palace of Progress. A complete tour of it took a couple of hours, nor was it possible to curtail the ex-perience, for movement inside it could only take place in one direction. An endless queue, shuffling in by one gang-plank, and out by another, was obliged to inspect

tier upon tier of galleries—up, up, up—down, down, down
—before getting away.

The exhibits were all intended to reassure the Common
Man, by presenting him with a gratifying picture of
what he was really up to. Most of them were concerned
with his conquest of Nature. Egalitarian touchiness was
uniformly respected; great names were seldom mentioned,
nor were many heroes set up for veneration. All this,
it was implied, had been achieved by nobody in particular. The arts, and the unpredictable phenomena of
inspiration, received a few vague and somewhat facetious
tributes. The inequitable distribution of genius, the er-
ratic proclivities of the Uncommon Man, do not easily
lend themselves to charts, graphs, diagrams and working
models; the Common Man can be more easily persuaded
that he will shortly, thanks to his own ingenuity, set off
for Mars, than he can be convinced that he ever wrote
Hamlet. A discreet cruciform object, in a secluded corner,
bore a placard which broadmindedly complimented him
upon his resourcefulness in having invented God.

Ivy's impressions of her visit to this place were confused, for she had found it exhausting. She knew that
she must have seen a great deal, because she had, for
two hours, inspected brightly illuminated objects and
listened to very simple explanations by loudspeakers.
She remembered best a giant model of the human brain
thinking a thought. It had looked uncommonly like tripe
and had pulsated in a nauseating way. But she could
never forget it because it had provoked her father into
making an awkward scene. He had demanded loudly
what thought this brain was supposed to be thinking;
one thought, he maintained, can be much more im-

portant than another, and an exhibit which ignored this point was an insult to the public. He stood there, fuming, while the loudspeaker, again and again, repeated its jocular and condescending little commentary. The people behind wanted to get on and could not, as long as Frank Toombs remained, outraged and stationary, in front of the brain. Some grumbled. Others suggested unseemly and flippant answers to Frank's question. The thoughts ascribed to this brain were getting quite out of hand when an official turned up and peremptorily moved them all on.

"Why are you laughing?" asked Conrad in surprise.

"I was thinking of Dad," said Ivy. "We all went to that place, that Palace of Progress, and he was awful! He groused from start to finish. He said it was nothing but a kindergarten and they were treating us all like kids. Well, it was, in a way. Everything done up to look like a sort of toy. But they meant it to be educational."

He looked at her doubtfully.

"Who were they?" he asked.

"The people who got it up? I forget. They were all very famous, educated people. You don't think they meant any harm, surely? You don't think they were wicked?"

"I knew one. I met him afterwards. I'm sure he meant harm. It was harmful to treat people like that. Your father was right. It was like a terrible toyshop. That dummy telescope!"

He seemed to be as much aggrieved over the telescope as Toombs had been over the brain. His objections, although more violent and incoherent, were upon the same lines. But Toombs had merely been irritated, whereas Benbow had been deeply disturbed. He looked upon the whole exhibition as evidence of some organised and deliberate attack on human dignity. He complained again that he had never been able to "see people" properly in consequence. He seemed to have brooded over the experience until it had become an obsession. The loudspeakers, in particular, had horrified him.

"Man! They kept on saying. Man! But they were really persuading us that there is no such person. We are not to see him any more, when we walk down the street. They pretended to be talking about us, but they were not. Thought and knowledge don't belong to us any more. All they offered was little jokes and a few hints about what is being done by people with no names and no faces. They hid themselves and shouted, so that we couldn't ask questions, even if we had wanted to."

"Dad asked questions all right. Don't get so excited, dear. They were only records. They made records beforehand. See?"

"How could they know beforehand what we might want to ask? They must really believe that we are worthless, imbecile creatures. Those records were made by people who secretly despise us."

"No. They were very nice ladies and gentlemen. Why should they want to do us harm?"

"I don't say it was intentional. That's the trouble. You see, this . . . this attack was first made on educated, intellectual people. They have lost their faith in man. They sincerely despise him; so now they can't help spreading it among us—the idea that we are despicable. They find it impossible to connect the thought of us with the thought of anything great. Did you notice the sculpture, outside in those gardens?"

266

"If I did, I don't remember it. Time we all got out, we were dead to the world."

"There were groups of men and women and children. Very large. Huge. To hide the fact that we were being made to feel small. They had the faces of idiots, cheerful and trusting, and not worried about anything. They all had very thick legs. Nobody hungry. Nobody sad. Nobody thinking. Nobody noble. And then amongst them, these vast *Things!* Shapes! Thought, they were called, and Knowledge, and Truth, and Courage, and all that sort of thing. But not in human form. No greatness must be shown in human form any more. Only imbecility."

"You really think they did it on purpose?"

"Who is behind it then? Who is the enemy? Who wants to convince us that we are all idiots?"

"Perhaps it's Satan," she suggested, feeling that she had better humour him.

"Satan?" He looked startled. "You mean . . . you believe in the devil?"

"I'm Church of England," said Ivy cautiously. "But they do say he's the enemy of mankind, don't they? They're always talking about the crafts and assaults of the devil."

"Perhaps you're right. But hardly anybody believes in the devil nowadays."

"I think it's much better than getting suspicious of people and calling them enemies. I must say, I think it's very unjust of you to have it in, like this, for those poor people, just because they went and got up an exhibition."

She looked at her watch and added, "We ought to be going, or we'll miss the bus back. I've been shopping in Beremouth, remember."

"Would your mother mind if we got married?"

"She'd create from here to Kingdom Come. But I'm not going to marry you, Conrad, until you're properly back in your seven senses."

It was the first time that she had ever called him by his name. They were both aware of the challenge which it implied.

"I am in my seven senses," he protested.

"No, you're not. You haven't answered two questions I asked you, before you started all this about Gressington, just to get away from it. And there's another one. There's somebody I haven't heard about yet. Somebody you never mention."

He got up again and looked down at Hodden Beach.

"I don't think I'll come back by bus," he said. "I think I'll try to get to the sea, and walk home tonight."

"Please yourself. Where's my handbag? Perhaps it's just as well we shouldn't arrive back the same bus. And I'm never likely to go to Hodden Beach with you, or anywhere else, till you've answered my questions. From now on, Conrad, you've got to stand on your own legs."

"Shan't you bring me tea in the mornings any more?"

"No. I shan't bring you tea in the mornings any more."

He smiled at her. They both knew that she would.

"You haven't been alone these last two years," she insisted. "Who was she, Conrad?"

The smile vanished. He turned and made off down the hill, throwing two words over his shoulder as he went:

"Frank's wife."

PART VII

To What Abode?

1

Just before dawn Christina heard a car drive up quietly and stop outside the gate. She was at the window in a moment. It was their car, looking strange and different, as everything did in that light, in the tender, mournful clarity which is neither night nor day.

The town, the sea, the hills, had the same unfamiliar aspect; they slept, the whole world slept, as though unwilling ever to wake again. High up in the sky, over Summersdown, the first rosy clouds heralded the inevitable recall. Only the dead may sleep on, untroubled and at peace, while dawn breaks, and those who have looked upon death during the night turn again to the task of living.

Presently Dickie got out of the car and shut the door very quietly so as not to wake people still sleeping, for so short a time, behind their drawn curtains. There was a remote dignity in his bearing, as he walked slowly up the path. For a few hours it would set him apart from other men, until the mystery which he had beheld should be obliterated by the clamour and bustle of the day. He was not yet a mourner, able to name a loss—not yet a bereaved son, interviewing undertakers and sending telegrams to distant cousins. Returning to his house, in this limpid quiet, he was simply humanity, reconciled for a while to its end.

Poor Dickie! she thought. But she knew that he was not, at that moment, poor Dickie.

She ran downstairs. They met in the hall.

"All over," he said.

"I know. I saw. I saw you coming back."

He stood looking at her blankly, as though uncertain where to go next.

"Go up and rest a little," she suggested. "I'll bring you some tea."

He plodded upstairs. She put on a kettle in the kitchen while the dawn light grew stronger.

The dear old man! He had been so kind, so kind always. Sad! Sad! But natural. Old men die. This one had died with little pain, with less suffering than is the lot of many. He had only been very ill for a couple of days and had never known that he was dying. His beloved Dickie had been beside him. But sad . . . sad . . . that people should have to grow old and die, and never hear the birds any more, the birds now sleepily chirping in the garden.

When she took the tray upstairs, Dickie was lying on their bed. He had removed his shoes but had not stripped off the candlewick counterpane. At any other time she would have made him get up while she folded it away, for it was one of her treasures. She let it pass, however, after a glance at his withdrawn face. Silently she poured out a cup of tea and gave it to him.

"Was it . . . how was it?" she ventured to ask, after a while.

"Peaceful. In his sleep, they said. But I think he knew.

He had my hand. He gave it a little squeeze, just before he went."

He drank half a cup of tea and then looked at her as if realising for the first time that she could not have gone to bed that night. She was wearing a dark grey suit.

"Have you been up all night?" he asked.

"Yes. I waited. I waited up. I didn't want to be asleep when you came back."

"Where's Bobbins?" he asked, looking round the room.

"Serafina and Dinah have got him. I moved his cot in there. They've been so sweet, trying to save me trouble."

She poured herself out a cup and sat down on the bed beside him.

"I'm very sorry I couldn't be with you," she said.

"You couldn't have left the children."

"No. But I was sorry not to be able to be with you."

It would have made no difference, as she knew, had she been with him, but she would have wished to be there. A husband and wife ought to go through these things together. Life was not so bad, death more endurable, when they faced it side by side. To go through things together was one of the reasons why people married.

There was nothing to be done for him yet. Later on she might say words of consolation; she could remind him of the happiness which he had always given to his father, and of the old man's delight in his first grandchild. Later on she could take her part in the many things which must be done. Just now he needed no comfort.

Her own weariness overcame her. She lay down on the bed by his side and gazed, as he did, at the bright clouds beyond the window.

"I keep seeing him lying there," said Dickie suddenly, "and at the same time I keep seeing him standing at the gate of The Rowans—oh, it must have been a long time ago. When I was a boy. Turning round and calling to me. I was late for something; church, I expect. A long time ago. Yet it seems as . . . as fresh as the other."

"I know," said Christina. "It was the same when Mummie died. All the old times seemed so near, as if they were still happening. It made one feel as if there's no such thing as time, really."

He turned his head and looked at her with faint surprise, as though he had not expected such a comment from her.

"I suppose," she said, "it's the same for everybody, when their last parent goes."

"Yes. Everybody."

The word seemed to go on in her tired brain like a distant murmur of waves: everybody . . . everybody. . . .

"I've got a lot I ought to see to," he remembered.

"Plenty of time, dear. Rest a bit longer."

His black shoes hurt him, she remembered. They were a size too small. She must make him get another pair before the funeral, because he would have to stand for a long time, afterwards, shaking hands with people. It would be a big funeral. The whole town would come. There was much to be foreseen; much to be done.

Perhaps I am hard-hearted to start remembering those things so soon, she thought. But it's not my father, and I am less sensitive than Dickie. He is thinking about death, now. Only death. He feels things so. It's funny. He must have seen a lot of dead people in the war. I suppose there wasn't time to think, then. It's when people

273

think that they feel. Dickie thinks a lot, so he feels the more. I won't bother him about shoes, and things like that, till he can attend to it.

She looked round at him and saw that he had dropped off to sleep.

So that's good, she thought tenderly. That's good for him, to get a little sleep, my darling Dickie. It's lucky for him he has me to look after him. I will try harder to make him happy. Never mean or petty. I won't think about that, because it is all over and we can forget it. We can't help being angry sometimes; that's human. But we need not be petty. That we must struggle against; that is the saddest thing to have to remember. And the curtains in the lounge here will do nicely for his new study at The Rowans.

Now that's hard-hearted! To be thinking of curtains already. I am very sad. I shall miss the dear old man very much. His twinkling eyes, when he peeped round the door, the day Bobbins was born! Oh, I shall miss him very much. I shall always remember him. And I shall tell the children about him, so they'll remember him, even after we are dead. He shan't be forgotten.

Dickie shall have exactly the curtains he likes in his new study. I won't decide everything without consulting him. He shall have all the room he wants for his books. What he'd really like is to have that thing that Mr. Pethwick . . . Oh, dear! Thinking of that makes me remember *the other!*

Why can't somebody take it away from there, where I have to see it every time I go to the café? Reminding me! How mean I was, not telling him, and I never can now.

274

He says it's got to stay there till an authorised person takes it away. I heard him going along the path with the watering can; I'm ashamed to think how mean and petty I was. Nobody will ever know I knew, though; even if it all comes out. A point from which we can't get back he said. Thank heaven we didn't get that far, and it's all over now. I can't think why I ever let myself get into such a state. What was it all about? *A poor little briary bush!* He was whistling that song, going down the path . . . when I didn't tell him . . . *and that will never be, be, be* . . . that man who never came back . . . Edward . . . Edward . . . never came back any more. . . .

Her eyelids fluttered and she too fell asleep.

As the first sunbeam shot over Summersdown, Mrs. Hughes came padding softly along the road and let herself into the house with a latchkey that Christina had given to her. She knew what had happened, for Dr. Browning had rung her up before he left The Rowans, as he had promised to do.

Her eyes were full of tears for the loss of a lifelong friend. But she was confident that he had gone to a better place and her mind was occupied with plans for helping the bereaved household. She also was thinking about shoes.

The little house was silent and sleeping. She crept upstairs and found their bedroom door ajar. Peeping in she saw them both, lying on their bed side by side, fast asleep, their young faces shadowed with fatigue.

In their dark suits, upon the yellow counterpane, they reminded her of something that she had seen once: two spars of wood washed up at haphazard on the beach, to lie like companions until the next tide came and swept them apart again for ever. It was as though they lay there together by chance, and only for a little while.

She stole away on tip-toe and went downstairs to prepare for breakfast. Tears were rolling down her cheeks now; she knew not whether she wept for the living or for the dead.

2

To be remembered and mentioned last had always been the lot of Dinah Swann. She had neither Joe's infant pathos, nor Serafina's vitality, to recommend her. Adenoids and very imperfect vision had dulled her wits. Nobody felt any impulse to talk to her, ask her questions, or tell her anything; she was merely a third child, stumbling awkwardly after the other two, so little aware of her surroundings that she scarcely knew herself to be deprived.

On the day before the funeral she stood in the Pattisons' front garden, vacantly staring at a blurred mass of colour which was all that she would ever see of a flower border, twelve feet away, until somebody had discovered that she needed glasses. Even so she thought it very pretty and continued to gaze at it, with her mouth open, until the gate clicked and an unfocussed figure came up the path. She could not be sure who it was until the person got quite close and evolved into a strange lady asking if this was Mrs. Richard Pattison's house.

"Yes," said Dinah, stirred by a vague memory of somebody else, long ago.

"And you . . . are you Dinah?"

"Yes."

"Oh!"

The lady plumped down on her knees, flung away a large bucket bag which she carried, and hugged Dinah, crying, "I thought so! Dinah! I thought so!"

She smells like Mummie, decided Dinah. Has she come for me?

"You're so like him. Oh, dear, I could laugh! You *are* so like him. I'd know, anywhere. Is Mrs. Pattison at home?"

"No. Have you come for *me?*"

"Oh, I will, love. Yes, I will. But not today, I can't take you. Quite soon, though. Where's the others? Serafina and Joe?"

"They've taken Bobbins for a walk."

"Bobbins? Who's that?"

"A little baby. He belongs to Aunt Chris."

"Got one of her own, has she? That's nice. She's been ever so kind to you, hasn't she? She must be a very sweet lady. Will she be back soon, do you know?"

Dinah remembered that Aunt Chris had only just gone down to the post office, so the lady suggested that they should sit on Bobbins' rug till she came back.

"This lady . . . Aunt Chris you call her? How long have you been stopping with her?"

Dinah could not quite remember. A long time, she thought.

"Before that, we were at Summersdown," she said.

"Oh, I know. I've been up there and found the house all shut up. Gave me such a turn! But the person in the next house told me where you'd gone. Is that your Auntie? The lady in black coming along the road?"

"I can't see."

"You must see. Just coming across the road now."

"She's too far away. I can't see who she is."

"Goodness! That must be attended to. I expect you need . . . yes, she's coming in here. Let me get up, love. I must go and say how do you do."

Dinah let her new friend get up, but retained a clutch on her skirts as they advanced to meet a blur of black.

"Mrs. Pattison?"

"Yes?"

Christina's voice was a little sharp. She was tired and dying for a cup of tea. Ivy stiffened.

"I've come," she said, "to enquire about Mr. Swann's children. My name is Mrs. Wright. At present. On Saturday I'm going to marry" —she glanced down at Dinah and spelt, with a meaning nod—"Mr. S-W-A-N-N."

"What? Their . . . ? You know where he is then? What's he been doing all this time? Is he here?"

"No. It's a long story. He couldn't come today. As a matter of fact he's been ill; *nerves!* He's a lot better, but not quite over it yet. So I thought I'd better come."

"It was quite time somebody came," said Christina coldly.

"That's right. But it's all been rather complicated. It affected his memory. How we shall ever thank you for having been so kind, I don't know. And I'm so sorry to hear about your sad bereavement. The person who directed me here told me about it. I'm afraid I've come at a very awkward moment."

"It is rather."

"I'm ever so sorry. But I'm only here for the day. I want to fix up about taking them off your hands as soon as possible. So, if you could spare a minute or two . . ."

"Yes," said Christina. "Now you're here we must settle

279

something. Come in, Mrs. Wright. You, Dinah, run along and play."

Dinah, however, refused to let go of Ivy's skirt. For the first time in her life she felt that she belonged to someone. A scene was averted by Ivy, who dived into the bucket bag and produced a small doll.

"Take her and sit in the sunshine," she said to Dinah. "All smothered she's been, poor dear, in my old bag. Find out what her name is, will you?"

"Is she mine?" asked Dinah.

"Surely, if you look after her. Air she needs."

Dinah returned to the rug, tenderly dandling the doll. Ivy, following Christina into the house, explained that she had brought one or two little presents for the children.

"Just to help make friends," she said.

In the lounge they sat down and took stock of one another.

Just a working-class woman, thought Christina. A nice person, and superior. She'll be all right with the children. But he could have married somebody better than this.

Not out of the top drawer, thought Ivy, whose social horizon was wider than Christina's. A nice person, but doesn't quite know how to behave. I'd imagined somebody older; not this little madam in her smart blacks. I hope we're going to get on!

When Ivy hoped that she was going to get on with people she generally meant that she had taken a dislike to them. She could be, on occasion, rather formidable, as several of her employers had discovered. In as few words as possible she gave an account of Conrad's arrival in

Coombe Bassett, his illness, and his recovery. All the trouble was attributed to nerves, but Christina understood that euphemism perfectly well and would have employed it herself. He was, said Ivy, very much better and had told her everything, but he still had a settled antipathy to the very thought of East Head. He would not even name anybody to whom she might write, so she had thought it best to come herself and have what she called a look round. If it was convenient to everybody she would return within a fortnight and remove the children.

Christina's feelings became more cordial as she listened to this narrative. The woman seemed to be honest, resourceful and independent. Conrad's nerves excused his strange behaviour, and it was excellent news that he would never come back to East Head. All his things would be sent away now, including that sinister memento of the past, which nobody had yet removed from the Pavilion vestibule. If only it could be taken away and forgotten!

She offered Ivy some tea, in a friendly voice, and rose to get it.

"Oh, I'll come too," said Ivy, also rising. "You mustn't trouble to bring it to me, really, Mrs. Pattison."

Before leaving the lounge she took a peep through the window at Dinah on the lawn.

"Playing with her dolly, as good as anything," she reported. "It quite knocks me over, her being so like her father. Made me take to her at once."

"You haven't seen the others yet," said Christina. "Joe is sweet. And Serafina's such a clever little girl."

"Oh, I'm sure I'll love them all. But I believe, somehow, Dinah's going to be my special girl."

281

This struck Christina as an odd preference, but lucky for Dinah, who was not likely to win hearts very easily.

In the kitchen the two women felt more at ease with one another. Ivy sat squarely on her chair, instead of on the edge of it. She surveyed Christina's arrangements with an approving eye; very nicely done, for what it was, she thought, with some condescension. No servant, obviously, and a good thing too; a person like Mrs. Pattison would be unlikely to secure one who would be of much use.

And then, quite suddenly, they knew not how, all social barriers fell as they struck up a duet of indignation against Elizabeth Archer. How anybody could be so wicked they did not know. It was like something you read in the newspapers, not something in real life. They had drunk two cups of tea apiece before finishing with her, since they repeatedly agreed with each other and said the same things several times over.

It was a real relief, confessed Ivy, to learn that Elizabeth deserved no consideration. That had been one of her reasons for coming to have a look round. She was not one to steal another woman's man. She could not have married Conrad with a clear conscience had Elizabeth been faithful and waiting for him at Summersdown.

"Though I was almost sure she wasn't, Mrs. Pattison. She sounded like the sort that thinks only of themselves, and it's plain to see he never got a decent meal. Not that he ever complained. But when that person next door told me she'd gone and deserted the children, I didn't feel she had any more claim. What they'd have done without you! Which reminds me, about the expense. We can't ever repay your kindness, but we ought to repay the expense they've been. He thinks he's got some things here that he could sell, perhaps. Some of these little statue things that he does. He seems to have been able to sell them in the past."

"Why yes," said Christina. "He . . . he's quite a famous sculptor, you know. Supposed to be a genius."

"I'm not surprised," said Ivy. "Though I didn't know how famous. But it's very good, what he does. You mean he's been in the papers?"

"Oh, yes. He got a prize in Venice."

"He never thought to tell me that. Well, anyway, you mustn't refuse to let us know exactly what we owe you, Mrs. Pattison. I know you'll understand how we feel about that."

"It's been no expense to us," said Christina. "Mr. Archer took care of all that. He came down here, you know, and took his own children away, and fixed up with me to look after the little Swanns for a bit."

"Mr. Archer? Frank? He's been here?"

"Why, yes. And I must write to him, the very next post, and tell him Mr. Swann is all right. You must give me the address. He's been so worried. They're great friends, you know. In spite of. . . ."

"Oh, Mrs. Pattison! That's wonderful. Oh, that will make a difference to Conrad. All the difference in the world. Losing Frank was like losing half of himself."

"Why should that awful woman part two friends?"

"That's what I say! Why should she?"

They went to work on Elizabeth again and were still at it when the children returned with Bobbins, over whom Ivy had the manners to exclaim, before attempting to make friends with Joe and Serafina.

Joe, to whom she presented a fish to float in his bath,

283

heard with unconcern the news that in a fortnight he would be removed to another home. Dinah demanded to be taken there at once. Their ready desertion to the new-comer was a little mortifying to Christina; neither of them displayed the slightest reluctance to leave her, although she had done so much for them. Only Serafina held aloof, scowling slightly and accepting a plastic purse with no more than a mutter of thanks.

The interview was a short one as Ivy had a train to catch. No sooner had she gone down the path, with the faithless Dinah and Joe fondly hanging upon her, than Serafina turned on Christina.

"Is that Conrad's new woman?" she demanded furiously.

"Serafina! That's not a very nice way to put it. They're going to be married."

"So we have to go and live with them?"

"I'm sure she's very kind and nice and ready to be a mother to you."

"I like Elizabeth better."

"Well! Really! After the way she treated you?"

"She didn't treat me badly. She used to talk to me and tell me things. She'd read books and met all sorts of people. This one . . . she won't know anything. There won't be any books to read. Oh, I wish I could stay here."

Christina kissed her, touched by the compliment.

"I never was in a house with so many books," lamented Serafina. "When shall I ever get to know anything? I'm not a baby. I can't bear to leave you and Bobbins and Uncle Dickie. He's such a wonderful man. He lets me take his books and tells me things, when I ask. He showed me how to read a dictionary. I do so love him. I perfectly worship him."

284

"Well, dear, he's very busy now, and very sad."

"I know. Till after the funeral. But I've got a whole lot of things to ask him, that I've saved up till he's happy again. When do I have to go? Will I have time to finish the book I'm reading before I go?"

"I expect so. What is it?"

"Paradise Lost."

"Good gracious! I should have thought that was rather difficult for you, with all those long words. You can't understand it, surely?"

"Oh, I like long words. And I hate understanding things; that's so dull. And if I don't know a word I can always poke my proboscis into a dictionary."

"Your what?"

"My nose," cried Serafina gleefully. "That's a lovely long word for a nose. I asked Uncle Dickie what a proboscis meant, and he gave me a little dictionary, and showed me how to read it. He said in future I could poke my proboscis into that, and not ask him quite so many questions."

3

The little handful of earth felt cold in Dickie's palm. As he scattered it upon the coffin it seemed to him as though he was consigning himself to the grave, that he too lay down there.

He put the thought from him and stood erect, staring across the heads of the crowd and seeing nothing. Now was not the moment to think of the future; there would be plenty of time for that when this ritual was over and all these people had gone away. But the small trickling noise of the earth falling continued to whisper in his ears, as he listened to the final prayers and bent, with Christina, to take a last meaningless look at the coffin, far below, before they turned away and abandoned the dead.

She took his arm and they walked slowly together towards the cemetery gate. The path was lined with faces, well-known faces; there was hardly one which had not been familiar to him since childhood. Since all bore the same expression they all looked alike—one face upon several hundreds of shoulders, one face over several hundreds of years. This face had looked upon his father once, as he came from paying a son's last tribute. Bobbins, in his turn, must see it: the face of East Head burying a well-loved townsman.

286

Christina was doing it all very well. She gave pale
half-smiles of recognition to right and left, as if thanking
people for their presence and sympathy. He realised that
he too ought to have looked about rather more, on this
walk to the gate. And he ought perhaps to have done
something, he did not know what, about Sam Dale in
his Mayor's rig; bowed to him in some civic way before
quitting the grave-side. But it was too late now. He was
handing Christina into the first of the waiting cars. They
were driving back to The Rowans, where hospitality was
to be provided for kinsfolk and intimate friends.

The streets looked quiet and empty. Most of the shops
were shut, out of respect. As soon as their car had passed
these would open again and the brief, solemn hush would
lift from the little town.

"The wreaths!" exclaimed Dickie suddenly. "Thousands of them! And we don't know who . . ."

"That's all taken care of," said Christina. "Mrs. Selby
and Mrs. Browning are getting a list made of all the
names on the cards, and notes about who sent what kind
of flowers, so we can write and thank people apprecia-
tively."

Not for the first time did he wonder what on earth he
would have done without her. She thought of everything.

They had reached The Rowans. She walked in the
same slow way beside him up to the door, but, as soon as
she was inside, she ran off to the kitchen, calling to the
housekeeper. He was left, for a moment or two, alone
in the hall of his new abode.

Of course this was to be his house, and he would
spend the rest of his life in it until he left it, decently, in
his coffin. There was no point in going anywhere else,

287

since he would be obliged to take Christina with him, wherever he went. He would be no less miserable elsewhere and she much more so. It had been madness to dream of escape, or to suppose that this marriage could terminate with his father's death. He could not possibly leave her. She had done nothing to deserve it, save bore him intolerably and exhibit justifiable resentment when that fact became apparent. No wife could have behaved better than she had during the last few days. He pitied and honoured her for the efforts that she was making, but he had ceased to love her. At some point, during their estrangement, that slender thread of continuity had snapped—the thread which runs through every happy marriage from the first vows to the final parting, which survives changes, storms, surprises, hazards, discoveries, quarrels and reconciliations, blending all into a single experience. There was, for him, no link between the past and the present. They had made a disastrous mistake, but he had no right to leave her unless she wished it, which she never would. Their union, no longer nourished by love, must be preserved in kindness, compassion and mutual forbearance.

Black figures were creeping up the path. He went into the dining room where substantial refreshments were set out. All this, too, had been very well done.

Soon the house was filled with a subdued yet festive murmur. It was, in its way, a pleasant funeral. The prevailing sentiment was warm and not too painful. Everybody had loved old Mr. Pattison but he could be mourned without extreme disconcertment, for there was nothing insufferable about his death, no sudden shock, no desolate widow, no helpless orphans, no work left half-finished, no life cut off in its prime. Since all must die, this was the best way to do it.

Dickie and Christina went about, dispensing hospitality and hearing the same things said, again and again. A few old men looked glum, as if listening to their own knell, until Dickie had filled them up with his father's whiskey; after that they brightened and put more faith in their individual constitutions. Pattison relatives who had not met one another for years got into corners and exchanged family news. It seemed to go on for hours, but Dickie was spared the latter part of it, for he was employed in driving convoys of guests, who had come from far afield, to catch their several trains.

From the last of these trips he came back to a silent house. Some rattling, splashing and chatter were going on in the kitchen regions: Christina was alone in the drawing room. They were to have a drawing room now; The Rowans was that kind of house. She had kicked off her shoes and was drinking a final cup of tea. They exchanged a look which meant: *Well! It went off all right.*

"Were your shoes comfortable?" she asked anxiously. "I got them a whole size larger than the others."

"Perfectly, thanks. Did yours hurt?"

"Agony! Oooooh! I'm tired."

"Let's go home."

"Goodness, no! There's all the washing up and the good china and plate to be put away. Allie and Mrs. Hughes stayed. . . . I ought to be in the scullery now. You go home, though, and hold the fort, because Mrs. Simpson may want to be getting away. Take the car. I'll drive back with Allie."

The Bay Hill house, when he reached it, looked small

289

and reproachful. He supposed that he must set about selling it. Christina wanted to move into The Rowans immediately. By the New Year other people would be living here and nothing would be left of the life begun two years ago, when he and Christina returned from Italy.

Serafina was in the lounge, reading, with her customary fierce concentration. She looked up as he came in and asked if it had been a nice funeral.

"How can a funeral be nice?" he asked, throwing himself into a chair.

"I mean, were the people satisfied?"

He considered it and said that he thought they were.

"They don't say *dead* in this town," observed Serafina. "They say *passed away*. I don't like it. It sounds like bath water."

He did not answer.

She got up, adding, "I'll go away. You're still sad and I mustn't be a nuisance."

"That's all right. I just don't want to talk."

"I know. We shan't talk any more, because you'll still be feeling sad when I go away. It's a pity."

He felt some compunction, remembering what Christina had told him of the child's reluctance to leave them and her strong attachment to himself. He had done little to deserve it, and was sorry that he had not taken more trouble to talk to her, had not given her more advice about books to read. No particular impulse of benevolence had inspired him; he had merely found her amusing, and had snubbed her without mercy as soon as she bored him. It was agreeable to be heard with such respectful adoration; her eagerness, her ignorance, her untrammelled imagination, her frantic hunger for mental nourishment, had not been without pathos. His curiosity had been aroused when he discovered that she genuinely preferred poetry to prose, but his interest in her had flagged when it appeared that she set more store by sound than sense. She did not really enquire into the meaning of what she read; her questions arose from her feeling for rhythm and metre. She mispronounced many words, but she never made mistakes in the scanning of a line. She had a voice of considerable range, and the unspeakable Elizabeth seemed to have taken some pains to train it.

"I'll send you some books," he said. "I'll send you the Oxford Book of English Verse."

"Thank you. I'll read it."

She spoke sadly. He surmised that there would be few books in the new Swannery, and nobody to tell Serafina what anything meant. For everyone else it would be a change for the better, to judge from Christina's account of Mrs. Wright.

"You'll go to school," he said encouragingly, "and get books there and learn a lot of things."

"That's not the same as talking to you. You know what I want to find out."

"And what is that?"

She gave him a blank, puzzled look.

"How can I know till you've told me? *Something!* When we are talking, I always keep feeling you'll say something. If I knew what it was, I'd ask you. If you could guess, you'd tell me. So that's why I keep on asking questions. It might come out someday. Something that explains why we were born."

"My dear Serafina! I don't know why we were born."

"I know. But you are the only person I've met who wonders about it."

"Do I wonder?"

"Oh, yes. Don't you remember what you said when you explained that poetry to me? That poetry that says it isn't safe to ask too many questions?"

"I don't remember. What poetry?"

She glanced at him reproachfully and said:

> "But ask not bodies doomed to die
> To what abode they go.
> Since knowledge is but Sorrow's spy,
> It is not safe to know."

When he had recovered from his astonishment she was gone. Her voice and her eyes had moved him deeply. She could not possibly have understood what she was saying, but he thought that he had never encountered such a gift of utterance. Nothing said that day would remain with him, save this. Yet she had merely repeated a verse which blew through her haphazard mind, delivering words to their target because she could speak, not because she understood them.

Later that evening he told Christina that he doubted whether the new Swannery would be congenial to Serafina.

"Of course it won't," said Christina. "She'll be bored to tears."

"She ought to get a first-rate education. She ought to go to Oxford."

"Oxford? H'm!"

Oxford, thought Christina, was Dickie's solution for every human ill, because he had been unable to go there

himself. Bobbins was to be sent there, at all costs, in order
to be happy ever after and never get toothache.

"Now I think," she said, "that Serafina ought to go
to one of those schools that teach children how to act.
I believe she might have a real talent. They look after
them very well at those schools and give them a proper,
ordinary education, as well as training them for the stage.
She has a way of looking at you and saying things: she
puts it over, as Mr. Prescott says. She does it, even when
she doesn't know what she's saying."

"There's something in that," agreed Dickie. "But I
don't know who'd pay for it."

"Mr. Archer will. Sometime or other I'm going to
write to him about it. He owes a lot to Serafina. You
see, she's tough. Nobody has ever treated her like a child.
I think it would be better for her to start earning her
living rather young. She's got a lot of far-fetched, fanciful
ideas. If you gave her a very . . . well . . . intellectual
education, I think she'd just go floating off out of this
world, and turn into a crank. But if she has to get down
to a good hard job, with a lot of strictness, but using her
gifts at the same time, she might turn out very well. I've
thought about it a great deal."

"It's a brilliant solution," he exclaimed. "Very, very
clever of you to have thought of it, Tina!"

His surprise was a little too obvious. She felt tempted
to say, *Thank you for a nut,* a sarcasm current at the high
school when over-patronising compliments had been
paid. But she refrained. He had grown so touchy lately
that she had to be careful what she said. A few months
ago he would have laughed.

In a spasm of anxiety she wondered just how long it

293

would be before they laughed again. How long must she watch her tongue and encounter this impersonal courtesy? Until he had got over his father's death, she supposed. It must be that which made him seem so distant, for he surely knew, by now, that everything had blown over, as far as she was concerned.

In any case, it was not, perhaps, an evening for laughter.

4

As soon as the children had been despatched to the new Swannery, Christina set about moving house. She began briskly. After a while she fell into a kind of languor, disheartened by Dickie's lack of interest. In vain did she endeavour to consult his taste at every point; he was determined to leave everything to her, was sure that he would approve her decisions, and did not care in the least what curtains he had in his new study. Nor would he go near The Rowans, unless she commanded his help in some task of heavy lifting or moving.

Sometimes she tried to believe that they were getting along better than they used to do. Over the Bay Hill house they had bickered a good deal. Their tastes had clashed. Now there was no occasion for argument. Their conversation was cautious and neutral; they had become unnaturally considerate of one another's susceptibilities. If this meant that they were getting along better, she could not like it. The joy and zest of the move began to evaporate. She asked herself occasionally why she should be taking so much trouble. This question had never occurred to her before and she found it dismaying.

Her plans were, as usual, sensible and economical. Very little had to be bought, since The Rowans was already well stocked with everything that they could ever want. They could lock the door of the old house any morning, and sleep that night in the new one, without chaos or exhaustion. Only their personal possessions, clothes and books, need be transferred before the move, and these she meant to take over daily, in instalments. Sam Dale would transport for her, sometime or other, a few large pieces of furniture, but she meant to sell most of the things at Bay Hill, since The Rowans had a better dining-room table, more capacious wardrobes, and a much handsomer three-piece suite.

Dickie passively waited to be told when they should go. The old house looked emptier every day and the new one, whenever he was obliged to go there, looked fuller. He therefore supposed that the date must be drawing near. Upon a Saturday afternoon he was instructed to bring over all their gramophone records; Christina had taken the cabinet that morning in Mrs. Selby's station wagon. They had a great many; he had quite forgotten how many. Instead of stacking them in the car and getting off immediately after lunch, he wasted time in looking them over and wondering why he had neglected certain old favourites for so long. He even played a couple of them over, for he would not have another chance to do so until Dale's truck transported the radiogram. He felt slightly aggrieved to think that some days must elapse before he could play them again, although he had neglected them for months.

At last he pulled himself together and carried them all out to the car, wishing that there were not so many. Christina could have thrown half of them away, for all he cared. She had, in fact, thrown out a good many,

296

because they were old and scratched, and with them one called *Edward! Edward!* which was in perfect condition but which she never wished to hear again.

When he reached The Rowans she was upstairs, putting clothes away. She heard him arrive and shrugged her shoulders resignedly, for she knew why he was so late. If she asked him to bring over books he just wasted his time, sitting about and reading them instead of putting them away on shelves.

He carried a first stack of records into the study, and there he got a surprise. Pethwick's gift stood in the window, gleaming in the afternoon sun, mysteriously animated, redeeming all the promises with which his memory had enriched it. She must have sent for it and put it there to please him.

Touched and grateful he walked round it, viewing it again from every angle. The glass had been carefully dusted and polished. Upon his desk he found a small bottle of surgical spirit which she must have got for the purpose.

For some time now he had been aware of her deliberate attempts at reconciliation, and he had been grieved at his own inability to respond to them. They could not restore the past; they had come too late. He had thanked her and had known that his thanks were not what she wanted. Now, however, he was so much delighted that he felt an impulse which could be expressed without any humbug. He bounded upstairs and found her putting clothes away in a large mahogany wardrobe.

"Tina!" he said, pulling her to him and kissing her warmly, "I've just been into my study. You *are* a darling girl!"

"I thought it would be a surprise," she said.

"It was. And so beautifully dusted."

"It looks nice there, doesn't it? I've got to like it, now I'm used to it. I've got to like it very much."

Poor girl! he thought. What a raw deal she was getting! With another man she might have been so much happier, a man who appreciated her many virtues better, and cherished her, and made love to her. He had not done so for a long, long time: not since some night before that storm which had marked the beginning of all their troubles. Even when they ceased to quarrel a tacit uneasiness had held them apart. He had not known how to end it.

Such a state of things could not go on forever. Their marriage might have been a disastrous mistake for both, but they were young, they were normal, and they could not spend the rest of their lives in a state of courteous celibacy. He must soon do something about it, yet he half dreaded an intimacy which might only reveal the measure of distance between them. He must try, he thought, to make her happy, to give her a good time. That used not to be difficult.

He watched her for a while as she took clothes from a trunk, folded them neatly, and stowed them in the bottom drawer of the wardrobe. Then he looked round the room, which had been his parents' bedroom in the old days. Since his mother's death it had been unoccupied, for his father had moved into a single room on the garden side of the house.

Everything reminded him of his boyhood. Upon the dressing table was a small china tree on which his mother had hung her rings. The same pieces of old English pottery decorated the mantelpiece: Wesley preaching to the blacks, and Grace Darling rowing towards a rose-embowered lighthouse. Above them was a picture of two Russians in fur caps driving over the snow in a sleigh. The large double bed was bare and heaped with pillows and bolsters in clean striped ticking. But there was plenty of linen for it in his mother's well-stocked cupboards, beautiful linen, so Christina said, the envy of every other woman in East Head. She loved all these good, solid things. Perhaps they might be of some consolation to her.

She continued to move steadily between the trunk and the wardrobe. He turned again to watch her, noticing the graceful stoop and curve of her body as she bent to lift the clothes out, her young energy, the swing forward of her bright hair over face and neck.

"What are you thinking about?" he asked suddenly.

She glanced up at him in surprise. This was not a question which he often asked, nowadays.

"Oh, lots of things," she said. "So many things at once that they really add up to nothing."

"Poor Tina! You'll be glad when this move is over."

"Shan't you?"

"Yes. I think so. I dare say we'll both feel better. I . . . I don't quite know what's got into me lately. . . ."

Yes, you do, she thought, as she began on the next drawer, which was to hold his shirts. You've been thinking it's hell to be married to me. And now you're thinking that perhaps it isn't so bad after all. You're right. We couldn't hurt each other worse than we have, so perhaps it will be better.

She half smiled to herself and went on with her work.

Her smile and her silence took him aback; they were almost like a challenge. After all, she was his, and had no business to be mysterious, when the gist of his complaint was that he understood her far too well. Disturbed, he continued to watch her, and told himself that she was really a most beautiful girl. It was ridiculous to go on like this.

Christina, aware of his scrutiny although she did not look round, knew what was happening to him. She could not decide whether she was glad or sorry. She ought to welcome any sign that she still had power with him, but her heart was heavy. She had hoped for something else, for some different kind of understanding, when she put that surprise for him in his study. This, the renewal of desire, would have been bound to take place sooner or later; she would have preferred to feel that they were completely friends again before it did.

"This will be our room, I suppose?" he said at last.

He went across to the bed and thumped the box spring mattress which was, like everything else in The Rowans, the best of its kind.

"Come along, Tina!" he exclaimed, almost impatiently. "Let's see if it's comfortable."

She turned and stared at him. Did he mean now? His face, flushed, a little blurred and blunted, left her in no doubt about it. Oh, well, she thought, going to him. It's one way of getting a man back. The only way, so they say. I must try to make him happy.

She supposed that she had when, after murmured words of gratitude, they fell apart again on that enormous bed. It had been all right, too much so, she thought, for people who were not really friends. And now they were once more thinking their separate thoughts. She mused upon a possibility which had not, it seemed, occurred to

300

him: this reckless, unpremeditated embrace might have given them another child, begotten in their new house before they had even left the old one.

She had no objection. She wanted several babies and she hoped that the next would be a little girl, a companion to whom she could talk, a little daughter whom she would call Anne. She did not want another boy, doomed to grow up into an incomprehensible, unhappy man. Always wanting something, they don't know what, she thought, and it wouldn't do them much good if they did, for it would turn out to be something quite out of this world, something nobody has ever had. Men! Oh, I wouldn't be a man for anything. Poor things, they're never contented with what they do; they're always thinking it might be better. Because they can never do anything so wonderful as have a baby. No. Not all the greatest discoveries and inventions and art and religion and everything, all the things they do, can be so wonderful as a perfect live human being. We know we just couldn't do better, when we've had a baby, which we do with hardly any trouble. Yes, and everybody praises us and congratulates us; while if a man wants to do something perfectly wonderful everybody laughs at him.

She turned to look at Dickie. His face was pale now, remote and grave. He is thinking about death, she surmised, and how soon we shall die.

He was. He had begun by remembering their honeymoon, and the folds of their mosquito curtain, and the racket the Italians kicked up in the street all night, under the hotel windows, shouting and laughing and starting up motor bicycles. From that his mind had leapt forward to the last time, years ahead; they would not know it to

301

be the last, perhaps, but there would be one. On this bed? In this house? The abode of bodies doomed to die. . . .

"Yoohoo! Christie! Yoohoo!"

A loud hooting from the hall shattered the quiet of the house. Christina jumped up with a startled cry.

"That's Allie!" she said. "I must go down or she'll be coming up. She's been wheeling Bobbins out with her Nancy and she said she'd bring him here at four o'clock."

Allie had brought the babies and the perambulator into the hall. She stood there and shouted and wondered why Christina did not come. Just as she was upon the point of exploring upstairs, her friend came running down, full of apologies, a little dishevelled, and making no attempt to explain why she had been so long.

"Has Bobbins been good?" she cried. "Hullo? Hullo? You Bobbins? Have you been good? Have you?"

What, wondered Allie, can she have been up to? She looks funny. If it was anybody but Christie, I'd think. . . .

"Are you going to keep this old wall paper?" she asked, looking round the hall. "Awfully old-fashioned, isn't it?"

"Wall paper is coming in again," snapped Christina.

Dickie now appeared on the landing. He came down the stairs, looking rather sheepish, nodded to Allie and went out to the car for more records. The situation became clearer to Allie. She grinned and turned away to inspect the Pattison umbrella stand, which was at present empty, since the umbrellas would not arrive until the family did.

That grin annoyed Christina. Allie could be dreadfully

common sometimes. Had it been herself, she would probably have made no secret of the strange way in which she had spent the afternoon; she would have retailed the whole episode with much giggling. Nor would she hold her tongue about this discovery. She would make a tale of it, to some of the younger matrons: Yes really! At four o'clock on a Saturday afternoon. No wonder we all sighed for Dickie! I always say Christie was born lucky.

For the first time in her life Christina began to comprehend a little of Dickie's dislike for East Head. She felt an impulse to get away and live among people who who did not inevitably know everything about their neighbours. This sort of thing would not be so likely to happen if they could select their friends and if intimacy was not simply imposed by habit. What had she, after all, in common with Allie? Why were they supposed to be such close friends? Propinquity had been the chief agent; they had some affection for one another but very little respect. In another place she might find a companion who was superior to Allie, whom she could admire, perhaps, and even imitate to a certain extent. There was nobody of that description in East Head, but there might be somebody somewhere else.

Allie was peering about into the rooms and taking notice of Christina's alterations. Presently she went into the study.

"My goodness!" she cried. "What on earth. . . ."

"Mr. Swann did it," explained Christina, joining her. "Mr. Pethwick gave it to Dickie."

"What's it supposed to be, then?"

"Nothing. Just what it is."

Allie shook her head and turned up her eyes.

"Weird," she commented. "Still and all, I like it better than the one we've got in the Pavilion."

"Yes. I wish they'd take it away."

"My dear! Haven't you heard? It's never going away. It's there for good. We're going to buy it."

"What! Buy it? Who's going to?"

"Town's going to. With the War Memorial money."

"Allie! No! They can't! They can't!"

"They're going to. Aren't they crackers?"

"But who! The committee! Why, Dickie's on the committee! He's never said a word about it."

"So's Mummie on the committee, and she ought to know. You know how she goes on about the younger generation?"

"But nobody else! Nobody else. . . ."

"Oh, yes, lots of people are very keen. Mr. Dale says it will give a big boost to East Head to be so modern. And then Sir Gregory interfering got into a lot of people's hair."

"Oh, dear! I've been so busy. I've hardly seen anyone, these last few days. I'd no idea . . ."

"Funny Dickie never mentioned it. Mummie says he's written to Mr. Swann about it, to ask if it's for sale. The committee asked Dickie to write."

"When? When?" cried Christina. "Oh, I remember. Wednesday. They met on Wednesday. But . . . but what does Mr. Swann say, then?"

"Why ask me? You're married to a member of the committee. You ought to know more about it than I do."

"Mr. Swann mayn't realise . . . mayn't know . . . what it is."

304

"Ha! ha! ha! That's good. Even Mr. Swann!"

Christina had rushed off to meet Dickie, who was coming up the path with an armful of records.

"Dickie! Dickie! What's this about the town buying that thing in the Pavilion? Is it true?"

"It's been proposed," said Dickie. "But I don't know if it will go through. I haven't heard from Swann yet."

"But he can't. You mustn't. It must be stopped. You don't like it yourself, Dickie. You know you don't."

"My dear Tina, I can't prevent the rest of the committee from buying what they want."

"You could. You stopped them buying the portrait."

"I had grounds. But this is a work of art. . . ."

"No it's not. It's rubbish! Ridiculous rubbish."

"If you want these records brought in, you must please let me get on with it."

She stood aside and let him go on to the house.

The shock quite confused her. She had been so busy lately that she had seen few people and heard very little news. Such an item would not, in any case, have excited great interest in her circle, and nobody had thought of mentioning it. They naturally supposed that Dickie had done so. She had believed all danger to be at an end; weeks had gone by without any discovery or exposure, and Swann's effects were shortly to be removed to Coombe Bassett. Now it was upon them.

And Mr. Swann, she thought, when he gets that letter, won't know what Dickie is talking about. He'll suppose it's the statue he really did. He may say yes. He doesn't know about that Thing, that wicked dangerous Thing!

She knew what it really was, yet she feared and hated it so much, it had been the agent of such double dealing,

305

that she almost felt it to be deliberately malign. Ever since it appeared it had worked on people, causing them to deceive themselves and each other, to quarrel, to lie, to desert one another, to pile betrayal upon betrayal. She was sure that some discovery of the truth had caused Martha to fly, leaving her friends in the lurch. Conrad Swann, for whom she professed so high an esteem, would inevitably suffer when it all came out, as it was now bound to do. Everybody would laugh at him and nobody would buy his work any more. His other supporters, Dickie, Nigel Meadowes, would, unawares, do him a great injury. Good, innocent citizens, like Mrs. Hughes, would be blamed for making a laughing stock of their town. Several people had undoubtedly done wrong, but she herself was worse than any, for she could have prevented the whole calamity, had she spoken in time. She could have stopped the exhibition. By her silence she had brought this trouble upon everybody and Dickie would never forgive her.

For a moment she glanced at the fact that she need not be involved. She could hold her tongue, allow things to take their course, and nobody need ever know that she had been to blame. But that would be to abandon all of them, Swann, Dickie, Mrs. Hughes, to a disaster which might still be prevented. If Swann were warned, he could turn down the offer, and the whole mistake might be hushed up.

Dickie would never forgive her if he knew. She could hold her tongue, but in that case she was not sure that she would ever be able to forgive herself. She felt quite unable to decide which was the worse alternative.

When he came out of the house again, she was still standing on the path where he had left her. He was looking rather black; that she should follow up their reconciliation with a fresh squabble over Swann augured badly for the future. She would seem to have learnt nothing.

"Why didn't you tell me?" she demanded. "Why did you say nothing about it?"

"Because," he said coldly, "it's not a subject upon which we can ever agree, is it? We've found that out by experience. We can't discuss it without getting angry, so we'd much better not discuss it, I think."

"But, Dickie . . ."

"I'm not going to talk about it. What do you think you're doing? Raking all this up just when we . . . just when . . ."

"I didn't know anything about it till Allie told me."

"It's no business of yours. I don't want to hear a word more from you about it."

"All right. All right. You shan't."

"That's a good girl!"

He smiled, relenting, and went on for the last stack of records.

5

And now he is happy listening to the radio. Just because he is listening to his favourite music he is quite out of this world, and has managed to forget everything for a little while. He has to forget everything, before he can be happy, because nothing in his life makes any sense to him. That is not happiness. He is not a happy man.

This afternoon. And immediately afterwards I made him angry because I started to argue again, and he was very gloomy all through supper. But now, for a little while, he is quite in a rapture. That is how he lives his life: either miserable or quite in a rapture. Sitting there and listening, and seeing it all in his mind, because he knows it so well, he can imagine it on the stage. And he smiles at me sometimes, because he knows I'm fond of Mozart, too. He's thinking it pays to be firm. He was firm with me, so I shut up, and now we are happily listening to Mozart together.

I shall never be able to hear this music again without feeling sick. It will remind me of this terrible night, when we were sitting here, and he was listening, and I was trying to find the courage to tell him.

But I'll let him enjoy it all to the end before I do. So now he is happy, looking at the score. He is listening to all those jokes and laughing at them. I never can like those bits where they just jabber, with little chords from the piano. Which bit is it? Those two men in a graveyard . . . I never know what it's all about, jabbering away in Italian, but they seem to have to have it. Does anybody know what it's about?

There is no escape. Nothing can stop it. Nothing! Nothing!

Whether I speak, or whether I don't, this blow must fall on him, now he's written that letter. Nothing can save him. I can save the others. I can stop it from getting worse. But I can't save Dickie.

This afternoon. He was so pleased when he found it in his study. Now he will never be able to enjoy it again, or take a pride in it. He will never be able to think of Conrad Swann again, without feeling humiliated.

Dickie sat up, his eyes bright. He was waiting for some special moment. He smiled across at Christina.

A tremendous voice rang through the room, like the tolling of a great bell:

"DI RIDER FINIRAI PRIA DELL' AURORA!"

Oh, that awful voice! It speaks, suddenly in the graveyard. You won't laugh tomorrow, it says, or something like that.

Why couldn't we laugh? Why couldn't everybody laugh about it? Why should that rubbishy Thing have the power to bring such misery? Who is behind it? Is there some cruel person who has done it all on purpose? No! How could there be? Nobody. All an accident.

It's so unfair. Dickie never liked it. He saw through it. How could I know Martha would run away and leave poor

309

Dickie to write her idiotic mistake in a letter to Mr. Swann?

Perhaps Mr. Swann will forgive him. But he will never forgive himself for supposing that silly object was the work of a great artist—a man he thinks the world of. He never liked it, but that won't make any difference. He will feel he ought to have known.

Why is he smiling now? It must be another of our favourites . . . he remembers it all so much better than I do. A man and a woman. . . .

Crudele! Ah no, mio bene!

Oh, yes! Yes! His favourite song of all, and mine too. He tells her she is cruel, and she says no, she is not. And it keeps breaking in, all the time while she is arguing and making excuses for her behaviour, that lovely tune keeps breaking in, the tune she is going to have to sing to him. So at last she has to sing it, because there is nothing else to say. So lovely! So lovely! He is in a dream, listening to it.

Tu ben sai quanto t'amai.

You know, she says, you know how much I love you. Just that. She need say nothing else but that. She sings and he listens, and everything is all right.

He will never forgive me. I should have thought that would be the worst. But it's not. I wouldn't mind what I had to bear if I could protect him from this.

I understand him better now. Better than I did when we were happy. It isn't that he will mind having made a stupid mistake. He is not conceited. But he is always searching for something. He is disappointed in his life. So he's always searching for something that he can feel is more important than just his little life. He wants something that he can admire so much that it will make living worth while. And this . . . this will make a mockery of something he admires. He will feel it's no use; there is no difference between true and false.

Not even God can help, unless it's to change Dickie into somebody different: somebody who wouldn't mind so much. God can't do that. It may be foolish of Dickie to mind so much, but that is the way he is made. Oh, you know, you know how much I love you.

He never will. He doesn't want to know. It would make him too sad if he knew. Everything is too late.

The music stopped for a moment. The great aria was over. For a few seconds, before the finale, there was no sound in the room save a faint humming from the radio.

"Very fine," said Dickie. "But she wasn't quite up to the second half, was she?"

"No," said Christina, who had not heard a note of the second half.

"We've got a terrific Commendatore, though. It's going to be a wonderful finale. I'm feeling cold already, waiting for the moment when he comes in."

She jumped up and rushed upstairs to their bedroom. Even there the music pursued her faintly, as it poured from the radio in the room below. She flung herself down on the bed, her hands over her ears, lost in panic and desolation.

The statue! She cried wildly to herself. The statue! Cowering as though she could hear it coming up the stairs. It was no accident. Something had been let loose; somebody was making use of this inane thing, this innocent bit of rubbish, which had already done so much harm and was bound to do more, because it was a fragment of falsity, and ought not to exist in the world for a single moment longer. To take it away, to destroy it, was the only remedy, but nobody would ever do such a thing unless she did it herself. Nothing could repair the damage already done, but the weapon could still be snatched from that mysterious, hostile hand.

She ran downstairs, and out to the garage, with no clear notion of what she meant to do. That might be manifest when she reached the Pavilion. The doors would be shut at eleven o'clock but she still had twenty minutes.

As she got the car out, a scheme solidified. She would tell Mr. Beccles that Dickie had sent her to take it away. He would probably give it up; everybody seemed to think that Dickie had power to act for Conrad Swann. And then she would contrive to destroy it—bury it perhaps in some place where nobody would ever find it. To Dickie, to the world, she would announce that she had done this because she did not happen to like it; other people did such things, for she had read about them in the newspapers. They went into galleries and destroyed statues or pictures which they did not happen to like. They were mad people and everybody was shocked at them. Prison or a lunatic asylum was probably their lot, and might be hers. The whole town would condemn her; they would pity Dickie because he had a mad wife. Her life was in ruins, but, by doing this thing, she felt as though she might draw all the retribution down upon herself and be the only one to pay, as she deserved to pay. The Thing would be no more; they should never find it or discover what she knew.

The streets were nearly empty as she drove down to

the Pavilion, for most of the cinemas finished their last houses soon after ten. In Market Square the country buses, brilliantly lighted oblongs, were drawn up in rows. Long queues were filling them before they set off, up and down the coast, or inland, over the dark hills. The wind was getting up; the first autumn gales were beginning, and ragged clouds sailed across the moon. Upon the deserted Parade an endless line of lamps stretched away beside the sea wall. A high tide boomed and dragged at the screaming shingle.

She parked the car and went towards the Pavilion which stood up, rectangular and aggressive, under the hurrying clouds. It was not yet shut. An unpleasant greenish light glowed through the ranks of glass doors. These vestibule lights had always caused controversy; they poured down, from some concealed source, pervasively bright but unflattering to the faces of people coming out of the theatre hall.

If Mr. Wetherby was a woman and had to make up, she thought, as she hurried toward the doors, he wouldn't like having to look like a corpse.

Alan Wetherby!

An unidentified figure took a step out of the shadows, in her mind. Whose name was invariably quoted as warrant for the Thing? Who had encouraged Martha to believe that it was wonderful? Did he know? He, of all people, was the best qualified to guess the truth. What part had he played in all this, and why had she not thought of him before?

Now that she had thought of him, she knew. He was the person behind it all; he had let it happen deliberately. And she knew why: it was his idea of a joke, his way of

enjoying himself. He liked to make people feel small
and foolish. He was looking forward to a grand spectacle
of general humiliation.

But he should not have it. For all his cleverness he had
not reckoned with mad Mrs. Pattison.

She went slowly through the doors. There had been a
picture shown in the hall, but the audience had all departed a quarter of an hour before. The vestibule was
empty, its glassy blue floor streaming away to that trans-
parent North wall and gleams of moonlight on tossing
waves. She had never seen it thus before, and was, for
the first time, impressed by its beauty. Even the strange
light, emanating stealthily from the fabric, was beautiful
in a cruel way; nobody else was there, no corpse face
looked at her, and this light was at peace with emptiness.

Treading with fearful steps over her own reflection,
soaring walls and arched roof below and above her, she
approached the space at the head of the stairs. The light
revealed dahlias and chrysanthemums and a square block
of marble in the middle of them. It was the pedestal
upon which the Thing had stood.

She stared, blinked, looked away, and stared again.
The pedestal was empty. The Thing had gone.

In that merciless light, amidst so many deceiving reflections, she could not immediately believe her own eyes.
It was some seconds before her brain received the message.

Gone.

The vestibule echoed with a series of clangs. A young
man had come out of the hall and was shutting its doors.
He said a word or two to an usherette, who came out with
him, and they laughed before she hurried off into the wind

314

and the night. Their laughter rang away, under the roof, as Christina hurried down towards the hall doors. These echoes were also only apparent when the place was empty.

The young man was Mr. Beccles' factotum and his name was Ernest. Nobody knew his surname. He looked a little startled, when she came up to him, for he had thought the vestibule to be empty.

"Where's that thing gone?" she demanded. "That thing they had in the middle of the flowers?"

"Why, it's there still," he said, with a glance toward the stairhead.

"No it's not. The stone is there. The statue has gone."

He took a step or two in that direction, gaped, and exclaimed, "That's funny! It was there this afternoon."

"When?"

"Between five and six, it was there still."

"Are you sure?"

He reflected and declared, "S'matter of fact, I am. There was a coach party in, and one feller was there taking pictures with this little camera, size of a button. I noticed that."

After further reflection he gave judgement: "Somebody must've taken it away."

"How could they? Without you seeing?"

"That's right. They couldn't."

"You've been out here all the time since six?"

"Naw. Seven to eight I was getting me supper, in the canteen. But Mr. Beccles, he was out here then. P'raps he knows."

She glanced at the glass door into Mr. Beccles' office. It was locked and dark.

"He's gone home this half hour," said Ernest. "But it

must of happened when I was off, see? Funny I didn't notice."

"Who could it have been?"

"I couldn't say, Mrs. Pattison. But it must of been somebody entitled to take it, or Mr. Beccles, he wouldn't of let it go."

Ernest glanced meaningly at the clock over the café entrance. Nobody could ever read this clock, which had no hands and no numerals, but the glance signified that he wanted to shut the main doors and go home.

"Very queer," said Christina. "Goodnight, Ernest."

"Goodnight, Mrs. Pattison."

They both took another stare at the empty flower bed. Then she went out into the darkness. The rising gale caught and buffeted her as she emerged from the shelter of the building. A light mist of spray blew over the sea wall into her face.

6

"Conrad!"

"Yes, Frank?"

"Have you been listening?"

"Yes, Frank."

"What have I been saying?"

"That I mustn't laugh," said Conrad piously. "Can we have some more marmalade?"

Archer snapped his fingers at the head waiter and pointed to the marmalade dish. This was his third descent upon the Metropole and he was, by now, regarded with some awe. More marmalade was brought immediately.

Conrad fell upon it, for he was very hungry. They had been out to sea before breakfast that morning. Moreover he was in tearing spirits; to find that he could return to East Head without uneasiness was an immense stimulant.

"And why," asked Archer, "mustn't you laugh?"

"Because it would do a lot of damage to your reputation if this story got out," said Conrad promptly.

"Yours, old man. Yours. Your reputation."

"Same thing."

This was true. Their reputations were inextricably involved.

"So you'll keep a straight face till we get home?"

"I'll try. But I think it's very funny."

"Funny my arse! A lot too funny. That's the trouble."

"Can I tell Ivy, when we get home?"

"You'll tell nobody. You'll keep your mouth shut and let me do the talking."

"All right. But I don't see why you should take me along, in that case. I'd much rather go for another sail."

"I take you along because I don't trust you out of my sight for five minutes, until we're clear of this town. I'm beginning to understand why it drove you crackers."

"Perhaps Pattison might like to come for a sail. It's Sunday, so he'll be free."

Frank gave Conrad a murderous look.

"I know you're a very, very simple person," he observed.

This jibe went home. It was not one which Conrad wished to recall. He winced and protested.

"Then don't treat me as if I was Martha Rawson. Pattison is going to need careful handling. We're in the dark. There've been some very queer doings here. We've got to walk on egg shells till we find out how come Mrs. P. knew, and he didn't."

"Huh! Huh! Huh!"

"Don't laugh, damn you."

"Sorry. But we aren't sure she knows, are we?"

"I'm ninety per cent sure. Every single question we asked, the children fetched up with Aunt Chris. Joe wouldn't have remembered, if Aunt Chris hadn't given him a chocolate biscuit. What got her so interested? Serafina told Aunt Chris a lie: said there was nothing in the shed. Why should Aunt Chris ask, if she hadn't smelt a rat. Obviously she was on to it."

"I expect she laughed," mused Conrad wistfully.

318

"She might. But she didn't hand the joke on to hubby. Why not? Why did she let him write that letter?"

"We can ask her."

"If we get a chance. I must sniff about and see how the land lies. If only she'll go on holding her tongue we may get by, for I don't believe anybody else knows."

"I think you're taking it all too seriously."

"You do? I'm going to have nightmares about it for the rest of my life. When I think! If I hadn't come down here, the week-end of the storm, and seen that thing, we'd be in the soup. I'd forgotten all about it, till you showed me Pattison's letter."

"Huh! Huh! Huh!"

"Now look here!"

Conrad pulled himself together and swallowed his laughter. He twisted his face into an unaccustomed scowl which he kept up for the rest of breakfast and on all the way to the Pattisons' house. He had a good deal of brow to knit and he looked so fierce that Frank had to remind him they were not on a lynching party.

Christina, who was upstairs, heard the gate click. She looked out of the window to see this disconcerting pair rolling up the path, side by side. They were formidable, and had always been so, ever since they descended upon Europe, a couple of grotesque adolescents from out back in Boogie Woogie or wherever it was. They looked more like men from some other planet than migrants from any known continent. Conrad wore corduroys and a tweed jacket. Frank's suit came from Savile Row. But these garments looked as incongruous on them as does fancy dress upon a civilised man. It was impossible to imagine what clothes they should have been wearing.

319

As they drew nearer she saw that terrible scowl and felt giddy with fright. Everything must have come out. She stumbled across to the bed and sat on it for a moment, trying to get her breath.

The doorbell chimed. She heard Dickie go along the hall to answer it, and knew that she must be there, beside him, to face whatever was coming, to draw their fire, if possible. She rushed down the stairs as Dickie opened the door.

"Are you busy?" asked Archer, as the two avengers surged into the hall. "We've come about your letter to Conrad. How do you do, Mrs. Pattison?"

"How do you do?" she whispered, shaking hands.

She looked so scared and so pretty that both Conrad and Archer felt anxious to kiss her. Conrad did so, and drew her arm through his as they all went into the lounge. His brows were no longer furrowed, and a little colour stole back into her cheeks.

"How is Mrs. Swann? How are the children?" she cried, in distracted tones.

Conrad, recollecting that he had been forbidden to utter a word, glanced at Archer, who replied that they were all well and sent their love. At this Conrad looked mutinous, for he liked the truth. They had done no such thing. The children had not known of this expedition and Ivy was far too well aware of her place to send her love to Mrs. Pattison.

"About your letter," began Archer, but was interrupted by Dickie, who wanted to get rid of Christina.

"I'm sure," he said to her, "that you're busy, and this is really a matter for the committee."

"I want to stay and hear about it," she said stubbornly.

320

He could not actually thrust her from the room, but he was terrified lest she should become contumacious, and gave her a look as quelling as that which Archer was, at the same moment, bestowing upon Conrad. Don't talk! was the tacit command to these two reprobates, who forthwith sat down side by side on a settee and prepared to hold their tongues.

"About the letter," repeated Archer, shooting out his eyes at Dickie.

Some things were already clear. Pattison knew nothing. No disclosure could have taken place since he wrote that letter; he could not else have opened the door in so placid a manner. Mrs. Pattison, on the other hand, knew everything. She was terrified. There might be very little difficulty in persuading her to hold her tongue forever.

"The fact is," continued Archer, "that the Apollo isn't for sale. Not at present. I've advised against it. Conrad very much appreciates your kindness in writing. He realises, of course, what an honour the town has done him. . . ."

"Huh! Huh! Huh!"

Conrad caught Archer's eye, heaved, and blew his nose.

"But I've strongly advised him to decline. I feel that, after Gressington, there'll be a good many Apollos about, don't you know. Some of them rather so-so. What with one thing and another, I think this one had better go into cold storage for a while. Perhaps you'd be so very kind as to tell your committee that?"

"I will," said Dickie, and added hastily, "though they'll be very sorry to hear it."

He was not a bit sorry himself and found it impossible

321

to say that he was. So he asked if they would now like to have it removed from the Pavilion.

"Thanks," said Archer. "We've done that already. We went there last night and saw the manager, and he handed it over. Everything is quite in order."

"Then . . . then where is it now?" breathed Christina.

Archer managed not to hear this question and explained that he was arranging to have all Conrad's property sent over to Coombe Bassett. But Conrad could not ignore the misery in her eyes; he said heartily, "It's at the bottom of the sea. We took it out in a boat early this morning, and dropped it overboard."

Christina and Dickie gave two gasps, one of relief, the other of surprise.

"You needn't have told them that," admonished Archer. "You're supposed to be out of the bin and of sound mind again. The fact is," he turned to Dickie, "Conrad has taken a sort of dislike to it. . . ."

"Huh! Huh! Huh! Huh!"

"He can't stand the sight of it. You know, he was a very sick man when he was . . . er . . . working for the Gressington competition, and the associations . . . well . . . they're painful."

"Huh! Huh! Huh!"

"Shut up, Conrad. But this is in confidence, Pattison. We'd just as soon not have it known."

"Oh, yes, I see," said Dickie, trying to look as if he did.

"I mean, the people here might think it a bit odd. They offer to buy it and he takes it and . . . and . . ."

A violent convulsion shook Archer. He realised that, in another minute, he would begin to laugh himself.

322

"So that's that," he concluded hastily, determined to get Conrad out of the house as soon as possible. "If you'll be a good fellow and say all the polite things? Put all the blame on me. You've been such a very good friend to us both. Sorry to have taken up your time. You must be busy. Come along, Conrad!"

But Conrad, who had suddenly grown serious, was looking searchingly at Dickie. Then he turned to Christina and said, "He didn't like it, did he? They made him write that letter? He didn't want to?"

"He likes some of your other things better," she said.

"I didn't understand it," said Dickie hastily. "I tried to, but . . ."

"You tried to?" cried Conrad in amazement.

"I wanted to like it, you know. I went and looked at it several times. I must say, it's a great relief to me to know that you . . . don't care for it so much yourself. I couldn't get anything from it, and felt that must be all my fault. I even started to read everything I could get hold of, about Apollo, to see if there was anything . . ."

Conrad's yelps were no longer to be stifled. He kept trying to apologise, but only went off into fresh convulsions every time he opened his mouth. Neither Christina nor Archer could resist the contagion. They were soon as helpless as he was. Dickie politely laughed, too.

"Books . . . books . . ." said Conrad, at last, with a violent effort at gravity. "I'm sorry. Books! You see Martha read me some books . . . funny . . . very funny . . . those books. . . ."

"They can't have been the same books that I read," said Dickie.

323

"Oh, yes," gasped Archer, coming to Conrad's rescue. "Girl turned into a tree. Must have been a sell for Apollo, that."

Conrad had fallen into a fresh paroxysm. He was trying to say something but could only hoot. At last he managed to articulate one word, "Thunderstorm!"

At this Archer and Christina nearly jumped out of their skins. Their laughter ceased abruptly.

"Just remembered it," explained Conrad, getting his breath. "Very bad thunderstorm, killed all the barbarians."

"Oh, I remember," said Dickie. "It's in Herodotus."

"You see," said Conrad, turning to Christina, "these barbarians, these Persians, they were marching on this mountain . . . what is it called? Apollo's mountain?"

"Parnassus," said Dickie.

"Where his temple was, at Delphi. So the local yok . . . the shepherds and . . . er . . . gro . . . farmers, and so on, they thought they had to fight. They went up to defend the place. But the priests, who worked the oracles, they weren't going to fight. They decided to sell out. They had some sacred armour that it was sacrilege to touch; they put it out in front of the Temple as notice of surrender, and announced that the God had moved it out by a miracle."

"Herodotus," interposed Dickie, "merely says that the armour was found outside."

"Does armour walk out of a temple on its own legs?" demanded Conrad. "It wouldn't now, and I don't believe it could then. You can see what Herodotus thought by the way he put it."

Dickie had taken a book from a shelf and turned up the passage.

"But when the barbarians were hurrying down upon the temple," he read, "a still greater portent befell. For it was marvel enough that arms of war should, of their own will, move out and lie before the temple; but thereafter occurred a second, of all prodigies the most worthy of wonder. For, as the barbarians were approaching the temple of Athena Pronaia, thunderbolts suddenly fell on them from heaven, and two crags were torn from Parnassus, falling in their midst and crushing many to death. A cry of triumph was heard from the temple of Pronaia. These combined events provoked panic among the barbarians. The Delphians came up and slew a number of them. The rest fled straight to Boeotia."

"You see!" commented Conrad. "And, that reminds me! Where's Martha gone?"

"Mrs. Rawson?" said Dickie. "I believe she's been ordered to take a year's cruise."

Conrad nodded and turned to Christina.

"Very good thunderstorm," he suggested. "Did a lot of good. They do, sometimes."

She murmured a faint agreement. He knew. This was his way of telling her that he knew exactly what had happened, and that she need not be frightened any more. She wanted to go away and cry, but feared that she might faint before she got out of the room.

"Hadn't I better," he suggested, "come and look at your baby? The children will want to know how he is. They'll be disappointed if I haven't seen him."

"He . . . he's in his play pen . . . in the dining room," murmured Christina, struggling to her feet.

Conrad rose too and helped her out of the room. Dickie made an effort to follow them but was detained by

325

Archer, who said that he wanted to settle the exact wording of Conrad's reply to the committee.

"Do you have any brandy anywhere?" asked Conrad, when they reached the dining room.

"There's some c-cognac in the sideboard."

He found it and gave her some, after which she cried for a little and he inspected Bobbins.

"Hasn't he got rather a long back?" he asked, when her muffled sobs had subsided.

"They all have," she said. "It's normal. Oh, Mr. Swann!"

"That's all right. Forget all about it."

"He would mind so much if he knew. He would feel that he hadn't appreciated you properly."

"He needn't know. Was that why you never told him?"

"Later on, yes. But at first . . . out of unkindness. Oh, but I am so glad you aren't angry."

"Why should I be?" he asked, in obvious surprise.

"It might have done you a lot of harm."

"So Frank says. But it hasn't."

"It was Mr. Wetherby's fault. I'm sure it was. He egged Martha on. I suppose it was his idea of a practical joke."

"It would be. But we've been too many for him."

Bobbins threw a coloured woollen ball outside his pen. Conrad stooped to retrieve it, smiling to himself and repeating, "Too many!"

"Mr. Swann. . . ."

"No hurry, you know. Forget about it for a bit, and then think it over."

"I'd feel more comfortable if I could tell him. But why should I upset him, just because I want to feel more comfortable?"

326

"Wait. Later on, it might not upset him so much."

"Oh, it would. Unless he changes a lot."

"Yes. But he might."

"Change? People don't change."

"Oh, yes. They change all the time."

"Do they?"

He did not answer that, because she was finding an answer for herself. Where was the furious child who had crawled about on this floor, looking for pins?

"I love him so much," she said, with a sigh.

When they rejoined the others in the lounge they found Dickie both composed and elated. Archer had explained Conrad's strange behaviour: there was still, he hinted, a certain amount of instability, although there was every hope of complete recovery. The Apollo could only be regarded as evidence of temporary insanity, so that it was good that he could now laugh at it. Dickie, by opposing Martha and preventing a hasty purchase of the thing, had done him an inestimable service.

"Thanks to you," Archer had said, "the whole business can now be hushed up and forgotten. If you hadn't used your eyes, and stood up to them, we should be in a God awful mess."

All this was balm to Dickie. To have been right in his judgement, to have done Swann a good turn, to find himself once more in accord with Christina, gave him considerable grounds for elation. And he was deeply thankful that Bobbins was going to be spared the Apollo.

After a cordial leave-taking Archer hurried his friend off the premises.

"I was a fool not to drop you into the sea, too," he said,

as soon as they were out of earshot. "You couldn't have behaved worse."

"I'm very sorry," said Conrad. "But I took her out of the room so that you could tell him I'm still a little mad."

"I did."

"And he looked quite happy when we came back. He's all right. We didn't really hurt his feelings. She's the one I'm sorry for."

"Did you talk to her? Will she hold her tongue?"

"I think so. She won't want to upset him."

"Yes. He takes himself rather seriously, I fancy."

"So he ought," said Conrad. "Nobody else will, if he doesn't. I think people should take themselves seriously. But I don't see why he should make such heavy weather over taking me seriously. If I take myself seriously, that's quite enough. Trying to . . . trying to . . . I'm sorry! I still can't help laughing. Why should he try so hard?"

"He's a disappointed man," said Archer thoughtfully.

He did not take Pethwick's view of Dickie. He did not assume that the choice of an easy life in East Head arose from any strong desire for leisure in which to appreciate Swann. On the contrary, he suspected that all this culture might have originated in frustration, and that Dickie would have preferred a more arduous career.

"He's got a lot to sit on and nowhere to put it," said Archer. "If his job gave him more headaches, he wouldn't take you so seriously. I know that type. You see them around, in the galleries, trying away. But they don't often have the cash to buy anything, so I don't have many dealings with them."

It is that type, he thought, the frustrated, the disappointed, the unsuccessful, which asks for most from art,

328

since it is continually haunted by questions which life has not answered. Who am I? What am I? What do I here? Is this my destiny, or have I made some avoidable mistake? Give me truth which disregards me, in which I play no part, but which stands unshaken and admirable, which I may contemplate and so forget my lot. Give me escape from hope and regret, anguish and solace; carry me into some other world where explicable laws prevail.

The assured, the successful men, to whom he sold his wares, had found their place in this world, had found work which absorbed all their faculties, which set problems serious enough to preserve them from the importunities of those other, unanswerable questions. They knew what they were buying and valued their acquisitions. They took pleasure in their aesthetic sensibilities. They snatched an afternoon, occasionally, to visit an exhibition; they took an evening off for a concert. Some of them might read poetry before they went to sleep. But certain transports were denied to them, since they were reconciled to life. These are reserved for the unreconciled—for those among the failures who refuse to wither, to rot, to drink, or to rail at fortune. Such men save their souls by turning to some great disinterested activity.

"You think he'd better be an appointed man?" asked Conrad.

"A what?"

"The opposite of a disappointed man. In a job which gives him a lot of headaches, so he doesn't have much time to be solemn."

"Possibly."

"Then I wonder he doesn't appoint himself, somewhere. What's to keep him here?"

329

"I dare say he's got into a rut. And I don't think his little Mrs. would like moving. She's got her roots here."

"She'd do anything in the world for him," said Conrad. "I think you ought to manage it, Frank. You know how to make people do things. We owe them both a lot. It would be a good way of saying thank you, if you kicked him out of here."

"I don't know," said Archer. "Sometimes I think the disappointed men get the best of it. That Fellow up there," he jerked his thumb skywards, "is a good deal fairer than you might suppose. There's an orange for most people—if only they have the sense to see it."

7

The young Pattisons moved into The Rowans at Michaelmas. Early in December they took a short trip to
London. Dickie had to go there for Chancery action, and
Christina, consigning Bobbins to the care of Mrs. Hughes
for five days, went with him. She had not been away for
eighteen months and felt that she needed a little holiday.

They went expecting to have a wonderful time, and had
the sort of time which is usually the lot of country cousins
in town for a week. On the night of their arrival they
dined in Bayswater with Christina's relations, the Barlows. It was a dull evening. The dinner was vile and their
hosts appeared to be overcome by the effort of producing
it at all. They had, they complained, no servants, and
they were still haunted by the memory of queues and ra-
tion books. Nobody in London, so they said, tried to enter-
tain any more. Things had become too difficult. Christina,
listening to the lamentations of the other women over their
tepid coffee, reflected that the same difficulties had prevailed in East Head, but had been defied by an endemic
neighbourliness which seemed to be lacking in Bayswater.
People in London did not enjoy one another's company;
the other guests at this dreary feast had obviously been
invited because some debt of hospitality was owing to

them, and they could be worked off together with the Pattisons. Everybody watched the clock, and at half-past ten they all trooped out together.

Dickie, on the drive home, refrained from crying: What a sluggery! He would have liked to say something appreciative, and racked his brains for a pleasant comment, but could think of none. Christina, however, was not offended by his silence. She was wondering why the coffee was cold; had people in London never got around to the idea of a percolator?

He was occupied with business during the day. On Tuesday, Christina explored all the shops in Oxford Street, bought some Christmas presents, and lunched with Mrs. Barlow in a well-known store. In the evening they went to a restaurant in Soho, of which Dickie had heard; the food was eatable, but only just, by Christina's standards. Afterwards they went to the current intellectual play. Christina, who did not attempt to understand what it was all about, enjoyed it, since the acting was first rate and several scenes were very funny. Dickie came away feeling that he must have missed something.

On Wednesday, Christina did the shops in Knightsbridge and Piccadilly. She explored the Burlington Arcade and walked up Bond Street. That night they dined with Frank Archer, who had kept in touch with them ever since his last visit to East Head. He and Christina had corresponded over the fate of Serafina Swann, and he had urged her to let him know if they ever came up to London.

He entertained them in a private room at a famous restaurant, and Christina was able to wear the dinner dress which she had hopefully brought to London. The food was

332

something to remember and so were the wines. But it was the company which impressed Dickie, for it included Sir Miles Corry, of Maxwell, Burke & Corry, a titan firm, in comparison with which Pattison & Pattison was as a minnow to a whale. Maxwell and Burke had both been cremated a long time ago, but Sir Miles was extant and had recently acquired a Mary Cassatt from Frank Archer. Both Christina and Dickie were struck by the difference in Archer's manners and appearance on this occasion; he did not look nearly so odd as he had at East Head. He seemed to possess some protean quality which enabled him to get by in any company.

The great Sir Miles was very nice to Dickie and talked to him a good deal after dinner, when they went into another room for coffee. Christina was gratified by this, and appreciated the food, but found herself a little shy with the other women. Lady Corry was very kind, they were all kind, they smiled at her, but they seemed to be at a loss for anything to say to her beyond enquiries concerning her baby, when they discovered that she had one. Since they were too good-mannered to raise topics from which she was excluded, she had no idea of the kind of conversation natural to them. She believed, however, that they would have gossiped about people, would have discussed births, deaths and marriages in their own set, and that they were a little sorry for her because she knew nobody they knew. This, she thought, was just like people in London. But it was a pleasure to see Dickie so animated and happy, discussing "take over bids" with Sir Miles.

On Thursday she had a hair-do, for which she paid double the price of a good permanent wave in East Head. She could not believe that she looked twice as beautiful,

333

but a new hair-do is an essential item in the ritual of a London holiday; she could not have gone home without one. In the evening they entertained the Barlows to dinner and a theatre. They had left the choice of a show to their guests, supposing that the Barlows must have seen a great many, and unwilling to make them see anything twice. The Barlows, who never went to the theatre, chose a musical of which they could not help knowing because it was advertised on such very large posters. Nobody enjoyed it.

On Friday, Christina lunched alone with Frank Archer, in a restaurant noted for the celebrity of its patrons. She hoped that he would point out a number of famous people, and came away without having gaped at one, not because there were none, but because of a conversation with Archer which put everything else out of her head.

That night she and Dickie set off to celebrate the end of their little jaunt. They went to dine and dance at a very special place, recommended by Archer, which turned out to be all that he had promised. It deserved the champagne which Dickie ordered, and the orchid on Christina's shoulder.

She let him get through one glass before she gave him Frank's message, but she was anxious to deliver it as soon as possible because he would need time to think it over, and, if he did decide to go and see Sir Miles, he must do it early on Saturday morning.

"Dickie!"

"Yes, dear?"

"I've got something rather important to say. I lunched with Frank, you know. It's about Sir Miles Corry."

Dickie, who had been watching some mysterious cooking operations going on at a neighbouring table, turned, and gave her his full attention.

"Frank told me . . . they want . . . Maxwell, Burke want somebody . . . a young man . . . a junior partner, really. A young man that was with them has decided to go to America. They want somebody instead. And Sir Miles liked you very much. And Frank and he have talked about you since: Frank told him that you are quite your own master and could come in, if you like the idea. I mean, if you sold the East Head practice, you'd have some money to put in. Frank says, if you like the idea, will you ring Sir Miles and go and see him tomorrow?"

She got it all out in a rush, giving Dickie no chance to say anything at all. Even when she had finished he was speechless for quite a long time. At last he said, "Maxwell Burke . . . me . . . but that . . . but that's the sort of chance . . . Maxwell Burke . . . anybody . . . *anybody* . . . they could pick and choose . . . me . . . Maxwell Burke?"

"Well, he liked you. And Frank talked to him."

"Maxwell Burke! Are you sure?"

"Yes. I've got a note to you from Frank. But I thought I'd explain first."

She fished the note out of her bag; he read it while their wild duck was brought to them and the orange salad was served.

"I could never have dreamt of such a thing," he said.

"But would you like it, Dickie?"

He looked at her as though he could not quite grasp her question.

"You've never been really happy in East Head," she

335

suggested. "I believe you might be happier in some bigger firm. What do you think?"

Dickie shook his head. He was still a little stunned.

"I don't know," he said helplessly. "It's so sudden."

"There's no reason you should stay in East Head. While your father was alive, yes! But now . . ."

"Yes, but . . ."

He tried to remember why he had thought that he could never get away.

"Of course, the work," he said. "I'd have to be a good deal more on my toes. Would I be up to it?"

"I suppose you'd have to work harder. Should you mind?"

"No. No. But it would be . . . an upheaval."

We've only just got ourselves into The Rowans, he thought. And now I'm to be shoved out of it. *I dread to be led from East Head.* What on earth is the matter with me? I should jump at it. I'm in a rut, and Tina is kicking me out of it. Tina!

"But you?" he exclaimed. "You'd rather hate it, wouldn't you? You don't like London. It would mean leaving all your friends and everything. You wouldn't want to leave the new house?"

"I should find that part rather hard," she agreed. "But I should get used to it, I expect. I've been thinking it over, ever since lunch. I should be . . ."

She broke off and spared him the knowledge of what she had been thinking ever since lunch. Her own happiness must lie in promoting his. She should be miserable unless she thought that he was getting the best possible out of his life. So long as he seemed to be doing that, she did not much care, now, where she lived. In East Head he

336

was perpetually confronted by his own mistakes; Maxwell Burke might give him less time to think of them. Should a removal to London turn out to be another mistake, that, she decided, would be just too bad. She must then resign herself to the fact that she loved a man who never knew what he wanted.

"I get rather impatient with East Head myself," she continued. "It's a pity, really, to spend the whole of one's life in one place, unless one has a duty to. It's a little cowardly; like a person who clings to their family too much, because they can't be bothered to make friends outside. I think a good shaking up is what we both of us need."

This rational answer contented him, and it was true, as far as it went. East Head had ceased to satisfy her. She had lately been very unhappy there, and none of her friends could do anything to help her. But of this grief, and its origin, she would not speak, because he did not want to see it.

"I believe you're right," he said.

"Your duck is getting cold, dear."

They both began to eat.

Tomorrow morning, he thought. But I mustn't begin, yet, to think of it as settled. I must see what he says. A lot of things must be thought of. The sale of the practice . . . the work . . . it will all be on a different scale. Another year or two in that hole, and I don't believe I'd have had the energy to tackle it. Thank heaven it's come in time. To get away! To get away!

Why shouldn't I make friends in London? she asked herself. People do have friends, in London. Eight million people. Walking about in London and not knowing anybody. Not in the shops. Not in the streets. No Mrs. Hughes, running in to help. No elevenses at the Pavilion, and hearing all the news. No news to hear, unless they write. Pushing the pram out every day with Bobbins and Anne. I'm glad I didn't tell him that I'm sure, now, about Anne. It might distract him. I will, when he's quite made up his mind, one way or the other. Nobody stopping to look in the pram and say how they're growing. But that's nonsense. I shall find some more friends sometime. If it was just going to another little town, I should soon pick up with things. Eight million people! How do eight million people ever get to know each other? They don't enjoy themselves in London. We've been out every night this week, but I haven't really enjoyed it. I get more fun in the Pavilion café. But I shall manage. I'm not a fool. I must manage. No use making him come to London and then sitting about with a long face, and grumbling.

"Let's dance," suggested Dickie.

They rose and went out onto the floor. They were good dancers and, in the past, had known some ecstatic moments, as they moved to the same rhythm in one another's arms. But now they danced rather badly because they were both pre-occupied.

"You're a very good wife," said Dickie, bumping her into another couple. "I'm not worthy of you."

"You aren't," agreed Christina. "You're walking on my feet."

"You do know I'm grateful?"

To hell with gratitude, thought Christina. Grateful men can't dance, it seems.

Having trodden a jerky measure they went back to their table and ordered *pêches flambées*.

338

"We could live in Bayswater," suggested the grateful Dickie. "Then you'd be near the Barlows."

Since the Barlows were her only friends in London it would be nice for her to live near them. Bayswater was, in his opinion, a sluggery, but he must do the best that he could for Christina's happiness.

"No," she said. "I want to live in Hampstead."

"Oh, do you? Why?"

"Well, it's nice there, isn't it?"

She chose Hampstead because she did not want to see too much of the Barlows. She did not mean to depend upon them. In Hampstead once, three years before, she had met a nice girl, of whom she sometimes thought and whom she would like to meet again. She had been taken there by the Barlows to walk upon the Heath, but she had somehow managed to miss them and to lose her way. So she had asked this girl, who was out with a dog and had been very friendly, not merely directing her but offering to go with her. They had walked for half a mile together, chattering gaily, until they ran the Barlows to earth in Ken Wood. Christina had never felt so much at ease with a stranger before, and the girl belonged to Hampstead, because she was married, and lived in a little old house near the Heath, so she said. There might be others like her: Hampstead might turn out to be a place where lonely women made friends, when they walked upon the Heath.

"We'll have some brandy," said Dickie, when their coffee came. "We must celebrate."

"You have brandy," said Christina. "I'll have *crême de menthe*."

A great big glass was brought for him, a little green one

339

for her. If they were to get their money's worth they ought to dance again, but they could not, at the moment, because the band was taking a rest, and the pianist was playing a solo.

It was a regrettably sentimental number, hackneyed and out of fashion, which he often played because he knew why it would always go down. His patrons, while affecting to despise it, listened; it sounded difficult to play but it was really a very easy piece and a large number of them had once played it themselves. The memory of this achievement gave them a certain satisfaction, although they shook their heads and raised their eyebrows. It had been, upon the whole, their most successful piece.

"Oh," said Christina, putting down her little green glass. "Liszt! I know this."

Her eyes clouded with memories. She was on the school platform at East Head, in her white organdie. Ten years ago! After that year she had given up learning the piano. Home! Home!

"It's got something," allowed Dickie. "But it hits below the belt."

"I played it once."

And were you killed upon the Capitol? he asked his *Döppelganger*, who would take the allusion.

This faceless comrade was now a man, and likely to remain one. Dickie no longer yearned for sympathetic female companionship. He would still have said that his marriage had been a mistake but he could say so without any very painful implications. The worst effects of it had been weathered and had worn off. He could now live with it very comfortably; he and Christina had grown sensible, they had learnt how to get along together, they had set-

tled down. He did not want any other wife. He had made
a mistake, but he had, upon the whole, done very well for
himself, could scarcely have done better. They would
never quite understand one another, but he preferred that
they should not. To understand Christina fully would be
to acknowledge himself the object of a love, passionate
and disinterested, which he had never, perhaps, deserved,
and which he was powerless to return. He could give her
gratitude, respect and affection, but love was not his to
command, once he had lost it. That she no longer depended upon it, but lived merely to see him happy, was
the most disturbing possibility of all; it exalted her to a
stature with which he could not hope to compete, and
gave a dire meaning to the conjecture that they were ill-
matched. He took refuge in the belief that they had settled down.

This tune, he told his other self, hits below the belt
because it has the nostalgic cadence; three notes down in
the diatonic scale. *Soh! Me! Doh!* All the great nostalgic
tunes are built up upon those three notes. *Forty Years On.
Linden Baum. Home Sweet Home. Swanee River. Dulce
Domum.* Sing those three downward notes to people and
they will sigh. Look at Christina! Sodden with sentimentality. But only in the West, objected the *Döppelganger.*
If we were Chinks, the nostalgic cadence wouldn't mean a
thing.

Dickie dropped the conversation. An imaginary friend
can always be shut up when we have had enough of him.
He began instead to consider what he should say to Sir
Miles tomorrow morning. It was a great advantage that
they had met already, in such pleasant circumstances. He
reflected, with a grin, that Sir Miles was also the owner of

a Swann, sold to him by Archer. But he would not mention this link tomorrow. Oh, no! Not for many years would he venture to talk about his own Swann; not until his professional capacities had been proved and accepted. A queer fellow, Swann! Attractive, but a little silly. Having spent months upon a particular work he took a sudden dislike to it, and dropped it into the Bristol Channel.

Liszt, after some noisy agitation, had got back to the nostalgic cadence, with an augmented diddle-diddle in the bass. Mummie was sitting in the front row, remembered Christina. Everybody I knew was there.

Dickie, smiling at his memories, sat up and straightened his waistcoat. There was upon his face an upshot light of years to come. For a moment he looked older, harder and more assured. Hope and regret, anguish and solace, were no longer to roam unchecked across his nights and days. They were to be kept henceforth in their proper kennels, recognised and ruled, brought firmly to heel by the appointed man.